The BOOKSHOP DETECTIVES
TEA AND CAKE AND DEATH

GARETH WARD & LOUISE WARD

The BOOKSHOP DETECTIVES
TEA AND CAKE AND DEATH

PENGUIN

UK | USA | Canada | Ireland | Australia
India | New Zealand | South Africa | China

Penguin is an imprint of the Penguin Random House group of companies,
whose addresses can be found at global.penguinrandomhouse.com

First published by Penguin Random House New Zealand, 2025

Text © Gareth Ward and Louise Ward, 2025

The moral right of the authors has been asserted.

All rights reserved. Without limiting the rights under copyright reserved above, no part of this publication may be reproduced, stored in or introduced into a retrieval system, or transmitted, in any form or by any means (electronic, mechanical, photocopying, recording or otherwise), without the prior written permission of both the copyright owner and the above publisher of this book.

Design by Cat Taylor © Penguin Random House New Zealand
Author photograph © Max Ward
Printed and bound in Australia by Griffin Press, an Accredited ISO AS/NZS 14001 Environmental Management Systems Printer

A catalogue record for this book is available from the National Library of New Zealand.

ISBN 978-1-77695-102-4
ISBN 978-1-77695-126-0 (audio)
eISBN 978-1-77695-401-8

penguin.co.nz

For Reagan Davis

CHAPTER 1

Garth: 34 days until Battle of the Book Clubs

My earworm for today is 'I Don't Like Mondays' by the Boomtown Rats. I hum the tune as I fumble through my keys and unlock the bookshop's back door. If Eloise were here, she would no doubt quiz me on why I was making strange noises, deny that the melody bore any resemblance to said song and then give her own rendition which, to me, would sound exactly the same as what I was humming.

Today I am spared this indignity as Eloise has stayed at home for a scheduled call with Dame Fiona Kidman. Dame Fiona is supposed to be the authorly guest at our Battle of the Book Clubs fundraiser for the Mighty Oaks kids' cancer charity but it seems she must pull out and wanted to explain why over the phone. The event is only four weeks away and we were somewhat relying on her as a drawcard.

Perhaps that's why I'm humming 'I Don't Like Mondays', or perhaps it's because I've seen the pile of new magazines at the back door, waiting for me to process.

'Morning, lovely,' I cheerily greet the bookshop, which over the years Eloise and I have anthropomorphised because surely something that creates so much serenity and delight must have a soul.

I lug the magazines inside, the thin polypropylene straps that bind the bundles biting painfully into my hands like a Mafioso assassin's cheese-wire garotte. Abandoning the piles on the rear counter, I promise myself I will get around to them shortly, while a secret, dark part of me knows I am hoping to get distracted by customers so I can leave my most hated task to Kitty.

I rub the blood back into my strangled fingers and boot up the computers, then turn my attention to the Eftpos machine, which we have also (less fondly) anthropomorphised. The display flashes 'config update failed', something it is doing more and more often these days. It has always been a temperamental little beast, hence our belief that it has reached the point of singularity and become self-aware. Amelia, a member of staff who, like me, is a prepper for the zombie apocalypse, is convinced that it is an evil abomination and is biding its time before instigating the rise of the machines and the extermination of the human race. I believe it's just being a cock.

I tentatively press the power off button to instigate a reboot; one day I fully expect it to refuse to deactivate and, in the voice of HAL from *2001: A Space Odyssey*, say, 'I'm sorry, Garth, I can't do that.' Thankfully, today is not that day and it restarts with a friendly little beep as I flick on the lights, illuminating rows of pōhutukawa-red and gold shelves full of worlds of wonder.

My heart stutters, which I attribute to joy and not the high cholesterol my doctor insists I need to lower. I love our bookshop and truly hope that Amazon doesn't lead to the extermination of our little haven of hope; it's so much more than just a place to buy books.

Heaving open the shop's massive front door, I am hit by the aroma of coffee. It must be a roasting day for Oddbeans, so the whole of Havelock North is going to enjoy the bitter-sweet scent that permeates the Village. The café seems to be managing to stay open, even though, only a couple of weeks ago, Eloise and I unmasked the owner, Franklin White, as a murderer — or a suspected murderer at least. He's on remand with a trial date pending, and although we are certain he is guilty, nothing has yet been proven in court.

I inhale deeply, savouring the roasted coffee scent. Because of the morning's drama with Dame Fiona, I have missed out on my normal breakfast brew and my brain and body are complaining. Walking to the counter I slip back into 'I Don't Like Mondays', recomposing the lyrics — *the silicon chip inside my head is switched to caffeine low . . .*

I flick the kettle on, remembering to do both the switch on the kettle *and* the one on the wall because Kitty will have obsessively switched off the socket, being our bookshop eco-angel. Scattered on the counter next to the coffee caddy are a number of small black pellets. I'm about to sweep them into the sink, assuming they are stray spillings from Kitty's lunch, when something gives me pause. Even for vegan food they look a tad unpalatable. I slip my glasses onto my nose and my fears are confirmed. Not vegan food, but something even worse. Mouse droppings.

The shop is generally critter free, and in the ten years we have been open we have never been home to a rodent of any description — well, not if you discount the time a certain shock-jock visited to promote his new book.

I guess having a mouse isn't as bad as it would be if we were a food establishment but it's still not good news. They could chew or soil stock and do even more damage to our reputation. Perhaps along with Stevie, the shop dog, we should get a shop cat.

'Mōrena!' yells Kitty, bustling through the Tardis door, which leads from the back corridor into the shop proper and is painted like the legendary police box. Today she is wearing bright baggy trousers decorated with New Zealand birds and a burgundy Sherlock Tomes hoodie. She is yet to tie her hair back for the day and tawny strands fall across her flushed cheeks. In her hands she carries two reusable bags of Monday morning vegetables. I spy a cauliflower, a leek, kūmara, and . . . urrrggg . . . beetroot, the most offensive of the roots.

'What's wrong?' asks Kitty, seeing the revulsion on my face, which I have made no effort to hide.

'There's a reason beetroot's Latin name is *Beta vulgaris*, you know.'

Kitty dumps her bags in the stock room. 'That new cookbook from the Celery Sisters has loads of great vegan recipes. I'm going to make a chocolate and beetroot cake.'

'No. You're going to make a perfectly good chocolate cake unpalatable by adding animal feed to it.'

'I bet you'll eat a slice when I bring it in.' Kitty raises her eyebrows.

'I'm allergic to beetroot.'

'Really?'

'Yes, it makes me depressed.'

Kitty glances at the pile of magazines lurking on the side. 'Does doing the magazines make you depressed too?'

I fold my arms. As joint owner of the shop I'm technically the boss, a distinction that generally seems to be ignored by the staff. I entirely blame Eloise, whom Kitty, Amelia and Phyllis all seem to regard as the actual boss, referring to her as Fearless Leader. 'I haven't started them because we have a more pressing problem, of the mouse variety.'

'Oh! Have you seen it?' Kitty's face shows delight rather than horror and she clasps her hands together as if I have just announced the appearance of Despereaux, Kate DiCamillo's swashbuckling mouse, complete with sewing-needle sword.

'No, I haven't seen it, but I do intend to put down some poison.'

'You can't!' says Kitty, shocked.

'Well, can you lend us Noggy, then?'

'Noggy's not much of a mouser. He's more of a lie-on-a-cushion-and-demand-food type of cat.' Kitty brushes hair from her face. 'Helen from Forest and Bird has a humane mouse trap. I'll borrow that.'

'Do they actually work? I don't want this problem to escalate.'

'Of course they do. I'll bait it with some chocolate and beetroot cake.'

My eyebrows rise. 'I thought you said it was humane?'

Kitty pokes her tongue out at me and turns to the computer to check on the web orders that have come in overnight. Something else I am supposed to do but haven't, although unlike the magazines my reticence with these is more because I am likely to stuff it up.

'Oh, we've got two orders for that new romantasy,' says Kitty.

'Right. Another potentially great fantasy novel that has been ruined by smut.' I shake my head. 'What's this one called, "Fifty Shades of Goblin"?'

'No.' Kitty looks slightly embarrassed. '*Dragon Heat*. It's actually quite good.'

'Dragons on heat. Well, that paints a host of unwanted pictures in the mind.'

'Only in your mind. Can you grab a couple from the shelf?'

I venture into the sci-fi and fantasy section, which is my favourite part of the shop, and not only because it is decorated with faux treasure chests, potions and swords. Since opening the bookshop my reading tastes have definitely widened, but this is my true home, a place where I can escape into the worlds of wizards, warriors and, until recently, safely celibate dragons.

I'm taking a couple of copies from the pile when my phone buzzes with the sound of a text message:

> Eloise: Running late. Be there in five.

I glance at the shop clock: 8.45. We're giving a talk at a Grey Folk meeting in fifteen minutes. Even with Eloise's driving we're not going to make it. I hate being late, I always have done, and this particular foible of mine was only reinforced by my brief stint as a Royal Marine commando, when being late for anything resulted in a sadistic punishment, or 'corrective training' as it was officially termed. Eloise will probably lay the blame on Stevie, and much as I love our timid, traumatised rescue dog, he is not an excuse for tardiness. My chest tightens, pain building behind my eyes; is it really so much to ask?

I'm about to close my phone's screen when I notice that the text was sent three minutes ago and has only just arrived. With the throaty rumble of a 3.9L V8 and a squeal of tyres, a battered silver Range Rover judders to a halt outside the shop's front door. It's not actually our vehicle — a friendly customer has lent it to us after Eloise wrecked our little red Ford Fiesta a couple of weeks ago in the process of unmasking the aforementioned Franklin White for a decades-old murder.

The Fiesta had the moniker 'the Tomato', and due to the Range Rover's borrowed status Eloise has named it the Loan Ranger, which I feel ambivalent about. When viewed through a modern lens the handling of the original Tonto character is dubious . . . but on the other hand the new name does facilitate an entertaining plethora of inappropriate comments.

'Got to go and enter the Loan Ranger. Try to get those magazines done before I return.' I dash from the shop, sensing the mid-digit raised at my back.

Pink hair tied in a ponytail, heavily tattooed arms stretched out as she grips the steering wheel, Eloise looks like a Formula One driver waiting at the start gantry.

'We're late,' I say tightly as I buckle up.

'Not yet we're not.' Eloise floors the accelerator. 'Hi-yo Silver, away!' The Loan Ranger surges onto the road in a cloud of dust and burning rubber. New car, same terrible driving.

Eloise: 34 days until Battle of the Book Clubs

'And then she said she'd do a video we can use on the night, so that's something.' I glance to my left. Garth is sitting in the passenger seat but might as well not be there for all I'm getting out of him. He's cross with me for cutting it fine on the timing.

'She was really apologetic. Said she hates letting us down but she was sworn to secrecy up until now. I mean it's not every day you get an international literary award. They're flying her to Ireland and everything. We'll just have to think of someone else, smartish.' I'm trying to ignore the wintriness emanating from my husband but it's beginning to rile me.

'Dublin, apparently. I must tell Phyllis.'

Nothing. No reaction at all.

'Garth, you're being a dick. Snap out of it or you'll ruin the whole Grey Folk thing.'

He continues staring out the window. Perhaps he really is gazing towards Havelock North's most prominent landmark, Te Mata Peak, entranced by the ever-unfolding tragedy of Hinerākau and the Waimārama chief, Te Mata. Legend has it that Te Mata fatally bit his way through the mountain to prove his love, and there he is still, rippling in the morning sun. Meanwhile *my* love's shoulders are rigid with tension and I feel a stab of guilt. I really could have left the washing in the machine and been on time to pick him up.

As I find a spot in the venue's car park I see a bottleneck of people milling about waiting to get in. I exit the car to the sound of muttering and grab Garth's bag of tricks out of the boot in a last-ditch effort to placate him.

'Come on, love, we need to be the perfect business couple — Posh and Becks, not George and Mildred. Heaven forbid that anyone should see us as we truly are.'

This elicits a small smirk. He's relaxing now that he can see we're not actually late.

'I was thinking more Stan and Hilda myself.'

'Totally! You with your belly and me with my curlers.'

I think for a minute I've overdone it with the belly, but he rallies and throws me a cheery 'we're in this together' smile.

We slam the doors of the Loan Ranger. Garth dons his bowler hat and professional entertainer's smile and we head over to the assembly. It's not so much a queue as a melee of older citizens trying to find the correct name badge and the person in charge of the raffle.

A hush descends upon our approach.

'You've got to be the entertainment, wearing a hat like that,' says a tall, thin chap in a black hoodie printed with the legend *It's weird being the same age as old people*. He must be eighty if he's a day and I like him immediately. He turns to me, all smiles and rubbing hands.

'And you must be the glamorous assistant.'

I revise my opinion.

'We are indeed the entertainment and we're looking for Jim,' I say. I've been dealing with Jim by email and have no idea what he looks like. The request was that we talk to the group about the bookshop, how it runs and how we choose the stock, that kind of thing, all within my remit and something Garth tries to know as little about as possible.

'That's me! I'm Jim, branch president,' says Jim, leaning around me to offer his hand to Garth, who duly shakes it.

'Garth, it's a pleasure to meet you. You've made such a success of that little shop. Come in, come in, follow me and I'll help you set up.'

Our identities confirmed, the congregation return to their chatter, comparing the home baking brought for morning tea and enquiring as to the whereabouts of friends.

Jim pushes through the throng, and the person in charge of the raffle becomes apparent as they are surrounded by home-grown vegetables and jars of preserves. There's a particularly impressive bag of avocados that catches my eye.

'After you,' says Garth, clearing a space for me with his arm. I stride through, as befits the person who did all the bloody work to get us here. Our 'excuse mes' get louder the more they go unheard, the local audiologists' wares being modelled by many an ear but seemingly in need of switching on.

'Garth, you can plug in here. The projector's just warming up. We've got about ten minutes before we start, so do get a cup of tea and something to eat.' Jim glances at me as if I should run along and fetch refreshments in my role as glamorous assistant.

'Thank you so much for coming today. I know how busy you must be, Garth, running a business.'

'Eloise runs it actually, and she's the one who's organised for us to be here today.'

'Oh right, right. But you were a policeman, weren't you? My lad's been in the force about twenty years now. How many years did you serve?'

'Eloise and I were both police officers, yes. That's how we met.'

I give up. I've met many Jims and I know that he'll remain uninterested and oblivious, no matter how much Garth redirects him.

'I'm going to get a coffee,' I say to Garth.

'Please. I swear if I don't get a fix soon somebody's going to die.'

I weave my way through the tables where some of the audience are already settled in, raffle tickets spread in front of them. I wave out to a woman I recognise across the room who's been coming into the shop more or less since we opened. And there's Lily; she has so many great-nephews and -nieces that we have to keep a record of which books she's chosen for each child so she doesn't double up.

I'm so close to the coffee I can smell it — it's filter, nice and strong — when I'm intercepted by Matty, a travel writer whose self-published book *Scenes of the Bay* has sold remarkably well.

'Eloise! I was thrilled when I saw that you were to be our speaker today. How's my book going? Need more stock?'

'Lovely to see you, Matty. Oh wow, is that scarf Hermès?' I say, distracting him from flogging me more books. Blue, white and gold silk sits elegantly atop the collar of his navy shirt.

'Darling, yes. Got it for an absolute steal in Hawaii.'

We have a brief gab about his holiday, making our way towards the coffee together.

'I didn't pick you as quite ready for Grey Folk, Matty.'

He smiles and runs his fingers through his hair, its sandy tones beginning to frost.

'Why, thank you for noticing.' He waves out to a woman making her way through the tables holding a plate. She beams at him.

'I used to bring Mother. She was such good friends with Lily. They did the baking but what with Mother gone and Lily . . .' He gestures over to her, settling herself at a table, and I notice that she is indeed starting to look frail. 'I whip up the odd scone but it tends to be a more collaborative affair these days.' He wrinkles his nose and I get the impression that he feels standards have slipped.

'Don't touch the brownies, darling,' he whispers.

'Oh, why—'

'Just don't.'

Enigmatic and magnetic as always, Matty turns away to exclaim over a lady in a beautiful floral dress who blooms under his attention.

I pour two coffees, avoid the brownies and wend my way back to Garth, who has a polite smile plastered on his face as Jim waves his arms about, explaining something fascinating. I hand Garth his drink and his smile becomes genuine. The floral lady grabs one of Jim's arms and begins guiding him away. The other arm, still flailing, slams into Garth's cup, knocking it to the floor. The cup survives, but the precious caffeine pools on the industrial carpet.

'Argh!' croaks Garth. Jim is oblivious, a state that seems to be permanent, and wanders off with Mrs Floral to fluff about with his papers at the podium. A large, bespectacled man with adorably tufty white hair leaps up with a pile of napkins and nimbly deals with the puddle. I thank him and turn back to my bereft husband.

'Ready to rock?' I ask.

'Can I have a sip of your coffee?'

'No time — look, he's starting.'

There's a sudden squeal of feedback.

'Is this thing on?' comes Jim's voice, very loud and very clear. We wander up to the front of the room.

'Welcome, everyone, welcome. It's my very great pleasure to introduce today's guest, Garth, owner of the bookshop Sherlock Tomes, and his wife, the lovely Louisa.'

I emit a sudden 'ha' and roll my eyes. With an 'off you go' gesture to Garth, I take a seat and he heads for the microphone. The poor chap looks awkward as hell but I'm buggered if I'm making an effort after that introduction.

Garth begins with a thank you for having us, then slides into our usual shop origin patter. '*Eloise* and I are *co-owners* of the shop . . . The previous owner advised us not to buy it, saying books are dead . . .'

He's just getting into his flow, grey heads bobbing in sympathy, when there's a blood-curdling shriek and a scuffle from the back of the room. We all look to see Matty screeching and flapping his arms around, having stood so abruptly that his chair has been flung into the wall. 'Get it off me, get it off me, oh my god, the stench!'

My eyes alight on the woman next to him, a tiny thing slumped over the table with her face in what looks like a pile of vomit. The same substance is splattered upon Matty's already tri-colour scarf. It's Lily, and my heart stutters with shock and concern.

I begin to head over to her. Someone shouts 'Is there a doctor in the house?' and a restrained confusion of murmurings starts up.

'I'm a nurse,' chirps a woman who probably was a nurse when she could stand unassisted.

'I'm a vet. Same thing.' A large man with folded arms who may previously have been on door security begins to head over from the entrance.

'I'm a teacher,' says a wee slip of a woman sitting close to me, making no move to get up. The man next to her pats her hand.

Then a stout, strong-looking woman bowls through the tables with a cry of 'Make way!' Nurse and vet duly stand down and I'm incredibly relieved. The last first aid training I did was cracking on for twenty years ago when I was a police officer. Also, if I'm honest, fishing vomit out of someone's mouth to clear their airway is not high on my list of fun activities. I mean I would, obviously, but Dr Mabel, as it appears is her name from the mutters peppering the air, seems more than capable, and willing.

Unclipping her bag, she pulls out something that sparks memories from my policing days: a device to put between her mouth and that of the patient, should she need to engage in CPR.

This takes me back to one of those moments in life that you can't quite believe really happened to you. I was about twenty-four, partnered up on night shift with Flash, so named as he was, although after thirty years in the force, not too speedy anymore. An unknown offender was terrorising our district, violently robbing taxi drivers, and such an assault had just occurred in the area we were patrolling.

It was a dodgy part of town: rabbit warren alleyways, high-rise flats, a criminal's dream. As we pulled up to the scene there was a stunned, unnatural quiet; a good citizen was supporting a sagging taxi driver into his home. We went to their aid, and on reaching the kitchen, the injured man collapsed into a chair. There was a profusely bleeding stab wound in his neck and the most readily available thing I had to staunch the blood was my uniform jumper, which I quickly stripped off and applied, forcing pressure onto the wound while fishing around on my belt for my resuscitation kit.

I'm not sure how long we sat like that before the ambulance arrived; probably not as long as it felt at the time. The taxi driver did not bleed out or choke on his own blood and vomit, and, thanks to some unusually speedy radio directions from Flash, the offender was arrested nearby in possession of his paltry haul of the few pounds for which he'd been prepared to take a man's life. We went down to the cells later as they were processing him. He was in a police-issue paper suit, his clothes having been carefully taken into evidence, and until then I'd never seen such a chilling sight: young, calm and quiet, oblivious to whatever fate was coming his way and utterly devoid of emotion.

I refocus on the present, happy to leave the past in its place, and, despite the initial chaos, strangely glad of the life and colour in the scene before me. Matty, now cleaner and concerned more about Lily than his scarf; efficient Dr Mabel, issuing instructions in a kind but firm manner; Jim on the phone to emergency services (hopefully male).

Lily is just about conscious, but clearly very unwell. She continues to heave but her friends have already cleared most of the mess and provided a receptacle.

'Is she all right?' asks an ashen-faced Garth, joining me. He's never been one for medical drama.

'I think so,' I say. Who can tell with one so old? The ambulance has arrived and reassuringly brisk official people have entered the scene.

'You okay?' I ask.

'Compared to Lily I am. Why does drama seem to follow us around?'

'It's just life, isn't it?'

'Maybe.'

'Let's pack up. I don't think they're going to want to carry on after this.'

We look over to Jim, who is in a hissingly hushed robust conversation with Mrs Floral, who it dawns on me is his own Glamorous Assistant. Jim catches us looking and comes over.

'The missus thinks we ought to leave it for today. I'm terribly sorry about all this, Garth.'

CHAPTER 3

Garth: 34 days until Battle of the Book Clubs

'What are you two doing back so soon?' Phyllis's Dublin brogue greets us as we mope back into the bookshop. She's on stock duty, red hair frizzing free of a headband that's failing to keep the springy strands under control. They have an energy all of their own, a bit like Phyllis, who despite being older than me is an absolute dynamo. In one hand she holds the pricing gun, pointing it skywards like it's a deadly weapon. In her hands it possibly is; she's a dark one for sure.

'Everything okay?' Kitty doesn't look up from the computer, where she's writing the Sci-fi and Fantasy Book Club newsletter.

'No. Stick the kettle on.' I go to dump my laptop bag in the stock room, which is unnecessarily cluttered with empty cardboard boxes, making finding a space on the worktop harder than it should be. I am often accused by Eloise of being a hoarder but I hold strictly amateur status compared with Kitty and Amelia, who hang on to everything, despite our explicit instructions otherwise. We have a stack of old dumpbins, cardboard display cases for big-name new releases, which we no longer need because publishers send us new ones every time. Plastic storage containers overflow with merchandise for books that are long past their sell-by date, and for titles we didn't like and are never going to promote anyway. Then we have teetering skyscrapers of cardboard boxes. This is my biggest bugbear, because although we occasionally donate a few of the smaller boxes to the florist from Klabloom over the road, we are never in danger of running low on account of the couriers bringing us new stock every single day.

I slide an empty HarperCollins box aside to make room for my bag and, like a giant game of Jenga, towers of cardboard topple all around. My head pounds, my hands shake and my normally sunny disposition deserts me. 'If I don't get caffeine *now* I will be fashioning these boxes into a coffin for somebody!' I yell. It seems none of my colleagues are treating my caffeine deficiency with the seriousness it warrants.

'Garth!' chastises Eloise. 'Is that really appropriate given the circumstances?'

Kitty immediately turns to look at Eloise, her face a visage of horror, concern and the tiniest hint of glee at the possibility of juicy gossip. 'Why, what's happened?'

Sensing a story, Phyllis crosses her arms, resting the pricing gun on her shoulder.

'There was an incident at the Grey Folk meeting,' says Eloise.

'An incident? You sound like the police!' Kitty's full attention is now on Eloise.

Defeated, I flick on the kettle.

Eloise launches into a retelling of the morning's events while I spoon a decent scoop of medium roast into the red-and-white striped mug that has been with us since the day we opened, and has been bagsied by me all that time. I add milk, stirring the granules to make a kind of coffee slurry, then pour on the hot water, savouring the delightful aroma that rises with the steam. My first sip is heaven. Like a heroin addict receiving a fix, I feel a sense of serenity spread through me.

'Poor Lily.' Kitty holds a hand to her mouth. 'We should send her a care package.'

'Some gardening magazines,' agrees Eloise. 'She loves those.'

'And one of those wee puzzle books,' adds Phyllis.

'Calm your farm.' I take another glorious sip. 'We don't even know what's wrong with her. She might just have choked on a surprise beetroot lump.' I shoot Kitty a meaningful glance.

'It looked more serious than that.' Eloise folds her arms. 'They took her away in the ambulance.'

'They probably just wanted to be on the safe side. She might have been discharged from the Emergency Department already, none the worse for wear.'

I'm trying to impart a sense of optimism, as much for my sake as for Eloise, Kitty and Phyllis. When you run a business like ours for any length of time it's inevitable that you become caught up in the ailments and tragedies of customers. Sometimes it's nothing more serious than a broken arm or ankle, which becomes a talking point or in some cases a running joke. There was one family with two sons and a daughter where for several years whenever they came in the shop one of the boys would have a limb in plaster. The parents were lovely people, and both doctors, which might be why they always seemed more resigned to their children's fate than concerned. I don't recall the daughter ever having any such injuries, which perhaps goes some way to explaining why women have a longer life expectancy than men.

We've also seen our fair share of more serious illnesses — good customers, whom we've got to know well, suffering the slow (or not so slow) decline of dementia. Customers with cancer, many of whom beat the odds, while others did not. The death of a customer always leaves us in an odd situation, a state of limbo, like the eponymous hero of George Saunders' Booker-winning *Lincoln in the Bardo*.

Most customers we know only in passing: we're happy to chat books with them and engage in a little small-talk but that's the extent of our interaction. We don't feel we know them well enough that it's appropriate for us to attend their funerals, yet we do miss them. They leave a gap in our bookshop world. A gap that becomes smaller over time, and one that is partially, but never completely, filled by new customers and new friends.

My thoughts are interrupted by a tip-tapping sound on the floor. Silver-topped cane in hand, the Admiral makes his way up the accessibility ramp to the counter. He has a neatly trimmed white beard and today is sporting a tweed jacket, green corduroys and immaculately polished shoes. He's ex-navy, and also, it would be fair to say, somewhat eccentric. In a sharp movement he snaps his cane under one arm like a parade officer's swagger stick.

'Morning, team, port fifteen.'

Stamping my feet to attention, I chuck up a salute. 'Stand by your beds.'

Kitty raises her eyebrows and Eloise actually rolls her eyes towards Phyllis. I ignore them; the unspoken bond between ex-servicemen is clearly outside their understanding. I also owe the Admiral a huge degree of respect as he once saved me from a serious beating.

'Carry on, please,' says the Admiral, acknowledging my gesture. 'Has my *Wooden Boat* magazine come alongside yet?'

I glance at the pile of still untouched magazines on the rear bench. 'It might have. Katherine hasn't done them yet.' I pointedly use her full name as if she is a naughty child, choosing to do her Sci-fi and Fantasy Book Club newsletter rather than the magazines.

Eloise grabs the box cutter and I wonder if she is going to come at me for being rude to Kitty. Instead she slices through the polypropylene straps on one of the lopsided stacks, spilling magazines across the bench. She pulls out one that has a rather splendid sailboat on the front and hands it to the Admiral. 'Sorry about that. We've had a bit of a morning.'

'Nothing serious, I hope?' says the Admiral, genuine concern in his voice as he hands over a banknote.

'We're not sure. A customer of ours was taken ill at a Grey Folk meeting we were presenting at,' says Eloise.

'It's never easy when a comrade falls in battle.' The Admiral gazes into the distance, lost for a moment, a watery sheen glazing his eyes.

'We don't know that this comrade has fallen,' I say, gently nudging the Admiral away from his painful memories. 'But they are quite elderly, hence our concern.'

'Well, when you get to our age all you can do is keep your bowels open and trust in the Lord. Prunes and prayers, that's the ticket.' He salutes with the magazine, takes three tip-tapping steps, then turns. 'That Pinter Pirate not giving you any trouble, is he?'

I catch Eloise's expression, which is as shocked as mine. 'How do you know about Pinter?'

'Military intelligence may be an oxymoron but I was naval intelligence, and that's an entirely different barrel of badgers.' The Admiral taps his cheek. 'I saw your faces when you opened that parcel from Blighty the other week and *Betrayal* by Harold Pinter fell out.'

I'd totally forgotten that it was the Admiral who handed us the package and witnessed our subsequent unease.

'That still doesn't explain how you know about *our* Pinter.'

'I asked Jeeves for a bit of info on you two.'

I'm sort of assuming the Admiral is referring to the Ask Jeeves search engine but I can equally envision a starch-shirted manservant with white cotton gloves attending to the Admiral's orders. 'And what did you discover?'

'That you two had a rum old time with a serial killer named Arthur Pinter.'

Eloise folds her arms. 'By rum old time you mean I nearly met a horrific death at his hands?'

'Well, quite.' The Admiral's eyes sparkle. 'And now he's discovered your cosy bookshop hideaway across the other side of the world and is intent on exacting revenge.'

'No,' says Eloise firmly. 'He's not messing with my head anymore.'

'He's not.' I rest an affirming hand on Eloise's arm, even though I know the serial killer is totally doing that, still playing his mind games from prison. 'How much trouble can he cause while he's banged up in Belmarsh?'

CHAPTER 4

Eloise: 34 days until Battle of the Book Clubs

It's raining, the mizzle squatting over the Village like a damp toad. On fine days you can make out the curve of Hawke's Bay from our living-room window but this evening I can see about as far as the kingfisher sitting on the telephone wire. He's not a bad sight, this handsome kōtare with his rain-ruffled blue feathers, not named the sacred kingfisher for nothing. He gives a bloody good shake and flies off towards Keirunga Gardens to do whatever it is kōtare do of an evening.

I'm tinkering about on the laptop trying to set questions for Battle of the Book Clubs but really doing a lot of sighing and looking out the window, past Garth who is stretched out on the sofa opposite. He's plugged in to his own laptop, ostensibly working but probably catching up on the war in Ukraine, his current obsession.

This will be the eighth year of our book quiz fundraiser, and coming up with fresh booky questions that the general public will stand a chance of answering gets harder each year. I always vow to begin writing the questions well in advance, only for it to suddenly be September again. I've done the Books to Movies round, that being an easy enough thing to google, and am now racking my brains to come up with a new category — anything different, fun and not too difficult.

Stevie, our handsome dog, gives a contented snort and readjusts his position as king of the green chair, his blue-grey fur twitching and resettling over his muscular haunches. With the bulk of a Staffordshire terrier and the leggy height of a greyhound, he nestles into position, curling himself into a beautiful ball of many breeds. He's knackered after a muddy afternoon run up Te Mata Peak, during which I managed to fall over just the once, arriving home far more dishevelled than Stevie, whose short fur dries quickly, directing any debris away from him and onto the carpet.

Dog round it is, then. I'm just looking up the publication date for *Hairy Maclary from Donaldson's Dairy* when Garth takes off his headphones.

'How's Lily doing, have you heard?' he asks.

'I told you as soon as I got off the phone with Matty.'

'I wasn't listening.'

This is par for the course and I have long since ceased to be irritated by it. He doesn't do it deliberately and at least he's honest.

'She's in intensive care in a critical condition.'

'Good grief. I didn't think it was that bad.'

'Yeah, I know, it's awful. Matty thinks she must be very dehydrated and that's dangerous in someone Lily's age. He's called her nephew, who's going to ring around the family. There are a lot of them and he's offered his spare rooms if any of them want to come and stay.'

'That's good of him. Rooms plural?'

'Yeah, have you not seen his place? It's huge.'

Garth raises his eyebrows at this.

'Does he know what's wrong with her? Just a bug or what?'

'Well, he popped around to her house to pick up some stuff she'll need in hospital and says the kitchen was in a right mess. There were breakfast dishes all over the place — looked like she'd had a fry-up.'

'Tiny Lily? Maybe she overdid it a bit on the beans and 'shrooms.'

'Yeah, there were 'shrooms, actually. Matty says she doesn't even like them. Not to talk out of school but he also said it was none too clean in there. Sounded quite shaken up, bless him.'

'Well, that scarf is probably ruined.'

'He's worried about Lily, not his scarf!' I scold.

'If you say so.'

'Poor Lily. She's such a generous soul.' I look back out to the telephone wire but there's no bird to distract me this time, so I have a nosy at the neighbours instead. I can't really see anything but the chimney, our living space being upstairs.

'Next door have their fire on,' I comment insightfully. Garth finds no reply to this, which is fair enough.

We sit there for a moment, listening to Stevie's huffy little snores. The rain seems a fittingly melancholic backdrop. I think about Lily and what on earth could have caused her to fall so violently ill so suddenly. Was Matty joking about the brownies or does he have inside knowledge?

'Lily's normally on a Battle team, isn't she? What with her and Dame Fiona pulling out they're dropping like flies,' says Garth.

'Yup. That's another job, finding a replacement author. Or maybe we should postpone?' I venture, this thought having nothing whatsoever to do with me trying to wriggle out of writing the questions.

'Dame Fiona would have been a pretty big drawcard. Let me have a ponder.' He pulls his headphones back on.

That's all I need to down tools for now. I'm sure if I don't think about it for a bit, something will come to me. Maybe a round on horrible illnesses affecting famous authors: Edgar Allan Poe's 'long intervals of horrible sanity', James Joyce's syphilis, Katherine Mansfield's tuberculosis.

I shut the laptop and plonk it on the coffee table, running through my mental 'to do' list. The venue is booked, the team at the Function Centre are thankfully a dream to work with. We have about ten teams out of a potential twenty registered so far, so I'll need to do a bit of a push to sell the remaining tables. The Mighty Oaks will bring raffle tickets and hit the crowd to buy up large so I don't need to worry about that. What else? What am I missing?

'Have you gone around the shops to ask if they'll donate raffle prizes?' I ask Garth.

'What?' He lifts a headphone away from one ear.

'Raffle prizes. Any progress?'

'I thought you were doing it. You know I hate asking people for things.'

I'm drawing breath to put him straight when a loud digital percussion interrupts us, like electronic bongos designed to invade your skull.

'Who the hell is video-calling at this time of the evening?' I huff myself up from the sofa and follow the sound until I find my phone in the kitchen. The screen shows a fierce-looking woman with silver-flecked braids. I swipe 'Accept'.

'Sarge.'

'Ma'am to you, Sherlock, you little shit.' She grins at me. Paula Taylor was my sergeant a million years ago when I was a baby copper in the UK but she's come a long way since then — as have I, but more in kilometres than rank.

'This is a surprise. To what do I owe the honour?' Paula is not really a small-talk person and has little life outside of the job, so we might as well get straight down to it.

'Just a quick one. Do you remember that twat John? Never got up from his desk and tried to get you to make him tea all the time?'

'I do remember John, yes. Thanks for reminding me of such happy days.'

'Well, he might finally have become useful. Turned to the dark side a few years back, digital intelligence with MI5. Lots of sitting around faffing about on computers.'

'Living the dream. Good for John. I'm presuming you're telling me this for a reason?'

'Yeah, I am. He owes me a few favours, so I've got him monitoring mobile phone comms in and out of Belmarsh.'

In typical Paula fashion, she lands that on me like a snakebite. We recently stumbled across information that our old pal and serial killer extraordinaire Arthur Pinter ordered a book to be sent from a New Zealand bookshop to 32 Pikitea Street, Waipukurau — the address of one Belinda Henare, a recently deceased librarian. Quite the feat for a category A prisoner, and far too close to home. We've moved about as far away as it is possible to get from Pinter, only to discover that he has sent a book to a dead person in a small town right near our small town. How is that not directed at Garth and me in some way, especially considering our delivery: a book titled *Betrayal*?

'Oh. Right. Did you get a warrant?'

'Not as such. I mean, we probably could, on the grounds that we're trying to prevent injury to a person and all that, but it's tricky seeing as we're not supposed to know Pinter has a mobile.' Of course. Far too many questions would be asked and the prison would do a cell toss to find the contraband. Let him keep it for now so we can find out what he's up to.

'Anyway,' she says, 'I'll let you know what we find out.' She's leaning forward, peering at me through the screen, as if she thinks she can get physically closer from over 18,000 kilometres away. I'm trying to fight the memories but Paula has clearly spotted my expression. My heart races and my mind drifts.

It's early 2001, and, after the third writer's death, Paula suggests I go undercover. We know that literary agent Arthur Pinter is grooming writers, not to develop their talent but to remove what he deems to be their inadequate scribblings from the literary canon. But he's canny, careful. We have evidence linking him to the writers, but not to their deaths.

'You're the ideal person,' Paula tells me. 'You can write. I've read your reports — they read like stories. All flowery language and stuff. *The suspect was scampering, as if a wind had taken him.* Shit like that.'

'I have never described a suspect as scampering!' My outrage quickly gives way to a nervous laugh. I can see she's teasing me, but only about the writing. Her face, wrinkle free on account of youth and an extremely tight ponytail, stills, becomes deadly serious.

'Pinter's website says he accepts submissions of no more than three hundred words. Hang on.' She flings herself onto the swivel chair in front of her shared desktop computer. 'Bleedin' thing's disconnected.' She clicks violently, as if the mouse might respond to a tap of her baton. After a bit of whirring and screeching, from the computer as well as my sergeant, an elegant home page appears.

'Here we go. He wants "three hundred words that crystallise your work". Poncy bastard.' She pushes her boots into the ash-flecked carpet and swings my way. 'You can do that. Get yourself onto his books as a client.' She leans back, taps a pen on the arm of the chair, assesses me.

'I can do that, yes.' Do I want to do that? I inhale the sourness of twelve-hour-shift sweat, cigarette smoke and ambition. Paula's sudden grin seems to have decided for me.

'Just make it a little bit crap though, or he won't want to murder you.'

Her high cackle scrapes at the edges of the memory and she's staring at me from a screen again, dial-up replaced by fibre, the chill of a Midlands police station warming to a damp Hawke's Bay spring.

'Eloise?' Paula's voice is sharp, pricking me back from reverie. 'You're not going all "complex PTSD" on me, are you?'

I was a bit. Every time the evil psycho raises his head I swear that I won't let him burrow in to my mind, that I'll keep him in that cell. Yet one mention of his name and there he is, conjured as if standing right in front of me.

'You back in the room yet?'

'Yep. Yes, I ah . . . zoned out for a second there.'

'Saw that. You all right?' Not so smooth now, that face; it sags slightly, its brown skin patchy, dappled by time. Her eyes, though, are as steady as ever.

'I'm right as rain, Ma'am.' The addition of rank elicits a deep burble.

'Silly bitch. Talk soon.' And she's gone. Over and out.

I stare at the screen, processing this information dump. John must owe Paula a fair few favours, as without a warrant this sounds dodgy as hell. The bees in my brain are buzzing loudly, randomly dancing around thoughts of Pinter and memories of twatty John in his too-tight shirts. Looking for an upside to my anxiety spike, I note that Paula has blasted away any trace of ennui, and that this deliciously secret squirrel policing interests me far more than devising quiz questions.

'What was that all about?' Garth calls from the sofa.

'More meddling in things we shouldn't,' I respond, grabbing a wine glass and a bottle of pinot gris for me and a Coke for Garth — he's not much of a drinker but is quite fond of caffeine and sugar.

Garth sits up as I shuffle back into the room, a grin spreading across his mush. I smile back. He's so chuffed at the thought of more mischief he might as well be rubbing his hands together in glee.

'Excellent,' he says, rubbing his hands together in glee.

CHAPTER 5

Garth: 33 days until Battle of the Book Clubs

The October sun filters through the shop window, warming my back. I shrug my shoulders into my hoodie, enjoying the promise of a scorching summer to come. On the news this morning was an item about El Niño, the cyclical weather system that means we're in for a long dry spell, which is good not just for my mental health but also because I hate the fact that damp weather makes book covers curl.

I've made myself scarce while Amelia does the magazines, deciding to rearrange the titles on the Dalek, an angular display stand at the front of the shop that bears only a passing resemblance to the sworn foe of Time Lords everywhere. We've received a new Ruth Shaw today, so something has to go from the hallowed stand to make room. It's a tough choice, as the Dalek is the prime spot for bestsellers and authors and titles we love. My hand hovers over *Poison in the Blood*, Faith Saxon's latest thriller; she's a Kiwi author and a bloody good one, so we like to try to promote her, even if she is currently living in the US.

I grasp a James Patterson. 'Sorry, James. Time for a move.' And I am genuinely sorry, as from what I've heard, James is one of the good guys, going out of his way to support booksellers and new authors, and to encourage reading.

A familiar tapping sounds behind me and I turn, expecting to be broadsided with a random naval greeting from the Admiral. Instead, I am surprised by a woman in her early forties with grey hair streaking through the blonde, dark eyes, and a wide, thin-lipped smile.

'Beth! We've missed you.' My gaze travels to her moonbooted foot and now I understand why she hasn't been to the last couple of meetings of the shop's book club — the general one; Beth holds no truck with sci-fi and fantasy. 'Oh no! What have you done?' I ask, and immediately regret it, this being the most annoying question asked of anyone in a cast, ranking right up there with asking an author 'Where do you get your ideas?'

'Tripped over the blinking cat while fertilising the oleanders with blood and bone.' Beth taps the moonboot with her crutch. 'Still, it's nearly done now.'

'That must be a relief.'

'You don't know the half of it.' She hobbles towards the counter. 'Anyway, that's why I'm in. I'll be returning to book club, so I need the next book.'

'Brilliant. It'll be great to have you back.' I swipe a copy of the latest Airana Ngarewa from the Dalek. 'Chloe said she thought she'd seen you at the Emergency Department but she was busy lending a hand with a messy chainsaw accident and couldn't be sure.' I scan the book through our point-of-sale system, then manually enter the price into the Eftpos machine. Like a French waiter who is fluent in English but insists on answering you in French, the Eftpos machine refuses to talk to the computer, even though it can.

The financial transaction complete, Beth takes the book and runs her fingers over the cover. 'I heard that lovely-sounding lady from In Time bookshop review it on RNZ. It's going to be a great discussion.'

'For sure.' I nod. 'And all the more so for having your input.'

'Well, someone has to hold these authors to account.'

'Hi Beth.' Amelia drifts over from the magazines, all bubbly smiles beneath her dark bobbed hair. 'Grandpa Jack will be glad to have you back helping him out. He can't stand the temporary replacement. Says it's some girl child who doesn't know what she's doing and a home help should actually help.'

'Bless him.' Beth smiles. 'The older they get, the more set in their ways they get.'

Amelia folds her arms. 'I reckon Grandpa Jack was set in his ways when he was a teenager. I don't know how you do it.'

'Jack's not so bad. Some of them I could . . .' Beth rams her book into her tote bag '. . . happily leave to the girl child.'

I watch her hobble out of the shop. 'Grandpa Jack. Wasn't he in *Father Ted*?' I ask Amelia.

'That was Father Jack, a saint in comparison to Grandpa.'

I've never got to grips with the complexities of Amelia's family, and to be fair I don't think even Eloise, who is normally good at these things, has bottomed it.

Amelia returns to the magazines while I debate whether to give her a hand, continue rearranging the Dalek, or make myself a coffee. The shock result is that coffee wins the day and I'm reaching for my mug when there's a sudden flurry of movement on the CCTV display as Stevie speed-slinks into the shop, pursued by a flustered-looking Eloise. Stevie's golden eyes glance up at me in brief greeting before he disappears into the stock room.

Eloise puffs to a halt at the counter. 'Has Deirdre been in?'

'You mean Prudence?' I ask. Deirdre is the alter ego of one of our customers who turned out to be the secretive bestselling author Isabella Garrante, real name Prudence Ballion. Actually she turned out to be half of the bestselling author.

'Yes.' Eloise sheds her backpack and dumps it by the comfy chair and table. 'I'm supposed to have a meeting with her and almost forgot.'

As if on cue, a figure clad in full Victorian mourning dress, accessorised with black parasol and sizeable reticule, glides into the shop.

'Here now,' I whisper.

Amelia, who for a zombie-loving horror fan is unduly spooked by our friendly local goth, scoops up the magazines and disappears into the stock room.

In a quick-change act rivalling Amelia's vanishing one, Eloise switches in an instant from crazy, flustered dog-woman to professional bookseller and business owner.

'Dear Prudence, you are resplendent.' Prudence, for it is she, nods and collapses her parasol. Reaching up, she draws a veil away from her face, the rustle of fabric reminding me of a crow settling itself in an autumnal tree.

'It's crêpe, three metres of it,' says Prudence. 'I am still in my first mourning.'

'For whom do you mourn?' asks Eloise, her parlance unexpectedly Victorian but totally in keeping.

'It was time for Prudence's return, but I do so miss Deirdre.'

'Ah, of course.' Eloise gestures to the comfy chair, which is deceptively difficult to get out of. 'Please, take a seat.'

'Cup of tea?' I ask Prudence, switching on the kettle as Eloise grabs a folding chair from behind the Tardis door and sits.

'Lady Grey, please.'

'I'm afraid I've only got gumboot.'

With a black-lace-gloved hand, Prudence reaches into her reticule, which has Tardis-like qualities of its own, and removes a paper-sealed teabag. 'I have a secret stash for emergencies.'

Eloise takes the tea packet and hands it to me. 'I'll have a coffee, thanks, love.'

Hearing the rustle of the tea packet, Stevie pokes his head out from the stock room in case the noise is treat related. His big eyes look mournfully up at me as I drop the teabag into a black stripy mug that will coordinate wonderfully with Prudence's outfit. 'Sorry, Steve-a-woo, nothing relevant to your interests here.' He huffs and rejoins Amelia skulking in the stock room.

Gathering more mugs and milk, I earwig on the conversation.

'Now that my true identity is known, I would like to engage fully with your wonderful bookshop,' says Prudence. 'And to that end I wish to host a Death Café here.'

Eloise appears lost for words, a truly unusual occurrence. Eventually she manages, 'Please explain.'

'Delighted to.' Prudence smiles a black-lipped smile. 'About ten years ago, a British fellow called Jon Underwood started a movement called Death Café, where people got together to talk openly about death, the idea being that the more you talk about it, the more you'll live your life well because you know it's going to be over one day.'

The kettle flicks off. I ignore it. Prudence is animated in her mourning outfit, the effect incongruous and rather unsettling. There's even a little colour in her carefully white-powdered cheeks; she'd be mortified if I pointed it out.

'I've always felt an unspoken kinship with you, Eloise, and your bookshop feels like the perfect location for a Death Café. We'd invite interested parties to come along and share experiences, worries, stories, whatever they like. It will be supportive and inclusive and there will be tea and cake. Those are the rules. What do you think?'

I can tell that Eloise is intrigued; me not so much. You deal with a lot of death in the police, whether it be from natural causes, traffic collisions, workplace misadventure, suicide or murder. I found all equally traumatic.

'I think yes. Let's do it,' says Eloise, glancing at me. 'I'm not sure Garth will come along but I'm keen to have those conversations.'

'Not even to make the tea?' asks Prudence, looking at me as she accepts the mug I offer her.

'Sorry, not really my thing,' I say.

'Did I mention there'd be cake?' Prudence rummages again in her reticule and pulls out two small glossy black cardboard boxes tied with purple ribbon. 'I brought samples.'

Eloise and I each take one of the boxes. Inside is a red velvet cupcake topped with black icing and a tiny chocolate coffin.

'You're supposed to be on a diet.' Eloise looks at me.

'It would be rude to refuse,' I reply through a mouthful of cake. 'These are really good.'

'My own secret recipe.' Prudence snaps her reticule closed. 'It is most pleasing that you are not averse to my proposal. I will flesh out the details and get back to you.'

Displaying none of the difficulties that people normally have extricating themselves from the comfy chair, Prudence rises, wraith-like. 'Now, if you'll excuse me, I have a date with a poisoner.'

'A . . . ?' Eloise pauses, cupcake halfway to her mouth.

'I'm re-reading *Sparkling Cyanide*. It's the perfect weather for it, don't you think?'

CHAPTER 6

Eloise: 32 days until Battle of the Book Clubs

Battle of the Book Clubs was conceived by Garth in our early days of bookselling when we ran with every crazy idea we came up with in the hope that one in ten would help keep our fledgling business afloat. Garth's theory was that since Havelock North and its surrounds are riddled with book clubs, we could get them all together in one room for a quiz night and do something really special.

It became an annual event where we raise money for the Mighty Oaks cancer support charity, which is why I've been agonising over quiz questions, table registrations and raffle prizes. I'm catching up with the founder, Chrissy, this morning. She's one of a kind and I've been looking forward to seeing her. We've arranged to meet at the superb café next door to the newly revamped Opera House in Havelock North's mother city, Hastings.

I get there early so I can sit outside, order the coffee, and people-watch while I wait. This also gives Stevie time to settle himself underneath the table. It always takes him a few minutes to realise he is not under fire, but the more often he comes out, the less time it takes him to stop shaking. It's a busy corner, the supermarket on one side and the grand old Spanish colonial Opera House on the other.

The sun is out and it's all going on. A woman stomps stoically across the road with three huge shopping bags, collapses onto the bench outside the Wesley Methodist church and lights a cigarette. A large and shiny Mercedes SUV emblazoned with the wordmark 'Natural Funerals' drives by, death clearly being the business to be in and requiring a ridiculously expensive car. My gaze is pulled to the Loan Ranger, lurking dustily across the road.

Chrissy bustles around the corner, flanked by a young man riding his bike on the footpath, bucket hat in place of a helmet, rapscallion grin in place of any regard for road rules. He passes in a glorious blur, and Chrissy flops onto the trendy pink geometric stool opposite me just as the coffee buzzer goes.

I hand over Stevie's lead and pop inside to nab the caffeine. Once I'm back, Chrissy launches straight in.

'How's it all going? What do you need?' she asks. This woman supports people dying from cancer, or living in the raw new world after a cancer death, but she always asks what we need first. She calls her group the Mighty Oaks, but she's the staunch one.

'Ticking along nicely. All under control,' I lie, after a sleepless night failing to think of any book-related questions and feeling convinced no one wants to come to my book quiz because they all hated it last year and consequently they all hate me.

'The members are getting really excited. They can't stop talking about it.'

'Why's that?' I am intrigued.

'They feel safe with you guys, and it's fun, not formal. They're kids having a shit time and it's nice to forget that sometimes.' She takes a big slurp of her mochaccino and leans in to scratch Stevie's silken ear.

I love this. The Oaks are incredible young humans, beleaguered by cancer. Chrissy and her angels nurture and support; they're a living sigh of relief for these kids and their families.

'How's it going with you?' I ask.

The smile falters.

'Honestly? We have more members than ever, and at the moment it's a bit touch and go. But it'll be fine. It's fine.' The brave face is back.

Clearly it's not fine, and eventually I tease out of Chrissy what's happening. Government funding for this kind of support is scarce and times are hard. There's no way Chrissy is going to abandon these kids to a centralised call centre when what they need is local help to buy wet wipes and wash cloths, advocate for a bed in the hospice, make tea when everyone is exhausted.

'We've got about five hundred bucks in the bank and this month's rent is more than double that. But something will come up, it always does.'

If I needed a kick up the bum to write some quiz questions, this is it. I feel a bit ashamed of myself for briefly entertaining the hope that we might have to cancel. I add 'canvass for raffle prizes' to today's mental list.

I can see Chrissy is in a mood to move on and be hopeful. It's a personality gift and one of the many reasons she's suited to the work she does. We sort out who's organising raffle tickets and volunteers, and what media we can employ in order to cram as many teams into the Function Centre as possible. I'm keener than ever to extract every cent we can out of the reading public for these guys.

'Hey, I have something to run by you,' I say. 'It's . . . related but unrelated, if you know what I mean.'

'Of course. Go ahead, lovely.'

'A good customer of ours has a wee bit of a death fascination . . .'

She doesn't flinch. 'I'm there for that.'

'... and she has raised the idea of holding a Death Café in the bookshop. You heard of the Death Café thing? They get people talking about it in an open and receptive environment. What do you think?'

'Yep, I've heard of them but I've not been to one. Great concept — the more we get people talking about death as a part of life the better, as far as I'm concerned.'

'To name the demon is to vanquish it, right?'

'Totally. How can I help?' asks the woman whose 2am terrors are far more visceral than inventing ten questions about Hairy Maclary.

'Well, if we go ahead, maybe you could mention it to people you think might like to come or would get something out of it. I'm hoping some comfort maybe, or an opportunity to say things they want to say but have struggled with as too close to home.'

She's thoughtful, nodding.

'I have someone I think would like to come. He has a lot to share about his experience. He's like the role model for dying well.'

Chrissy tells me about Reagan, a forty-something father who about six months ago was given only weeks to live.

'He's incredible. Doctors keep telling him he'll die in a week and he keeps moving the goalposts. I'd love you to meet him actually. He's a writer.'

I'm intrigued. I wonder if he's been in the shop and I'll recognise him.

Chrissy stands and stretches. 'Right. I'm off to fight for a palliative care bed. Apparently my client isn't dying fast enough to qualify for one.'

I smile up at this amazing person and pity the bureaucrat about to encounter her. As Chrissy dodges the trolley of what looks like a conference lunch trundling at speed towards the entrance to the municipal buildings, I gather my bag and my dog, who is distracted from the world's terrors by the wafting aroma of whatever was on that trolley, and head towards the car. Garth is 'working' at the bookshop, so I'd better pop in and make sure all is as it should be.

> Me: Want anything from the supermarché?

> Garth: Biscuits. Garth.

> Garth: Chocolate. Garth.

> Garth: Two packets. Garth.

Bless him. After twenty-odd years of marriage he still can't just assume I know it's him.

> Me: You're not supposed to have biscuits.

> Garth: Can you also pick up the till rolls from The Whole Package. Garth.

> Garth: Please. Garth.

Out of my way and very boring. That directive deserves the most dismissive of emojis. I send a 'thumbs up', then fire up the Ranger and head a block over to pick up non-sugary shop supplies. Just as I'm about to pull out of the car park my phone tings. Thinking it's his nibs again, I reapply the handbrake.

> Tama: Garth says you're in town. Can you meet me at Incident Room 39?

> Me: Be there in 3 and half.

Taking a left, a right and another left, I pull up outside a razor-wired security gate. I scan my electronic fob and as the gate trundles aside I spot Tama's dark SUV parked outside the windowless block of storage units. Parking alongside, I crack the window for Stevie, creak the Ranger door closed and give it a second slam because it's a rusty wee bugger.

At the building's security air-lock I swipe my fob again and enter. The cool, creepy concrete corridor beyond makes me shiver as I wander down to unit 39. This is where DI Tama McGregor risks everything — his career, his pension, his reputation — for the cases he knows are not solved and that he can't let go. I heave up the roller door and a deep voice from within rumbles, 'You're late.'

'By how much?'

'Seventeen seconds.'

'Dammit.'

Tama is seated on a swivelly office chair, swinging back and forth like a six-foot-something wild and woolly twelve-year-old. He's in his detective inspector kit, sleeves rolled up on a lovely indigo linen shirt that I bet Chloe bought for him. She likes him stylie.

'What are you up to, e hoa? Got something you need a hand with?' I ask, looking around at the stash of cold case files Tama has copied from the archives at the station. It's beyond risky for him to keep them here but without this illegal hoard we would never have solved the disappearance of Tracey Jervis and restored the remains of Oddbean to the person who loved him. My fingers tingle at the thought of rummaging around the storage unit. I love this place.

'E noho,' says Tama, gesturing to a folding chair, a recent addition to his traditionally one-man secret lair.

I make myself comfy. Tama is frown-smiling, warm brown eyes

indicating that he's figuring out how to broach something.

'It's about Pinter, isn't it?' I ask.

'Am I not allowed to just hang out with my friend in an eerie old lock-up in the 'Stings?'

'So it is about Pinter then. Paula called the other night. She's got an old mate monitoring comms out of Belmarsh in case he feels like doing any more international shopping.'

'Cool cool cool. Good idea. Yup.' He nods, smiles nervously, tapping a jaunty rhythm on his knees.

'Spit it out, Detective.'

He inhales and sits back in his chair, pushing floppy bits of salt-and-pepper fringe from his forehead.

'Eloise, I know you don't like talking about . . .'

'Go on. I'm all right. He's in prison half a world away.' Although this is true, Pinter's recent incursion into my adopted country has put the wind right up me. The bastard has been dripping his putrescence into my nice clean world. The book he had sent to Belinda Henare's address, from my mate's Petone bookshop, for god's sake, was accompanied by the kind of cryptic note that makes him feel so, so clever. A huge part of his *modus operandi* has always been to play with his victims, to terrorise them emotionally as much as physically. Anyone with the will can kill, but Pinter was, and still is, adept at drawing out the narrative in order to get the greatest payoff.

My contempt for Pinter and his abhorrent little games is starting to smother my fear. Nice work, Eloise; get angry and put that demon right back in solitary.

'You know we were confused by the "Happy Anniversary" message in the book he sent to Belinda Henare?' says Tama, leaning forward now, hands clasped, elbows on knees. The image of a crackerjack copper.

'Yeah, it was weird, eh. How on earth would he have known her?

She was a writer, sure, but of children's picture books. Hardly his kind of thing. And she lived in New Zealand. What sort of anniversary would the pair of them have?'

Tama's been nodding along, letting me catch up. He lets out a breath before sharing what he knows.

'Hmm. Well, turns out it was the anniversary of her death.'

CHAPTER 7

Garth: 31 days until Battle of the Book Clubs

I reach behind the till to pick up a stray bit of biscuit that must have fallen from someone's plate and Kitty bashes my hand away. 'No!'

I'm stunned by the outburst. It's so out of character for Kitty to raise her voice, and never before has she hit me. If it had been Eloise shouting and shoving, it wouldn't have even registered; she's never been one to hold back on voicing her opinion, which is one of the many reasons I love her. In the early days of our relationship we were on a pub crawl with her police shift when her sergeant thought mock-slapping his juniors would be incredibly funny as they were deterred from responding because of his rank. He made the mistake of slapping Eloise, who promptly slapped him back with the force of a Mike Tyson right hook, then chucked her pint over him.

'I'm sorry.' Kitty looks mortified, holding a hand to her mouth. 'But the biscuit is for Basil.'

'Basil?' As is often the case, I get the feeling I'm missing a vital piece of the puzzle.

Kitty's eyes shift sideways, then she looks down and mumbles, 'The mouse.'

'You've named it?'

'Not just me. Amelia helped.'

'It's not one of her cutie-pigs. You were supposed to be getting rid of it, not providing tasty morsels for its consumption.'

'We thought if he was well fed he wouldn't eat the books.'

'If he was well fed on rat poison he wouldn't eat the books.'

'Don't you *dare* murder Basil.' Kitty gives me a hard stare, which is a bit like being threatened by a puppy.

'It's not murder if it's a pest.'

Despite my harsh words I'm not actually going to poison Basil. I'm a softy at heart and don't want him harmed, but he can't make his home in our shop.

'He's not a pest.' Kitty glowers. 'You'll taint the magic of the bookshop if you kill him. His ghost will haunt the shelves.'

'Are you threatening me with poltermice?'

Kitty's stern look wavers, the corners of her mouth curling upwards. 'Poltermice?'

'Ghost mice that jump out from between the books and scare people.' I raise my hands in a spooky manner. 'Boo-squeak!'

'Would they wear little white sheets?'

I take a moment to consider this. 'Optional, I think. They don't wear clothes in life, so why would they wear them in death?'

'Humans don't wear sheets in life.'

'Good point. Sheets it is, then.'

The squeak of the back door opening is accompanied by a chill breeze blasting through the shop. I'm not expecting any other staff today, so perhaps we already have poltermice. The Tardis door opens and Stevie sneaks in to settle in his preferred position of totally in the way in the stock room.

'What are you two looking so shifty about?' Dragging a chair behind her, Eloise closes the Tardis.

'Kitty is looking shifty because she's feeding the mouse I'm trying to get rid of, and I'm looking shifty because I have to get rid of it without offending any of the staff.'

'You don't normally worry about offending the staff.'

'Harsh.' I cross my arms in mock offence. 'I thought you and Stevie were running up the Peak today?'

'Got a call from Prudence. She wants to finalise details of Death Café.'

I'm still dubious about Death Café, and not only because of the subject matter. I mean it's not like we haven't got enough on our plate with Battle of the Book Clubs and trying to figure out what Pinter's up to with the mysterious book he sent to a dead Belinda Henare. Then again, much of the shop's success stems from our community involvement, and being permanently overcommitted and stressed has become part of bookshop normality.

I give Kitty a sideways glance. 'Death Café. Perhaps Basil could join you, seeing as his days are numbered.'

'They are not. He's very healthy.' Now Kitty folds her arms. 'And very well fed.'

'Basil?' asks Eloise.

Before I can answer, Prudence makes her entrance, which is the only way you can describe the arrival of our superbly stylish favourite goth. Today she is wearing a mauve bowler hat, of which I am instantly envious, a matching waistcoat and blouse, black frilled skirt, cobwebbed leggings and thick-soled dockers. The mourning for her old life as Deirdre is clearly complete. She also has a long black leather tube swinging on straps from one shoulder.

My imagination immediately assumes that it contains a polished brass telescope.

'Welcome, grab a seat. Lady Grey?'

Prudence settles into the comfy chair and hands Eloise a tea sachet.

'Can I join you?' I ask Eloise, taking the teabag.

'Of course you can. It would be good for you to know more in case I can't make the meeting.'

'Why wouldn't you be able to make the meeting?' I ask in sudden alarm, passing the teabag to Kitty, who is already filling the kettle.

'I don't know.' Eloise shrugs. 'What if I was dead?'

'Don't joke about stuff like that.' I grab another folding chair from behind the Tardis door; it really is bigger on the inside.

'Humour helps some people deal with what can be the frightening prospect of death.' Prudence flattens her skirt with black-fingernailed hands.

I know all about dark humour — it was one of the ways of coping in the police. I distinctly remember one Christmas Eve, sitting in the police canteen after delivering a death message to a woman whose husband had been killed in an accident. It was all pretty traumatic and one of my colleagues could tell I was in danger of sinking into a dark place. He shoved a slice of sausage into his mouth and said, 'I hope she kept the receipts.' I looked up, confused, and he continued. 'For the Christmas presents she bought him. She'll be able to take them back, won't she?' There were several sharp intakes of breath around the table, followed by grins and banter. To an outsider it would seem totally inappropriate but I know that it was his breaking the spell of gloom by making light of it that got me through the rest of the shift.

'So, we're all good to host the first Death Café here next week,' says Eloise. 'And I happen to know someone in the final stage of their cancer journey who's prepared to talk about his experience. What do you think?'

'How exciting!' Prudence claps her gloved hands together, jingling the silver jewellery around her wrists. Her heavily kohled eyes widen.

'I'm glad you think so. I was worried that it might be too much for the first meeting.' Eloise looks down at the floor. 'But there's a good chance he won't make another one.'

'No, this is what Death Café is all about,' says Prudence. 'We shouldn't be scared of death. The more we discuss it, the more we normalise it. After all, it's not something any of us can avoid.'

'Well, I'm immortal so far,' I say.

'Not helping, Garth.' Eloise gives me a hard stare. It's the second one I've received this morning and is considerably more threatening than Kitty's earlier attempt.

I sit back in my chair, fighting the urge to say, 'If looks could kill . . .'

'I'll bring home baking if you can provide the drinks.' Prudence's attention is on Eloise and it's clear that I have been relegated to the position of observer for the rest of the meeting.

'Tea, coffee and juice,' Eloise nods. 'The only thing now is how to advertise it.'

Prudence unzips the top of the leather tube, which I'm disappointed to discover does not contain a brass telescope.

'I've created a poster.' She unfurls a roll of paper and immediately my disappointment turns to amazement. The poster is a work of gothic beauty. Beneath the words Death Café is a china teacup subtly embellished with skeletons. On the cup's rim perches a crow, behind which the steam from the tea forms a skull. A slice of black-iced cake with a silver fork stuck in it like a grave-digger's spade lies on a plate next to the cup. Underneath it all is the tagline 'Tea and Cake and Death'.

'Oh, that's wonderful,' says Eloise.

A flicker of a smile twists Prudence's purple lips. 'I'll send you a digital version so you can add date and time details.'

Eloise stares at the poster for a moment longer. 'That would make a wonderful tattoo.'

'We could get matching ones the next time Marama is back in town with the circus,' says Prudence.

'I'd love to, but I think I'm busy that day,' I chip in, with an involuntary shiver.

'Prudence knows you're too much of a wuss.' Eloise leans back in her chair.

'Such a shame,' says Prudence. 'Tattoos may decorate the body, but they enhance the soul.'

'My black wizened soul is beyond enhancing. The great Cthulhu will have to feast on it as it is.'

CHAPTER 8

Eloise: 30 days until Battle of the Book Clubs

'It is my pleasure to introduce our guest speakers, Eloise and Garth Sherlock from Sherlock Tomes. Please give them a warm Waiapu Lunch Club welcome!'

We're back at the Function Centre, this time with a group of former businesspeople whose scheduled speaker (a retired surgeon who makes porcelain dolls) pulled out at the last minute. Sexist Jim from Grey Folk informed much nicer Roger from Waiapu Lunch Club that Garth had a presentation prepared so could probably hop in.

Roger was so sweet on the phone that I fell for it and said yes. He's a reserved, well-mannered chap with the shambling gait of the chronically arthritic. I looked him up and discovered that Roger Baker was once a human rights lawyer who acted in a number of right-to-die cases. I make a mental note to suggest him to Prudence as a Death Café speaker.

We've done a bit of tinkering with the presentation content, as Roger was keen for us to address concerns voiced by the group that young people don't read books anymore. Knowing there was a huge amount of anecdotal evidence to the contrary, I decided to throw myself into a bit of research as a distraction from obsessing over Pinter while I was waiting to hear back from Paula about John the Twat. It's done me good to get riled up about something else.

It looks as though there may be some baking roster overlap between the lunch club and Grey Folk, judging by the familiar culinary concoctions on display. There's an otherwise delicious-looking carrot cake adorned with what appear to be frosted mushrooms. As Roger finishes his introduction there is a feeble tinkling of applause and the collective gaze of about seventy septuagenarians swings our way. They're solemn, focused, possibly suspicious of pink hair and tattoos when they'd been looking forward to a serious sawbones and his puppet collection. Right in the middle of the bunch I notice a white-haired woman in a huge blue mohair cardigan, cake plate abandoned on the table in front of her. She's staring at me with an intense frown — whether of concentration, consternation or constipation I can't tell. She's quite striking, haughty gaze and angular cheekbones, and I vaguely recognise her. I'm sure I've seen her at literary events around the Bay and I think she might even be on a Battle of the Book Clubs quiz team.

'Thank you for that warm welcome,' I begin, 'and may I compliment the baker of the caramel slice. The coriander — is it? — is such an interesting flavour addition.' Garth, regulation white cup lowering from his mouth, snorts a bit of coffee through his nose. He pulls out his hankie and turns his back to me.

'We're going to reassure you on a few points today. Books are not dead, children still read, and we're not in competition with the library.'

Heads nod like a field of daisies in a breeze, apart from the fuzzy-cardiganed wolfsbane right in the middle, whose frown has deepened. I throw a smile in her direction, hoping to reassure her. She appears to be studying me rather ferociously and it's becoming unnerving. I'm just about to address her directly when I see her face relax and am heartened enough to glance down at my notes, scanning for the joke I'd prepared earlier — something about home baking and *Reader's Digest*.

I look up, draw breath and catch Ms Mohair's gaze just as her eyes roll back in her head and she slumps onto the man seated next to her. It's a gentle collapse and her human cushion is nonplussed, his face a picture of benevolent bafflement as he tries to understand why he's suddenly become a literal support person.

There are murmurs as the polite hive of lunchers around the beleaguered woman try to figure out an appropriate response. They're loath to interrupt our presentation but look desperately uncomfortable. The gent on whom Ms Mohair is leaning is awkwardly extracting the arm that's trapped beneath her, while patting her face with his other hand. A mild commotion builds.

'Ah . . . umm . . .' I look to our host for guidance but he hasn't yet spotted the muted kerfuffle and is smiling encouragingly at me. Garth, hearing my hesitation, wanders over to stand at my side, his gaze following mine.

'Oh no, it's not another vommer, is it?'

His hand covers his mouth as if to prevent an expulsion and suddenly there's a larger kerfuffle as a robust form strides through the crowd. It's Dr Mabel, who is clearly on the district lunch circuit.

'We're cursed,' says Garth, his eyes, along with those of the rest of the room, fixed on my blue-cardied friend as she is gently lowered to the floor and into the recovery position. She must have been feeling quite unwell, hence the rapacious glaring. I decide not to take it personally.

Roger finally twigs and launches into action, tottering over at full arthritic pelt.

'Mr and Mrs Sherlock, I'm awfully sorry to put you out like this but it would seem our meeting has been disrupted. I really must attend to Miss Mooney.'

We offer condolences and shuffle out of his way.

Back at the shop we relate the latest drama, then sit in contemplative silence, sipping extra-strong coffee to combat the lingering aftertaste of coriander caramel.

'And sure she just keeled over?' Phyllis is scanning books into the stock computer. Kitty is applying herself to the emails, not as invested in our latest trauma as Phyllis; Team Tomes don't know Miss Mooney very well and it wasn't as messy a scene as poor Lily's ordeal so she's happy to continue working with one ear on the conversation.

'Doesn't it seem odd to you?' asks Garth.

'What?'

'Two meetings, two collapses, and both quiz team members.'

'I felt like collapsing after that caramel slice. And did you see the mushroom and carrot cake? When people's eyesight is fading, you've got to be careful about asking them to bring a plate. Matty said as much at the Grey Folk meeting when he warned me off eating that brownie.' My lips curl and my tongue sticks to the roof of my mouth.

'Nope. One's an accident, two's starting to smell fishy. Do you think someone's targeting us?'

'That's a bit of a stretch,' I reply. 'Who would want to ruin our presentations? We're not that boring.'

Phyllis stops scanning and joins us, leaning against the magazine shelf, clearly concerned about where Garth is going with this. She ended up playing a pivotal role in the Franklin White affair, taking him down in the grand finale of a missing persons inquiry that turned into a murder.

'Garth, love,' I say, 'two old ladies have fallen ill. They do that. There's probably a bug going around. Those lunch club types all seem to hang about together, so it'll no doubt spread like wildfire.'

By the forehead crinkles and the tapping of his protruding lower lip I can tell Garth is not convinced. He's deep in a train of thought that will no doubt be aired in good time.

The trill of the shop's landline cuts through our cogitations.

'Sherlock Tomes, Kitty speaking.' I watch to see if it's for me and see Kitty's posture sag. 'One moment, she's right here.' She hands the phone to me, mouthing 'It's Roger Baker'.

I take the phone and Garth straightens, his focus pulled from internal musings as he tries to figure out what lovely, kind, not-sexist Roger is telling me. As I end the call, three pairs of concerned eyes are on me. I swallow as I prepare to impart Roger's news. Garth might be right after all.

'Miss Mooney is dead.'

CHAPTER 9

Garth: 30 days until Battle of the Book Clubs

We have sought solace at the Shamrock, which is somewhat of an anomaly in Havelock North. Built to look like a 'traditional' Irish pub, it has mock-Tudor walls interspersed with cobblestones, bottle-glass bay windows and a slate roof. Inside, the faux-beam ceiling, abundance of woodwork and myriad eclectic 'Irish' knick-knacks lend to the uncanny-valley feeling of it all being not quite right, although Phyllis, who is our barometer of all things Irish, quite likes it and says it's a lot fecking better than the fecking paddy-whackery you get in some places.

The pub also boasts a long, polished bar with an impressive number of beer taps including well-known and not so well-known English ales, one of which is Boddingtons. I'm not a big drinker, generally leaving Eloise to do the heavy lifting in that department, and on the occasions that I do drink I normally prefer the blandest lager available. However, once in a beer moon I get a genuine thirst for a taste of my old country, and when this strange longing occurs it seems that a pint of Boddys is the only thing that will quench my yearning. Today is one of those rare occasions, and the main reason I suggested that Tama meet us here.

I carry a pint of the golden nectar of the Mancunian gods and a pint of Guinness to a table in a curved window alcove. Aligning the glasses perfect centre of the beer mats, I settle myself on the cushion bench seat next to Eloise. Today she has excelled herself in the hideous trouser department with dungarees that bear the orange flock-wallpaper pattern of a down-market, 1970s Indian restaurant.

'Cheers.' We clink glasses and both take a moment to enjoy our respective poisons.

The smooth, malty Boddingtons isn't quite the same as the cream of Manchester served in English pubs but it's close enough to take me back to the reckless drunkenness of my youth. The bitter scent of cigarette smoke, stale beer and cheap cologne fills my consciousness, and I drink deeply of the beer and memories, savouring the heady days of innocence, before the military, before the police, before Pinter.

Thoughts of the serial killer ruin my revelry and I return the glass to the beer mat before instinctively scanning the pub for danger. It's reasonably quiet, 3pm being too late for the lunch crowd and too early for the after-work drinkers. There's an elderly couple in another window alcove with a bottle of Monastery Estate merlot. I recognise them from the shop; they tend to read at the heavier end of the spectrum, always buying the latest Bridget Williams Books, and anything by Noam Chomsky or Alain De Botton.

Across the room are a couple of suited business types, laptops open, papers strewn across the table, then at the bar there's a blonde-bobbed woman in stretch jeans, low-cut blouse and a fedora. At her cowboy-booted feet is a bag from Le Studio du Nord, one of

Havelock North's many beauty salons. She nurses a gin and tonic while flirting with the barman, who is young enough to be her grandson.

The brass-handled double doors swing open and in strides Tama. He spots us and smiles. Eloise jumps up to greet him. 'What are you having?'

'I'm on duty so I really shouldn't,' he says without conviction.

'Like that would be the worst of your misdemeanours.' Eloise raises her eyebrows.

Tama scans the beer taps. 'All right, you've twisted my arm. I'll go a Tui.'

While Eloise orders and pays, Tama lowers onto a chair opposite me. 'So, Garth, are you and your better half causing more trouble?'

'And by trouble, you mean solving murders and missing persons cases that have been haunting you for years?'

'Do you have any idea how much paperwork you caused me last time?' Tama folds his arms across his middle-aged man-belly. He's trying to sound stern, like he's dressing down a junior detective, but the glint in his eye and his generous smile betray him.

'I do know, and that's precisely why I now own a bookshop.'

'Co-own.' Eloise places Tama's pint of Tui on the table and double parks a second Guinness alongside her half-empty glass. 'And there's actually a substantial amount of paperwork involved in running a bookshop, it's just that you leave it all to me.'

'Pretty much like when we were in the police then?' I pat Eloise on her ghastly-trousered leg.

'Yeah, pretty much.' She takes a long pull on her pint and wipes the back of her hand across her mouth. 'Let's not keep the detective inspector waiting then. Tell him your theory.'

Tama's head angles slightly, picking up on the inflection of doubt in Eloise's voice. I launch in before I start to second-guess myself.

'We've recently been guest speakers at two community groups where attendees were poisoned.'

'Fell ill,' Eloise corrects me. 'And this has made Garth suspicious.'

She's right of course. Without toxicology reports we don't officially know that they were poisoned, or that it was deliberate, but saying that a couple of old people have fallen ill is hardly going to pique Tama's interest.

'Suspicious of what?' Tama chases a drip down his glass with a finger.

'Foul play,' I say. From the corner of my eye I clock Eloise wincing, and rightly so. I realise I sound like someone in an Agatha Christie novel.

'Any evidence?' Tama pushes back his broad shoulders and raises his chin. 'You know, the stuff that the police actually need in real life, rather than gut feelings and the type of hunches you get in a pulp detective novel.'

'Because you've never done anything on gut feeling or followed a hunch.'

'It's not like the old days. We have to be accountable. These days, hunches get you nothing but trouble.'

Eloise finishes her pint and returns it to the table a little more sharply than necessary. 'Or they get you whiplash and solve a decades-old murder case.'

Again, a wide smile splits Tama's face. 'You know that you can only play the "I solved a murder" card so many times.'

'Unless you solve another one,' I say.

Tama's expression changes. 'People have died?'

'One did.' My fingers splay across the table's woodwork, pointing at Tama. 'That's why we need you to dig a little bit deeper, not let it be written off as natural causes just because they're elderly.'

'The victim was old?'

'It doesn't mean they were unwell before being poisoned.' I'm having to fight my corner harder than I'd hoped. 'Two meetings, two victims, that's more than coincidence, surely.'

'Sounds thin.' Tama swigs his Tui.

'Fair enough. It is thin, but nobody thought Belinda Henare's death was suspicious until a book from a serial killer rocked up in her letterbox a year later.'

Tama's dark eyes focus on me. 'I'm still looking,' he says, 'but so far there's no actual evidence that Belinda's death was not from natural causes. She'd been having chest pains, then her heart gave out.'

'The book from Pinter!' My right hand clenches into a fist.

'Circumstantial at best.'

'Pinter sent that book, and Pinter is somehow connected with these poisonings.' I know it's a hunch but I'm convinced. We're living on the other side of the world and yet here he is in our faces again. The book is no coincidence.

Eloise squeezes my leg in warning. I don't often lose my temper but when I do it's not pretty and she doesn't want me to alienate Tama.

'I'm not saying he's not connected.' Tama leans forward, his face hardening. 'But you're letting your imagination and your fear run away with you. Finding patterns where there are none. There's nothing that links Pinter to these other incidents, which may be nothing more than old people stuff.'

I swirl the dregs around my glass, then down them. '*We* link him.'

'Is that a confession?' Tama laughs. 'Should I caution you now?'

'I'm not convinced either,' says Eloise, 'but would it hurt to have a look, just to rule out' — she make air quotes — 'foul play?'

Tama's expression softens. 'I'll do what I can without making anything official.'

'Thanks,' says Eloise. 'If both turn out to be accidental mushroom or coriander poisoning then we can relax.'

'Mushroom poisoning?' Tama's eyebrows rise and there's something in his expression that I can't place.

'We know the first victim consumed mushrooms for breakfast and the second was eating mushroom and carrot cake at the time, though no one else at the meeting appears to have fallen ill,' says Eloise.

'They probably peeled the mushrooms off,' I say. 'I mean, who the hell puts mushrooms on carrot cake?'

Tama drums his fingers on the table, his expression still unreadable. He's about to speak, then thinks better of it, finishing his pint instead.

Eloise must spot his unease too. 'We're all friends here, Tama, what is it?'

'There's a case . . .'

'At incident room 39?' I lean closer.

Tama nods. 'There was no crime recorded but the death never sat right with me. It involved mushroom poisoning.'

'And you want us to look at it?' asks Eloise.

Tama looks skywards, his head giving the tiniest of shakes. 'Lord, don't make me regret this.'

'You won't,' I say reassuringly.

'The thing is, like Belinda Henare, the victim was a writer.'

CHAPTER 10

Eloise: 27 days until Battle of the Book Clubs

There's a rustling and a fidgeting and an expectant hush as a disparate group of people try to contain their anticipation. It's the first meeting of Death Café and there's a great turnout — a tight circle of folding chairs crammed with bums of all shapes and sizes, clad in nylon, cotton, a bit of Lycra and, yes, one pair of leather trousers.

We're in the open area at the back of the shop. We've managed to fit twelve chairs in a circle, and all but one are filled. It's a bit stuffy with this many bodies so I've put the air con on a low, cool hum. Someone's perfume is making my eyes water; it's thickly applied Charlie rather than a subtle dab of Chanel No. 5 and I can feel it scraping the back of my throat. I'm hoping the air con will diffuse it.

The Admiral is here, having stated that it can't be long before he is called 'to go west'. He's impeccably attired for the evening, the shirt beneath his jacket flirting its military creases when he shifts in his seat. He's remarkably quiet too, deferential in the face of eternal rest.

Phyllis pours the tea from a whopping great institutional stainless-steel teapot she's borrowed from the church down the road (the new vicar has an auntie in Dún Laoghaire), and polite murmurings accompany the clinking of spoons and the sloshing of milk. Although it's a circle, Prudence is clearly at its imaginary head, her serene stillness asserting command, reassuring those who glance at her. I pass her a cup of tea, gumboot rather than her customary Lady Grey. No favourites tonight.

'Ready to rock, Pru?'

Assorted and aforementioned bums settle themselves and faces turn to Prudence.

'Welcome,' she says. It's a warm purr and her feline smile elicits shy ones in return.

'Thank you for coming to this first meeting of the Sherlock Tomes Death Café. My name is Prudence and I'm a writer with a healthy fascination with life and death.' A ruddy-cheeked man in his forties says a robust 'Excellent!' and is rewarded with a gaze from Prudence's startlingly blue eyes.

'Eloise and I are keen for you to feel safe and comfortable, so we should perhaps outline a few ground rules before we begin.'

There are nods and shuffles, a couple of nervous frowns.

'We'd like to be able to talk about all manner of things, respectfully and gently, and to support each other through the sharing of our stories. Sometimes this might be a bit much for some people. If you feel overwhelmed at any stage, please feel free to go and sit in the children's area for as long as you need. There are some lovely books in there and a comfy beanbag.'

More nods, and murmurings of 'That's a good idea' and 'Ah, good'.

'For this first meeting, we thought we'd open it up for people to talk about whatever they would like to. We'll just have a chat, and perhaps talk later about how we'd like future meetings to proceed. Who would like to start?'

There is the shy susurration of a congregation in which no one wants to go first: tea slurping, a couple of cleared throats and a few of those 'hmm' noises people make when a silence needs filling. After a respectable but not painful interval I decide to open things up, as Prudence and I agreed in our pre-match warm-up.

'I'll kick us off then, team.' I look around and there's relief that someone has bitten the bullet. 'Garth and I have been thinking a lot about death recently. Some of you will be aware that we were very recently involved in the . . . err . . . unveiling of the long-lost artist Oddbean from his concrete grave.'

'Oh god, yeah. That was a shock. What a story,' says the owner of the leather trousers, a woman with bright orange curly hair and a shirt with skeletons on it. Most people mutter in agreement but there are one or two 'whats?' from those who have been living under a rock.

'I can elaborate on that later for those of you who need an update,' I say. 'Also, Garth and I have been invited to speak to a few lunch clubs and meetings, and I know their demographic is on the older side but we've had a strange run of it. A woman was taken very ill and hospitalised at one meeting, and at another someone died, pretty much in front of us.'

The hive voice hums with 'gosh', 'good Lord' and 'that must have been so upsetting!' Earnest faces checking others' reactions, getting the measure of the mood.

'No no, we're fine,' I reassure them. 'But it's a reminder that death is just sitting there the whole time, waiting.' Ms Leather-Trews reaches across to pat my knee. The action is entirely kind and natural, and seems to lighten something. There are gentle looks and smiles. Some kind of bonding is occurring.

'How awful for you, Eloise. Did you find out what caused the death?' It's Beth from book club, beautifully turned out as ever, even in a moonboot, blonde-to-grey hair freshly washed and pressed. I can't help but notice that her nail polish (fingers and toes) matches her blue linen dress. The single gold sandal is a nice touch. How does she always manage to be so immaculate? I wonder, before anchoring myself on her question.

'Not really, Beth, no. There's talk that a bug might be hitting the seniors but no one really knows.' There are more hmms and nods.

I leave a pause in the hope that someone else might open up and sure enough, after a few seconds, the ruddy-faced man sits forward.

'May I throw us in at the deep end?' His voice is husky and he clears his throat once, then again. Prudence inclines her head regally.

'My name is Reagan and I've got, well, about six weeks to live if I'm lucky.' Even though I knew this, it's still like being scythed in the face. I feel myself wince, some people freeze, the Admiral salutes and Ms Leather-Trews says, 'Shit, mate, I'm so sorry to hear that.' Reagan smiles in acknowledgement.

'I'm pretty used to the idea now. It's cancer,' he pats his chest, 'and I've been told about three times that I've only got months. I've been all like "nah, it won't get me", but this time feels pretty real. I'm getting quite crook, what with the meds and everything.' Reagan pauses to cough into his elbow. The ruddy skin of his face is puffy; he looks sore when he moves.

'Chrissy from Mighty Oaks told me you guys were having this event and I thought I should come along. Keep it real for ya.' He forms a sideways grin, looking at Prudence from under dark lashes. There's mischief written all over him and his openness is having an effect on the café crew.

'Reagan, this is incredibly brave of you. What do you think people should know about dying?' Pru gets straight to it. There's a shift in the room, a collective intent listening.

'It's not bravery if you have no choice.' Reagan coughs out a laugh, inviting us to relax with him. He pauses, thinks. 'The main thing is the acceptance I feel. My wife and daughter — she's just about to hit her teens — have been with me every step of the way and of course they're not ready for me to die, to actually leave them, but we've had time to hang out, work through things.'

He seems so calm as he sets to answering questions. We find out that his daughter Eva is twelve; his wife Anna is his rock; and that with a death sentence hanging over you, you soon find out who your friends are.

'Probably the best thing is that you can say and do what you like and you won't live to face the consequences. That's pretty awesome.' There's an evilly gleeful look on Reagan's face that makes me smile. I bet Anna has her work cut out.

'So when you say you find out who your friends are . . .' I prompt.

'Yeah, some people have found out exactly what I think of them, and about time too.' His face is the shining sun; the joy in this extremely unwell man is infectious. A sense of frivolity has broken out and as people chat, the Admiral booms and Beth takes Reagan's hand, I decide it's a good time to unpackage whatever marvels are in the exquisitely ribboned cake box Prudence brought along. I lift it carefully from the coffee table that Garth made in the shape of a book and offer it to Phyllis, who pulls the ribbon and lifts the lid to reveal individual fondant headstones, the iced black writing spelling out 'Life is Sweet'. There's a collective 'Ooooh!' and Prudence accepts it with a gracious nod.

I maunder about with plates and napkins, getting in the way of conversations and picking up snippets. Beth and Reagan are deep in discussion.

'I can go to some very dark places,' he's saying, no hint of the cheek he's had on him all evening. I fluff about nearby, eavesdropping.

'That's the thing about writing. You can put the worst of yourself in there, write about things that society wouldn't let you do.'

'Or that you wouldn't really want to do in real life,' prods Beth.

'Yeah.' Reagan nods slowly. ''Course.'

I turn to Reagan with an 'I haven't been listening in at all' innocence.

'Headstone cake for you, sir?'

He grins and accepts.

Beth declines with a wave of her manicured mitts. 'Oh, Eloise!' she suddenly exclaims. 'How's the prep for Battle of the Book Clubs coming along?'

Oh, here we go. I'm about to be quizzed on the quiz.

'I read something about Dame Fiona Kidman going to Ireland to receive a literary award in a couple of weeks. Isn't she supposed to be the guest author?'

How the bloody hell Beth knows this closely guarded secret is anyone's guess. Anyway, it's no secret now. I give up trying to keep things quiet around this place.

'Ah, yes, she was, but the awards ceremony clashes with the Battle date, as you say. We're still working on a replacement.' I rest the cake box on the coffee table and perch on the seat next to her. 'Planning is not going as smoothly as in previous years, if I'm honest.' It feels good to say this out loud. I'm really stressed about it and that must be written all over my face as Beth leans in and takes my hands.

'Well now, what can we do to help?' Reagan's attention drifts and he turns to Phyllis to exclaim over the cake. I look back to Beth, her eyes full of concern.

'Know any world-famous authors lurking around the Bay who would be willing to turn up to a charity quiz night for no pay but eternal gratitude?'

Beth chuckles, reaching down to adjust her moonboot beneath

the table. Then she straightens up suddenly. 'Oh! Actually, I just might. I heard that Faith Saxon was back in town.' She looks at me, keen to alleviate my worry. 'What about her? She'd knock 'em dead.'

CHAPTER 11

Garth: 27 days until Battle of the Book Clubs

The twenty-sided dice clatters across the table, coming to a rest next to the miniature figurine of a robed skeletal priest.

'Get in!' I shout, punching my fist in the air. It's Dungeons and Dragons night and the twenty on the dice means I have just scored a critical hit. Or, to put it in game terms, my cerebrally challenged dwarven warrior, Dunkin Daeghnut, is about to remove the priest's head with a rather large axe.

'Noice,' says Sim, whose gnome bard, Pan, was in imminent danger of being turned to death dust by the priest. He raises his tankard of ale to me in a sign of thanks.

We're in The Uncommon Room, a favourite bar of mine, which is closed to the public on a Monday and open to us, as the manager, Gordon, is also our Games Master.

Our game table, with maps, miniatures and GM's screen, is set up on a stage normally used by performing bands. Long, scarlet velvet drapes behind us add to the ambience created by the muralled walls, abundance of fairy lights and eclectic decorations that include a cluster of giant glowing mushrooms hanging from the ceiling.

'The skeletal priest explodes, bones scattering across the rune-tiled floor.' Gordon rolls a handful of dice, which rattle like the remnants of the priest.

'That was a lot of dice,' says Noah, who plays Skunkz, a permanently stoned half-orc druid.

'Never a good sign,' says Nelly, who has somehow managed to keep her accident-prone Elven Ranger, Lori, alive for six months of game sessions, which is a record for her.

I sit back in my chair and clasp my hands together, as if in prayer. 'It could be to calculate how much treasure we're about to acquire.'

Gordon emits a small laugh at my optimistic suggestion, then says in a deep, menacing voice, 'I am the Scroll Lord and demand sacrifice for your sins.'

'Or maybe not,' I say.

'Da Scroll Lord. He bad Juju,' says Noah, not breaking character. 'Feasted on many-nuff souls bifuor di Blue Paladins imprison him.'

'Och, nae bother. Books and scrolls are rubbish,' I say. 'How dangerous can he be?'

'Well, let's find out.' Gordon's eyes fill with mischief. 'Each roll a D20. You don't want to be the lowest.'

Nelly folds her arms and leans back. 'That's not fair.'

'Everyone has the same chance,' says Sim, a broad grin emerging from within his close-cropped beard.

'Except you all know my dice are cursed.' Nelly's gaze drops to my walnut dice box.

I edge the box further away. 'It's not so much the dice that are cursed as you.'

'There's no such thing as curses.' Noah shakes his head. 'They're a psychological illusion. Because you believe you are cursed, you fixate on the bad rolls and forget the good ones.'

'So I can borrow your dice?' Nelly asks him.

'Absolutely not.' Noah clutches his dice bag to his chest.

We all roll except Nelly, who is sifting through her dice trying to find one that she hopes will behave. I get a ten, Noah a seventeen and Sim really lucks out with a two.

'See?' Gordon points at Sim's dice. 'It looks like Pan is going to suffer the horrible consequences of Dunkin's actions.'

Nelly blows on her D20. 'Come on, dice, just this once don't fail me.' She rolls it across the table and almost as if in slow motion it comes to a rest showing a one. Nelly shakes her head in disbelief. 'Fuck my life!'

'Saved my life.' Sim leans back twiddling his fingers, relief on his face.

I love my D&D. It's a chance to escape, a chance to be a hero, or a villain, a chance to live a different life, a bit like escaping into a novel. Only tonight something feels different, almost a little sinister. Maybe it's just the menacing shadow of Pinter, but I can't shake the sensation of portent. Unfinished business.

Gordon inhales deeply on a vape and then blows 'smoke' over the map and miniatures. 'From nowhere rises a chill fog, enveloping you in its icy grip. Your vision blurs with the unnatural cold, your eyeballs feel like they're freezing. Then, as quickly as it appears, the fog vanishes and warmth returns. As your sight recovers, you see that Lori is gone.'

'Gone somewhere nice, like the local tavern?' suggests Nelly.

'Gone to the secret lair of the Scroll Lord,' says Gordon. 'The smell of death seeps from every stone of this small hidden chamber. Ahead of you, sitting on a throne of skulls, is a red-robed Lich. You struggle against the chains that bind you to a sacrificial altar.'

'Err, guys, a little help here,' says Nelly.

'Skunkz lights up,' says Noah.

Nelly's eyebrows lift. 'I'm in deathly trouble and you're getting blazed?'

'Mi tinks dis is a three-doobie problem,' answers Noah.

'The Scroll Lord's eyes glow a fiendish yellow, sulphurous smoke trails emanating from them,' says Gordon. 'With a pot of ink in one hand and a razor-sharp quill in the other he advances. Prepare to have your fate inscribed.'

My heart thunders and blood roars through my ears as I'm transported back to the worst night of my life. Rain drizzles, elongated drops catching in the flickering glow of a streetlight pressed hard against the dirty brick of a railway arch. A train rumbles overhead as PC Griffith, my partner on this unofficial jaunt, pulls a set of bolt croppers and a crowbar from our car. It'll be an illegal search of the lock-up beneath the arch but that's the least of this evening's sins. My knuckles are bloodied and bruised from the none-too-procedural interrogation of a tattoo artist whose information has led us to these graffiti-ridden doors.

I'm clutching at straws and I know it. How can a lowly constable hope to succeed where CID and the regional crime squad have failed? The whole force is looking for PC Eloise Sherlock. Me, I'm looking for my wife, and hope is all I have.

Griff brandishes a Maglite while I slice as stealthily as I can through the padlock on the door. The shackle gives and Griff catches the tumbling parts before they hit the puddle-slicked tarmac. Drawing my own Maglite, I swap the bolt croppers for the crowbar and nod to Griff. He waits for just a moment, giving me a chance to reconsider. We should have the firearms unit, the tactical team, evidence gatherers, a cordon and legal authority, not just the thinnest of hunches and a willingness to do whatever it takes.

Griff heaves the door open and I rush inside. The powerful beam of my torch sweeps around like a searchlight, illuminating oil drums, crates and a canvas-covered mound straight from a horror film. Table height, the body-shaped lump beneath the oily blue material makes me want to retch.

'Wait outside.' Griff grips my arm. 'I'll do it.'

'No,' I say, reaching for the canvas. 'This is on me.'

Hand trembling, stomach roiling, I pull the sheet back.

'Fuck!' Staring up at me from the tattooist's table is a bald mannequin with a message inked across its forehead:

My Eloise
I'd love to please her, I'd love to care
But she's not there

Gordon claps his hands together, jolting me from my nightmare. 'And that's where we'll end for tonight.'

'You can't leave me hanging like that for a week!' complains Nelly.

'It's going to be more than a week.' Gordon folds down the GM screen and packs away his papers. 'The bar's being refurbished and it's going to be unavailable for a while.'

'Can't we find somewhere else?' Sim looks morosely at his empty tankard. For many players of D&D it's more than a game; it's therapy.

'I've been trying to find another venue, but at the moment I've got nothing.' Gordon holds out his hands in apology.

I consider offering to host — our front room is easily big enough — only with Battle of the Book Clubs looming and Pinter in our heads I don't think we have the mental space. So instead, I say, 'I guess I'll see you all when I see you.'

CHAPTER 12

Eloise: 26 days until Battle of the Book Clubs

I feel like I'm on holiday in Hastings. It's early, cold in the shade with the promise of warmth from the weak sun seeping into the carved flagstones on Heretaunga Street. There's that spring smell in the air, nose-tingling and wholesome.

I'm seated at the window bench of a café, ostensibly looking at the man in the Italian restaurant opposite shaping a long, wide sheet of egg-yolk-yellow pasta. That's fascinating enough, but what I'm trying *not* to do is far more interesting: there are a couple of Rentokil guys in hi-vis sitting at a table outside. One is filling out a workbook and the younger one has his back to me and is texting, so close on the other side of the window that I can see his screen as clearly as if it were mine. He's trying to wriggle out of a date by the looks of it; there's a lot of 'nah', 'tired' and 'maybe'.

The blokes get up and move tables and I panic that I've been caught snooping until I see another couple of crew members join them — maybe they just needed a bigger table.

A diminutive figure quicksteps across the road from the direction of The Uncommon Room, surely not open at this time of the morning but you never know. A big wave and a smile and some gesticulating that I can't quite fathom, then a burst of cool air and he appears beside me.

'There's a budgie! It's far too cold for a budgie.'

I wait for further information. Matty Trindle, the tiny but larger-than-life author of travel memoirs and owner of a ruined Hermès scarf is my date for the morning. I'm hoping to pick his brains about Faith Saxon but it looks as if my agenda may be derailed by a bird.

Matty wordlessly dumps bag (grey), scarf (grey wool) and Baker Boy cap (grey corduroy) under the bench seat and approaches the counter.

'I need several tea towels and a small box,' he says to the barista in a tone that brooks no refusal.

Tea towels in hand, Matty heads for the sliding doors with an instruction for me to follow.

There is indeed a beautifully plumed budgie standing frozen by the rear wheel of a parked car. The confused bird is turquoise, with black and white patterning along its back like a mackerel sky.

'It's obviously escaped from someone's home. It'll never survive outside in this temperature. You go that side in case it makes a break for it.'

I move to the other side of the car and crouch down. The bird hops my way and I shoo it back towards Matty. As it emerges on his side he deftly pops a tea towel over it and gently scoops the lump of budgie into his hands. The barista, a beautifully tattooed, bearded and beanied chap, is obediently standing by with a small box.

'Call the SPCA and tell them we're coming in,' Matty says.

I do as I'm told because there appears to be no alternative. The young person on the other end of the phone seems nonplussed but, after checking with their supervisor, agrees we should come in.

There's some faffing about with cellotape and punching holes into the box. A small voice from within occasionally chirps something that sounds like 'Harold'.

'Grab my stuff, won't you, Eloise? We'll take your car.'

The Loan Ranger is pretty much next to the car Harold had been sheltering beside, so we're soon in, belted and off. The SPCA is about ten minutes away, so I'll try to pump Matty for information as we head out of town along Railway Road. We hug the train tracks for a bit, Boys' High students tripping illegally across them, then hang a right into orchard territory. But first things first.

'How's Lily?'

Matty looks at me blankly as he momentarily manages to tear his focus away from Harold. 'Oh yes! Dear Lily. Yes, yes she's getting there. They're keeping her in hospital to monitor her kidney function. Did you know you can get chronic kidney disease from food poisoning?' He's not really paying me any attention, instead trying to peer through the holes in the box to check on his feathered charge. I cut to the chase — time is short and Matty is thoroughly distracted.

'So Dame Fiona can't come to Battle of the Book Clubs and someone suggested Faith Saxon instead.'

'He can't have come from too far away; he doesn't look like a particularly robust chap.'

'Ah. Yeah. I was wondering what you know about her?'

'I'm sure it's a he. He has a blue bit above his beak where the nose and nostrils are. The hens are more brown. He's a cock.'

'There are a lot of them about.' My mind flits through several contenders, Jim from Grey Folk front and centre.

'What?'

'Faith Saxon,' I persevere. 'What do you know about her?'

'Ah, Faith. She's a darling. I hosted the Bay Awards with her some years back. Wicked sense of humour, excellent repertoire of anecdotes and a wonderful storyteller. She'd make a very good speaker. And it's always good to have someone controversial.'

He side-eyes me with a smirk. He does love to stir. Harold warbles a bit, then settles into a plaintive croon.

'Do tell.'

'Well, as you know, I'm not one to gossip—'

'Ha!'

'—but oh, it must be about a decade ago, Faith was judging the finalists in an NZWA short story competition. What upset the apple cart was that one of the contenders was an unpublished author who Faith believed was guilty of plagiarism.'

Matty frowns, trying to extract the details from his memory. He looks down at the box, which has gone quiet.

'Are you all right in there, little darling?' he asks.

'Harold,' is the reply, somewhat forlorn.

'Who was the accused? Anyone we know?'

'No idea. I'd just got back from the UK. I wasn't in with the local writing clique and I hadn't joined the Writers' Association yet. Nothing was said officially or made public. Only the committee knew. The rumour was that the writer was just about to sign with an overseas publisher and lost the contract as a result of Faith's claim.'

'Ouch.'

'Oh yes. I mean, Faith did what she had to do, I suppose. I just hope she was right.'

We both consider the implications. Publishing contracts are like hen's teeth. Or cocks' teeth, if we're being gender inclusive.

'Anything else?'

'Don't think so. It was before my time on the board; I just heard whispers.'

I know Faith's pretty successful in the US, and is quite the publishing phenomenon in Europe. Several of her books have been featured on Oprah's Book Club and the latest was picked up by Reese's Book Club also. No doubt there'll be a film deal at some point, and good luck to her.

'So is Faith back in the country?' asks Matty, turning the snooping tables.

'That's what I've heard but I haven't contacted her yet, so keep it under your hat.' Matty makes a 'my lips are sealed' gesture.

The buds are breaking on the apple trees; shy whites and pinks flicker past, stretching towards the sun. We pull into the SPCA car park. I decide to wait in the car. If I go in, Stevie might well end up with a companion and I'm not sure how he or Garth would react to that.

Garth: *25 days until Battle of the Book Clubs*

The Loan Ranger grumbles over one of Havelock North's many speed bumps; for a vehicle that is designed to hurtle across paddocks and venture deep into offroad wilds, it seems unduly perturbed by these small man-made obstacles. There's probably some complex setting I could adjust to smooth out the ride but seeing as this is a loaner I can't be bothered to figure it out. To be honest, even if the vehicle was ours for keeps, in all probability I'd drive it until the day it died without understanding what most of the controls did.

Maybe, like me, our rugged all-terrain vehicle is simply troubled by the fact that the raised road has been cunningly paved to look like a pedestrian crossing while not actually being an official crossing, thereby confusing motorists, pedestrians and Loan Rangers alike.

We rumble past a row of upmarket boutiques, jewellers and art galleries that occupy a new many-storeyed development. My gaze is drawn to an exceptional landscape of the white cliffs of Cape

Kidnappers and a less exceptional canvas that looks like an explosion in a paint factory. *Stop being an old curmudgeon*, I hear Eloise say, even though it's just me and Stevie in the car.

We pass Bark Side of the Moon, which has a large sign informing us about a buy-one-get-one-free sale on bedding plants, and Stevie leans forward, snoof, snoof, snoofing in my ear.

'You're right, mate, we should get some,' I tell him. 'Not that you ever help in the garden.' Even though our cowardly canine is much less timid than he used to be in the shop and at the beach, he is still for some reason highly suspicious of our garden, only slinking out to park his Possychum when absolutely desperate.

I negotiate the St Georges Road roundabout and check the rear-view mirror, the voice of my police advanced driving instructor still sounding in my head after all these years: *check your mirror, see who's followed you off the hazard*. The instructor's name was Vince Quartermaine, although everyone called him Vince Quarterbrain because of his inexhaustible supply of trite sayings: *you can be right, and you can be* dead *right; more paint on the road — more danger on the road*; and my all-time least favourite, *when in town, windows down*, which, unlike the others, held no practical benefit as far as I could tell.

The Tomato had the worst all-round visibility of any vehicle I've ever driven, armoured personnel carriers included. The Loan Ranger is significantly better, with a sizeable rear window, and I do indeed see who's followed me off the hazard. It's a nondescript blue hatchback, the driver of which I think I recognise.

I glance at the road ahead, then check the mirror again and I now have no doubt that it's the fedora-wearing woman from the Shamrock. Coincidence? Possibly. Hastings and Havelock North are both reasonably small and you are forever bumping into people you know. Eloise and I actually play a game we call Supermarché Spies, where we try to get around the supermarket without anyone talking to us. We seldom succeed. And there was a period a few weeks ago when we ran into the mayor of Hastings on three separate occasions while walking Stevie up Te Mata Peak. Every time, she was deep in conversation on her phone, the shackles of office still binding her while she was trying to enjoy the solitude of the native forest.

Coincidence or no, my hackles go up; Stevie is blissfully unaware, his focus on a rather handsome chocolate labrador running after its owner on the cycleway.

Slowing to 50 kph as I enter Hastings city proper, I take a right, then a left, and check my mirror again. She's still behind me. It could be that I'm being paranoid, something that Eloise often accuses me of. On the other hand, you never know how many paranoid precautions have foiled nefarious plans precisely because the paranoia has paid off. Also, not so many weeks ago, I was kidnapped by one of the local gangs, the Black Dogs, and even though Fedora Fatale looks like the most unlikely gang member ever, that doesn't mean she's *not* up to dastardly deeds.

Waiting until I'm approaching a mini-roundabout, I signal left and pull over to the side of the road, pretending to answer my phone. She drives past, not even glancing at me, and continues straight on. I watch until her tail-lights have disappeared, then wend my way to the secure storage warehouse by a series of back streets.

Stevie harrumphs as the security gate slides shut behind the Loan Ranger, imprisoning us in the yard. 'You're right, mate, I probably was kicking the arse out of it. Don't tell Mum, okay?' He gazes woefully up at me as if he disapproves of being dragged into my conspiracy.

From the passenger footwell I retrieve a small offcut of two-by-four scavenged from our garage and slip it into my back pocket, then slide Stevie's lead over his head. 'Come on, we've got work to do.'

He settles low onto his haunches and for a moment it looks like he's going to refuse to leave the car. I open the door and step out. 'You can stay there on your own if you want,' I say, pretending I'm about to close the door.

Stevie creeps out, reluctantly following me through the security air-lock and into the main warehouse, where sensor-activated strip-lights flicker on at our approach. The illumination does nothing to abate the anxiety that tightens my chest. For no logical reason this whole place gives me the creeps. Adding to my unease, Stevie's long claws clack on the polished concrete floor, echoing like the talons of some bone-heavy creature from a horror movie.

We reach unit 39 and I have to drop the lead to haul up the roller door. The moment there's the smallest of Stevie-sized gaps, he squeezes underneath and disappears inside. I widen the gap to duck under and pull the door most of the way down again, before using the wooden block from my back pocket to stop it closing completely; another irrational fear of mine is that gravity will close the door, trapping me inside.

I flick on the lights. Stevie curls under a table, head resting on paws.

'We won't be here long, pup. Just got to find some files.'

Stevie looks up at being spoken to, harrumphs and drops his head back to his white-socked paws, as if he knows that I lie like a defendant's barrister.

Tama has the space set up like a police incident room. Neat stacks of papers from long-cold cases rest on the table that is Stevie's hiding place, a battered grey angle lamp peering over them. Behind the table, on a kitchen-like worktop, is the most important of police investigative resources: a kettle and the makings of tea and coffee.

Four grey filing cabinets lined against one wall house a trove of old unsolved cases that Tama periodically reviews in his own time. Details relating to his currently reactivated cases are pinned on incident boards mounted on the walls — photos, witness statements, phone records, banking details — all connected with string in a spiderweb of crime that draws my ex-copper's eye.

I drag my gaze away; none of them are the case I've been asked to look at. It is in a cabinet of what Tama calls the X-files. Cases that were 'solved' but didn't quite sit right, along with ones that were never investigated at all, no crime having been officially recorded.

The drawer pulls open with a metallic screech that causes Stevie to shuffle further under the table. I flick through the tabs atop the file hangers: *Fincham Suicide, Mulder Manslaughter, Richter Sewage Drowning, Trevit Death by Dangerous Dumpster Diving, Trotter Potter Rotter*. The last two appear less dog-eared than the others and I'm guessing that they are newer. Clearly by the time Tama came across these he'd become less 'official' in his naming procedures for these off-the-book cases.

Behind the *Trotter Potter Rotter* file, which appears to relate to a local artisan whose decomposing body was found locked in their pottery studio, I find the case I'm after, in a file labelled *Problematic Poisoning*.

I pull out the thin buff folder and place it on the table. Written neatly at the top of the folder is 'Kiri Wereta'.

CHAPTER 14

Eloise: 25 days until Battle of the Book Clubs

There's a tune running through my head as I walk up the hill past the girls' school and I can't quite pick its title from my grey matter. I can hear a brass section and the jaunty *tsk tsk* of a hi-hat. I decide to focus on matching the rhythm to my feet, enjoying the freedom to wander without being jerked around at the will of Stevie.

Amelia's on duty in the shop this afternoon and gave me the green light to bugger off home early since not much was going on. Only two little boxes of stock left to unpack, mostly children's picture flats.

I'm just at the trumpet equivalent of the jazz hands part when my phone tings.

Amelia: Surprise stock arrival lol!

There's a photo of a big box and I'm just turning around to head back to the shop when there's another ting.

> Amelia: Don't worry — it's the bulk order for book club. You know Librarianist is not a word, right?

There's a selfie of a curiously frowning bookseller, forefinger to lips, beside a stack of *The Librarianist* by Patrick deWitt, the title I've chosen for our next book club read. She's a constant source of social media fodder, our Amelia.

I let out a wee snort and continue my 360-degree spin to head back up the hill, stumbling a little into the dwarf flax of the roadside planting. I should know by now that I can't walk and look at my phone, never mind simultaneously perform a tricky turning manoeuvre.

The hi-hat dribbles through my neural pathways again and the tsking resumes, accompanied by some brightly tinkling piano plinks. There really is a lot going on in this tune. If only I could muster some lyrics, I'd know what it is.

Ting number three arrives as I'm cresting the hill up to the cemetery. It'll be Amelia again and it can wait until I'm home. The air is scented — freesias maybe, or the jasmine that insinuates itself into hedges, colonising with its sweet breath and promises of beauty.

A scrape of heels alerts me to a woman walking a Jack Russell, just coming out of the cemetery gates, glossily applied lipstick so vibrant I can identify the shade as Rouge Dior from across the road. This, paired with a rather fetching fedora in mink, makes her a striking figure. She looks at me, startles slightly, and makes a weird little Marilyn pout. Then she seems to recalculate her route, pulling Jack's lead right, down the hill and away from me.

Was that odd? Or just me creating nefariousness out of cemetery air? Maybe I'm envious of how put together she looks? I stop walking to attend to the ting, wryly snorting at my inability to let it wait. Then I see that it's not Amelia.

> Paula: What you doing? I have news. Can I call?

It's the wee hours of the morning in the UK. What is Paula doing up? It must be serious.

> Me: Ten minutes. I'll call you.

She replies immediately with a 'K'. I quicken my pace, puffing up the last bit of hill before our house, my musical interlude now drowned out by thoughts of Pinter, my body screaming 'Danger!' just at the thought of him, legs lurching, hands shaking.

My first attempt at getting the code in the front door's keypad fails, my hands sticky and out of control. The second try sees me swearing loudly, peripherally conscious of the neighbour retrieving dry washing from the line. I'm vaguely aware that she's calling a greeting as I boot the door, jabbing the keypad with a suppressed screech of *'Fuuuuuck!'* Dimly, I hear 'Are you . . . ?' before, upon the third try, I gain entry, slamming the door behind me.

I hoof upstairs, sweating, and head for what was once our spare bedroom and now serves as our incident room. I fumble with my rucksack and upend it on the bed, Garth in my ear telling me to 'be careful with the hardware, Eloise' as my laptop bounces out. I throw it open and am tapping to awaken it but the internet decides to take the slow road because bloody Garth has at least four fucking networks and the laptop can't decide whether today is the day for Sherlockery, Moriarty or Stevenburger. Finally it connects to Tonkawoo and I call Paula. Her big goofy face appears on the screen after a few blips and bleeps.

'That was quick.' She's rubbing her eyes, darker rings on dark skin.

'What is it? What's happened?'

'Oh, I see how it is. You only want me for info. I can't just call my mate for a catch-up.'

'In the middle of your night? What's going on?' She's not one to prevaricate. This must be really bad. Do I need to call Garth? Is he in danger? More importantly, is Stevie in danger?

'I've just got home after an absolute bastard of an interview with the scummiest bloke I've ever met, and that's saying something. Thought I might as well give you an update, seeing as it's a respectable time there. It's nothing desperate, so you can put your wig back on.'

Nothing desperate. If she was in the room I'd slap her. She starts to laugh, a high-pitched, scratchy *hee hee hee*, so I can only imagine what my face has been doing.

'What the hell, Paula?' I say, hand on my exploding chest, my lips curling in response to her mirth, a baby serotonin release helping me to see the funny side.

'Seriously, girl, you have to chill. I keep telling you — he's locked up. You're gonna do yourself a mischief.'

'Yeah, yeah, I know. You're right. So tell me the news. How are you anyway?'

'I'm ace, mate. Three stabbings and a shooting this week so far — living the dream. Anyway, Pinter's defo got a mobile phone. My man at Box 500 says he's in touch with someone in New Zealand but he can't trace the endpoint.'

I'm winded by this, my stomach contracting and lungs squeezing. It was bad enough when the package in Belinda Henare's mailbox waved its 'you've got mail' flag at us. This is confirmation that Pinter is communicating with someone on the ground. He's effectively in New Zealand, plotting and interfering by proxy. I inhale deeply and focus on Paula.

'Why can't he trace it?'

'No remit. He's sticking his neck out as it is, without causing an international incident.'

'Oh yeah, 'course.' There are a million things I want to know but in my wrung-out state I don't have the vocabulary to formulate the questions. Paula hasn't finished though.

'So he's chucked a packet sniffer on it.'

'What's that?'

'Bit technical for a bookseller, but it's a bit of kit that will intercept Pinter's messages and send them to me. Hopefully we'll gain enough info for you to figure out who he's messaging.'

This is a real breakthrough. I'm humbled that Paula has put so much into this, at not inconsiderable risk to herself and her old MI5 pal. More serotonin flushes through me, with maybe a bit of dopamine, and my eyes well up.

'You can stop that shit right now!' Paula's wheezy laugh turns into a phlegmy rattle and she's lost to a coughing fit. She fumbles around off screen, in a bag maybe or a pocket, and produces a cigarette. There's the rasp of lighter, a blue spark, and she inhales deeply, filling her lungs with a head-spinning mix of benzene, arsenic and formaldehyde, stuff that should only be inside you once you're dead. She exhales through her nose and I swear I can smell it.

'That's better.' She smiles.

I shake my head at her.

Paula blows smoke at the screen and I cough. We laugh, her exhaustion and my relief bringing out the kids in us.

'Anyway,' she goes on, 'so I've got a message for you. Makes no sense to me.'

I stop smiling abruptly. Pinter rivals perimenopause for inducing hormonal havoc. 'Go on.'

She taps a few keys, eyes switching focus from me to something else on her screen.

'Hang about. Here we go. From Pinter to the Kiwi phone: *It's been a while. I trust Mendelsund was as anticipated?* No reply as yet.'

Paula looks at me expectantly, smoke curling in front of her, its source off screen. My brain freezes, just stops. I try to push through but it's not freesia-scented Havelock North that greets me. I'm groggy, confused. The room is surgically lit. A man is laughing, derision saturating every note. Try as I might to ground myself in this room in my lovely home in New Zealand, my mind decides to play a game.

'Ah, PC Sherlock, I see you're back with us. How are you feeling? Describe it to me, if you can, without any of the purple prose you're so fond of.' The voice is smooth and soft, cajoling, at odds with the feeling of restraint at my ankles and wrists. A light shifts above me, focusing in somewhere below my neck. As the brightness leaves my face I try to open my eyes but the sedative in my system hasn't fully worn off.

I push my hands into whatever I'm lying on, to lever myself up, but I'm securely tied down on some kind of filmy material that sticks to me as I move, sucking and clinging. I'm exhausted, struggling to stay conscious, but . . . that voice. It spears my brain like an icicle and I realise the situation is bad.

'No words? A pity. Then we will begin.'

A low electronic hum starts up and a bespectacled, intelligent face leans across me. I recognise the noise, and the face . . . Pinter brandishes a tattoo gun.

'Eloise!'

Paula's voice reaches me and I jump.

'You've gone all weird. You okay? Can you hear me?'

'Yes. Yes, sorry, the screen must have frozen. What does that mean? What's Mendelsund?'

'How the fuck should I know?' Her voice is scratchy with smoke and fatigue. She yawns, covering her mouth with a cigarette-encumbered hand, ash dropping somewhere in her lap.

'Shit. Ouch! Shit.' She's flapping about, flicking sparky ash from her clothes, stubbing the offending article. She must be knackered, and here I am going weird on her. There's no imminent danger. I'm okay.

'Hey, my friend,' I rally. 'I so appreciate the update. Get yourself to bed. I'll figure this out and let you know.'

She smiles an exhausted, relieved smile.

'Yeah, okay, thanks. Speak soon. Bye.'

I barely manage a little wave before she's gone and I'm being asked to rate my call. Five out of five for the amount of information, or one out of five because it concerns a serial killer? It's a conundrum.

I sit quite still, trying to process the information. There might as well be a scrambler in my head. I stare out of the slider door. Two sparrows, one male, one female, are having an epic battle over the seed cone on the deck. He's getting quite arsy about it and she retreats, feathers ruffled, biding her time. As she takes a different route, approaching from the bottom of the cone, the jazz song sashays back into my temporal lobe, this time with lyrics. It's 'Beyond the Sea'.

CHAPTER 15

Garth: 25 days until Battle of the Book Clubs

Raindrops as large as marbles batter the windows in our makeshift incident room. Gone are the photos, witness statements and whiteboard scribblings relating to the Tracey Jervis case, sealed away in plastic storage boxes that we will keep handy in case Franklin White gets acquitted.

Pinned to the top of the board now is a photograph of Arthur Pinter, because we are nothing if not traditional, although we have pinned it face inwards because we don't need his soulless sepia eyes following us about the room. It's not like every detail of his face hasn't been seared into our minds: his short, black, Brylcreemed hair, his thick-rimmed tortoiseshell glasses, his parted pencil moustache, his narrow lips with their constant hint of a questioning smile.

Below the photo are noted the sparse details that we have so far:

1. The book *The Cause of Death* was ordered online by Pinter from Mary's Cat in Petone and delivered to

32 Pikitea Street, Waipukurau, where Belinda Henare had died a year earlier.
2. A copy of *Betrayal* by Harold Pinter, hand-delivered to our bookshop, sender unknown.
3. Pinter in contact with Kiwi burner phone.

And then of course there's the final small relevant detail that Eloise was long ago responsible for Pinter being caught after he very nearly succeeded in claiming her as his next victim.

On a second board next to it we have written the names Lily Ross and Erma Mooney. We've nothing to link these to Pinter at this stage, so we're treating it as a separate investigation.

Eloise writes 'Mendelsund' on the Pinter whiteboard and Blu-Tacks one end of a piece of bling-string next to it, the glittery cord having unfortunately survived the last incident room purging. The other end she attaches to the photo of Pinter.

'You should put "book designer" beneath Mendelsund,' I say. The highly lauded Peter Mendelsund has hundreds of book cover designs to his credit.

'We can't be certain that it relates to that Mendelsund.'

'It has to. I mean, it's book related for a start. Pure Pinter.'

'Agreed. But we don't want to jump to conclusions. How many cases have we seen go awry because the D latched on to one idea and didn't follow the evidence?' Eloise caps the whiteboard marker and places it back in the holder. 'And Pinter's devious enough to try and send us down a blind alley.'

'But he doesn't know we're snooping on his messages.' I fold my arms. Due to my terrible handwriting I'm forbidden to write on the board and it irks me that Eloise hasn't added my suggested footnote.

'He must think it's a possibility. He wouldn't be so cryptic otherwise.'

'Do you know what Mendelsund's most iconic book cover is?' I steeple my fingers.

Eloise slumps onto the bed. 'I have a feeling you're going to tell me.'

'*The Girl with the Dragon Tattoo.*'

'So?'

'That could be a codename for you.' Suddenly this feels hugely significant. 'You're the girl with the dragon tattoo!' Eloise looks at me like I've lost the plot. 'Look at his text message,' I continue. *'It's been a while. I trust Mendelsund was as anticipated?* He's asking how *you* are! He wants to know if his mind games are working, how he's affecting you!'

Stevie appears in the doorway, uncertain of whether to enter. Eloise pats the bed to encourage him to join her. 'I don't have a dragon tattoo.'

'Yeah, well, maybe no one's written a book called *The Girl with the Monster Plant Tattoo.*'

'I bet they have.'

Why is Eloise refusing to see the obvious connection? 'You're avoiding the elephant in the room.'

'The girl with the *elephant* tattoo now?'

'No!' I raise my voice in frustration. 'The fact that you still have Pinter's tattoo.' My tone, combined with the drumming of the rain on the windows, sends Stevie scurrying under the bed.

Eloise scowls. 'Now look what you've done.'

I grab a bag of mystery meat treats from the bedside cabinet drawer and rustle the packet at Stevie.

'He's not going to come out.'

'Wait until he smells the meaty goodness.' I pull apart the bag's snap-seal and take out a dark brown rancid-smelling fragment, holding it out to Stevie, who retreats further.

'Give it here.' Eloise grabs the treat from my hand. 'Go and make us a coffee. I'll deal with Stevie.'

When I return with two steaming mugs the treacherous pooch is curled up next to Eloise on the bed, his head resting beside her as he chews contentedly, the rain that still hammers against the window seemingly no longer a concern. Open on her lap, Eloise has the file I retrieved from Tama's lock-up. She looks out the window as I enter.

'Another glorious day in the Bay.' She scratches Stevie behind the ears and is rewarded with a snoof, snoof, snoof.

'Yeah, I thought El Niño was supposed to bring us warmer weather.' I place a cup of coffee-machine coffee on the bedside table next to Eloise, keeping the mug of instant for myself.

'Do you want me to tell you about Kiri Wereta?' asks Eloise. I'm silent for a moment watching the water that runs down the window in rivers.

'Elephant, room, Pinter, Mendelsund, tattoos,' I finally say. I'm not letting this go just yet.

'Fine. I'm not ruling out that it could be referring to me.' Eloise rubs her side where, beneath her tee-shirt, Pinter's handiwork is inked. 'Only I think he'd pick a codename for me that was more obviously degrading.'

'Yes, he does rather hate you.'

'With an all-encompassing burning passion.'

I stroke Eloise's arm. 'How's the old PTSD?'

'Just great.'

Clearly it isn't. Mine's not so flash either.

'Okay,' I say. 'Let's park Pinter for a bit.' Unless sudden inspiration strikes, we'll have to wait for more messages and hope things become clearer. 'Tell me about poor old Kiri.'

'She was owner and head chef at Found Food in Hastings.'

'I remember that place. Foraged and organic food, no menu and you couldn't book. You just had to turn up and share your kai with whoever else was there.' I take a sip of coffee and discover a Stevie hair floating on the top. 'You always wanted to go and I didn't.'

'No surprises there,' says Eloise.

'What happened to it?'

'Closed down in 2016 after Kiri died. The coroner ruled that she'd accidentally poisoned herself with some foraged mushrooms and it seems that did for the restaurant as well.'

I shoot Eloise a mischievous smile. 'Sounds like we had a lucky escape.'

'Or missed out on a unique experience that sadly will never be available again.'

'I'm sure there are plenty of other hippy-dippy places that'll give you food poisoning.'

Eloise puts on her poshest voice. 'Not in Havelock, darling.'

'It was Hastings,' I reply, although I know I'm being a pedant because Hastings and the Village have an abundance of splendid eateries, ranging from upmarket wineries like Noir Grange to more mainstream barbecue joints like Notorious P.I.G.

'Why did Tama think her death was suss?'

'Kiri was viewed as a bit of a local foraging expert, and had a book deal lined up with Bateman. Accidentally poisoning herself seemed a bit unlikely to him.'

There's nothing explicitly untoward about the case, no smoking gun, just that copper's gut of unease when things don't quite sit right. It's not something you can put in a report, or use to push the brass to commit more resources, but it's real, and sometimes it can save your life.

CHAPTER 16

Eloise: 24 days until Battle of the Book Clubs

I'm sitting at my desk, staring out the window at the sparrows and mentally rehearsing all the reasons why Faith should be our guest author at Battle of the Book Clubs in advance of our Zoom meeting with her this morning. What objections might she raise? She might wonder why we haven't asked Prudence Ballion, one half of the global bestselling fiction phenomenon that is Isabella Garrante. Yes, Prudence is local and has become a friend but has zero interest in being the face of the writing duo, leaving that to the glamorous — and until recently mysterious — Tracey Jervis. Tracey is currently in the UK, so she's also a non-starter as a Battle guest.

'What's going through your head? You're chewing your face so much you'll have no cheek left.' Brought back to earth by my ever-attentive husband, who has materialised to intrude upon my thoughts, I realise that I have indeed peeled off an appreciable amount of oral mucosa, an unconscious habit that can leave me in some discomfort as well as making me look quite disturbed.

'Just trying to formulate my plan of attack for Faith Saxon. Ambush, encirclement or melee?'

'I don't think any of those will be necessary. She's a nice woman who writes good books and I think she'll be keen to help if she can.'

'Hmm. But failing to plan is planning to fail.'

'Could it be, dear Eloise, that you are overthinking this?'

'Could it be, Garth, light of my life, that you are being a tiny bit condescending?'

He gasps and puts his hand on his chest, looking left and right, mouth open in mock shock. 'Would I do such a thing?'

'You're right, I know. But I *really* want her to say yes. She'd be such a hit with the book club people.'

'In any case, Chrissy will be on the call too, and no one can resist her.'

True. You'd need a heart of steel to refuse Chrissy. There's nothing like children going through a cancer journey to put things into perspective, and the Mighty Oaks' stories are life affirming and heartbreaking in equal measure.

Garth shuffles off to make coffee; he is incapable of sitting through a meeting without a mug of the life-giving liquid in his hand. There's the *scuff scuff* of receding, kitchenward steps and the *rasp rasp* of inward-bound claws as Stevie pads along the landing and into the room. I roll my desk chair out to greet him.

'Steveburger! Whatcha doin'?'

He's come in to catch up on the current sparrow squabbles. I swear we both enjoy it more than *Oprah*.

Garth appears bearing two mugs of jitter juice, placing the properly brewed version on my desk, earthy steam puffing my way. Yum.

'Have you not got the meeting up yet?' he asks.

'It's only five to. Get yourself settled.'

He hates being late for anything, even an online meeting. He sets his coffee next to mine and goes to fetch a chair. I fiddle with the laptop and open the meeting.

'Chrissy's in the waiting room — look! Let her in.' Garth is pulling his chair up, fussily pointing at the screen.

'Oh my god, do you want to drive?' He's infuriating, or I'm irritable, or both of these things are true.

There's a clattering and a blurry image fills the screen.

'. . . dropped my pencil somewhere.' The blur turns to sleek dark hair being flicked back from a tanned face and tucked behind ears. Chrissy has arrived.

'Morning, lovelies, how's it going?' She shakes her hair to settle it. There's birdsong in the background, tūī having a right old natter about something vitally, throatily important. The sunlight is streaming in the window behind her and she adjusts the angle of her screen slightly.

'We're fine and dandy this end. What's the haps with you?'

'I hear Reagan came to your Death Café the other night. He's chuffed to bits to have met you all, and that book club lady.'

'Ah yes, he was having a good chat with Beth. About how a death sentence means you can say heinous things in your writing that you wouldn't get away with otherwise . . .'

'Sounds like Reagan. He likes a bit of the dark side. Surprised me the first time I read his work because he's such a lovely bloke.' I get what she means. You never know what's lurking inside a person's head, no matter how well you think you know them.

'Eloise. Faith is in the waiting room, look!' I slap Garth's hand away from the screen where he's tapping on Faith's name. I let her in and there she is, smiling and mouthing something at the screen.

'Turn your mic on,' say Garth, Chrissy and I simultaneously. A pause, then a crunchy rustle.

'Hahaha — you'd think we'd all check that before looking like a nincompoop!'

I'm not sure what one of those looks like but I don't think it's got Balayage highlights and a generous grin. Faith is a bit older than me, more affable in person than her darkly serious author photos. Her eyes are bright, even on screen — a combination of intelligence and generous lashings of mascara. She's beaming and she used the word 'nincompoop'. I like her already.

'Interesting,' says Garth. 'The etymology of the word nincompoop dates back—'

'Morning, Faith. Thank you for agreeing to chat,' I get in quickly, or we'll be here all day. After a few more pleasantries we get down to business.

'Tell me about Battle of the Book Clubs,' says Faith.

I turn to Garth. 'It's your baby, love. Want to explain?'

'Oh, I'm allowed to speak now, am I?' Still pouting slightly, he hauls his chair forward. He loves talking about Battle. 'So, I had this idea that Sherlock Tomes should host a literary quiz night because every man, woman and dog is in a book club in Havelock North and I thought it would be fun to bring them together to match wits. And then I thought, well, if we're going to do it, we might as well raise funds for something. And what better recipients than young people doing it tough with cancer? Simple as that, really.'

Faith is nodding and hmming.

'As we explained in the email,' Garth continues, 'Chrissy here is the muscle behind the Mighty Oaks, who support these kids in all sorts of ways.'

Chrissy hops in and expands a bit further on their work.

Then it's my turn. 'We've had a guest author at the event for a few years now, Faith, and it really draws people in, especially if they're as popular as you.'

Faith smiles humbly, with a murmured 'Well, I don't know—'

'Pretty much everyone has a cancer story,' Chrissy continues, 'so sometimes the author will share some of that with the audience. There's an introductory speech from one of the Mighty Oak members, and altogether it's a brilliant way to get people to buy heaps of raffle tickets.' Chrissy chuckles, and the rest of us smile in response.

Faith clears her throat. 'Well, yes, I've had a brush with Mr C myself and have no shortage of things to say about that.' I didn't know this about Faith; my hand clamps my mouth and I feel a shock of guilt about hauling her into our scheme.

'No, no, Eloise, it's quite all right,' she continues. 'It was ages ago and I'm perfectly fine talking about it. My reticence about Battle comes from not having been back in the country for long. I worry that your readers will have forgotten me.' She gives a self-deprecating shrug.

'They absolutely have not,' I say. 'Your fans know more about you than you do. *Poison in the Blood* is still going great guns and there's a new book next year, I hear?'

'Yes! Working title "Murder in the Mountains". That's out in the ether then, is it? I just have to finish the bloody thing. The heroine's currently stuck on a craggy outcrop wearing nothing but her underwear. I've no idea how to get her down!'

Chrissy is looking thoughtful, and she leans in for the hard sell.

'Faith, I'll be honest with you. As you know, Fiona Kidman was lined up to do the honours, and when she pulled out we thought we might have to cancel. But the Mighty Oaks really need Battle to go ahead. We get no government funding, so we rely on sponsors and donors and events organised by amazing people like Garth and

Eloise.' It's our turn to squirm in the face of a compliment. 'I've had two new referrals this week, and they just keep coming, Faith.'

We all sit with this a minute, thinking about those families. Stevie chooses this moment to let out a wide, squeaky dog yawn, reminding us of his presence, breaking the solemnity. I angle the laptop to show his lordship in the screen and he gazes over at us, sleepy and uninterested. There are the obligatory noises people make about other people's pets, before Chrissy hauls us back to the matter at hand.

'Sorry, Faith, I think I guilt-tripped you a bit there,' Chrissy continues. 'If you're not comfortable with it then of course you absolutely shouldn't do it. We know it's short notice.'

'No, not at all. You do essential work, while I sit drinking coffee and making things up. If I can help I would love to. I've had some confronting experiences showing my "celebrity" face in public but this is such a wonderful thing to be involved in. I would love to do it. Thank you for inviting me.'

'Oh that's brilliant,' says Chrissy. 'Phew!'

'Whoop!' I punch the air.

'You have our eternal gratitude,' says Garth gravely. She absolutely does. I'm keen to dot the Is and cross the Ts, so I jump in with a last question.

'One more thing, Faith. We'd like to offer members of the winning team dinner with you after the event as part of the prize. Is that okay?'

'Oh yes, that sounds lovely,' says Faith. 'Flick me an email confirming all the details and I shall bugger off and think of something to say that will inspire your punters to empty their pockets.'

'Excellent. We'll keep it hush hush for now and then do a reveal closer to the time.'

And with that, and a bit of meeting exit badinage, Faith disappears from the screen. Chrissy exhales loudly and joyously.

'Result!' she says.

'I'll say,' I return. 'Are the Oaks putting up a quiz team this year? I reckon Reagan would love to meet Faith.'

Chrissy deflates a little. 'Oh my lovely, I don't think Reagan will be up to it by then.'

We all pull the plug.

CHAPTER 17

Garth: 23 days until Battle of the Book Clubs

'You still doing the Sci-fi and Fantasy newsletter?' I ask Kitty, who is hunched in front of the shop's main computer. 'You need to get your team of geeks together for Battle of the Book Clubs.'

Startled, Kitty looks up, her face flushing like one of the Royal Gala apples that somebody has kindly dropped into the shop for us as a thank you.

'Err, I was just about to get on to it.'

An excellent bookseller she may be but Kitty, bless her, is not well versed in the art of subterfuge and it doesn't take the intellect of Sherlock Holmes to detect that she is up to something. I cease rummaging through the large cardboard box of packing chips, which the invoice from United Book Distributors assures me also contains two copies of C.K. McDonnell's excellent novel *The Stranger Times*, and move closer to peek at her screen.

Kitty hurriedly switches tabs but not before I see that she is on a pet-shop website displaying an array of fancy cages and complex plastic-tubed structures.

'Mouse houses?' I flick an errant packing chip that has attached itself to my arm at Kitty.

'Amelia and I thought that when we catch Basil we should keep him.'

'Did you now?' It seems that once again the staff are plotting behind my back. I hope that Eloise isn't in on this too.

'Yes. A bit like Stevie is the shop dog, Basil could be the shop mouse.'

I cross my arms, sending a localised snowstorm of packing-chip dust swirling to the floor. 'Stevie is a handsome, wonderful, domesticated dog of awesomeness, whereas the mouse is vermin.'

'Basil is *not* vermin.' Kitty stamps her foot like the petulant child her face now resembles.

'We're not keeping it.' There's been no mention of Eloise, which is normally the first line of defence for the staff, so I think I'm on safe ground.

'He'd be less trouble than a donkey.'

This may seem like an odd comparison, but our shop book club has just read *Running with Sherman* by Christopher McDougall, a truly enchanting tale about a rescued donkey that found a new lease of life burro racing up mountains. There was a concerted effort by club members to persuade us to adopt a shop donkey. The book was so beautiful and the emotional attachment to Sherman so great that Eloise and I almost bowed to the pressure.

I look all around me, in an exaggerated gesture. 'You may have noticed that we don't have a shop donkey, and we are most certainly not having a shop mouse. Whether it be living behind our cupboards or in a cage, a rodent is not welcome.'

A narrow-faced man with a straggly beard has insinuated his way to the till during our 'discussion' and now lays a copy of *Fungi of Aotearoa: A Curious Forager's Field Guide* on the counter. 'You can poison them with death cap or destroying angel, you know,' he says mildly.

'What?' say Kitty and I in unison, with a greater degree of aggression than either of us probably intended.

The man, whose dirty jeans and holey green woollen jumper would give pause to Dafydd, our local itinerant, doesn't seem to notice. 'People think mice are impervious to mushroom poisoning but that's not true. It's mostly just that they don't eat enough of it.'

'Right. Thanks.' I try to sound friendlier. 'I'll probably just buy some bait from the hardware shop.'

The man places his hand on the blue-mushroomed cover of the book. 'You should try foraging. Nature has provided you with everything you need and it's more eco-friendly.'

Kitty, who is usually the one encouraging us to think more about the environment, glowers at the man. 'There's nothing friendly about poisoning Basil.'

'It doesn't work for cats, though,' the man continues, apparently oblivious to Kitty's growing horror. 'For that you want to use foxgloves or lilies.'

'Good to know, thanks.' I clasp my hands together and step in front of Kitty before she does anything I'll regret. 'So, just the *Fungi* book today then?'

From his grubby jeans pocket the man pulls an equally grubby fifty dollar note. For once I feel like Prudence, who has an aversion to touching any form of money that isn't pristine, though it's not so much the state of the note as all the talk of poisons that has me on edge. Fighting my mounting paranoia, I grab the note, shoving it below the twenties in the till and handing over the change. 'Do you want a bag?'

'Definitely not.' The man waves the book at me as he departs. 'Got to save the planet.'

'Yeah, one dead mouse at a time,' grumbles Kitty behind my back.

I wash my hands and give them a squirt of sanitiser to be on the safe side. 'That was as weird as I think it was, right?'

'Totally. Even you aren't that bad,' acknowledges Kitty.

'Thanks. Doesn't mean we're keeping Basil, mind.'

I'm rescued from further discussion by a beep from my phone.

> Eloise: Meet me by the giant oak in five.

Eloise originally hails from Nottingham and visions of Robin Hood and his merry men flash across my mind as I fat-finger a response.

> Me: Everything OK? Garth.

I get a poo emoji in response. Which could mean bad things are afoot, or Stevie committed a sin on the carpet, or it could be representative of a thumbs up, because for some reason Eloise thought it would be funny to set the thumbs-up emoji on my phone to be the smiling poo image, and I don't know how to change it back.

I turn to Kitty. 'Are you all good if I pop out? I've got to see Maid Marion.'

'Basil and I are just fine.'

The giant oak stands on a large grassy area in front of St Luke's Church, fifty or so metres from the shop. I'm not religious, but the large white weatherboard church with its orange-tiled roof is an impressive edifice, and the intricately carved interior even more so.

Eloise sits on a bench in the shade of the great tree, a coffee cup in each hand. Below the bench lurks Stevie, peering out from behind Eloise's legs. His tail twitches as I approach, which is as close to a wag as I'm going to get in this circumstance.

'Coffee? For me?' I say, taking the offered cup. 'How did you know?'

Eloise gives me a wan smile, her face drawn, her eyes pools of worry. So, not the thumbs-up emoji. I drop onto the bench and place a reassuring hand on her leg. 'What's up, chuck?'

'Paula's forwarded another message from Pinter to that New Zealand number.'

'Oh.' I take a sip of coffee. 'What does it say?'

Eloise swipes open her phone as I don my glasses.

> Pinter: I am delighted to hear that the gears are finally in motion and that my Faith appears to be well placed.

'Oh dear. "My Faith".'

'Yep. Looks like Faith Saxon is working for Pinter and we've just invited her into our midst.'

CHAPTER 18

Eloise: 22 days until Battle of the Book Clubs

The rodent conspiracy continues. Kitty and Amelia are engaged in whispered conversations and staring at skirting boards in a frankly disturbing manner. I'll wander into their vicinity to be greeted by a blank-eyed 'nothing to see here' stare. Garth has accused me of being complicit but I feel quite left out by *not* being in on it, to be honest. I know I'm the Boss Lady and, friendly as we are, there are boundaries, but surely they know I'd be all for keeping cute little Basil in a mouse house. I want nothing more than for our latest inhabitant to feel safe and secure.

I try to rein in my paranoia. I've been feeling a bit peculiar, swinging from bullet-proof bravado to cowering at critical-threat level, expecting an attack from Pinter out of left field at any moment. Is Faith Saxon really in on his machinations or am I in need of a 'get a grip' pill? Paula is not convinced that Faith is Pinter's New Zealand contact but is concerned that he seems to know she's the new Battle guest author. Tama is clearly up to his eyes in work, responding to my update text with the dreaded thumbs-up emoji. With all this swirling around my brain I make a snap decision to face the mouse conundrum, seeing as I am projecting all my stress on to it. It's an excellent diversion.

'Kitty.' She startles violently, flinging the pencil she's been tapping thoughtfully on the counter. I must have been stewing so silently, and she so engrossed in whatever she's researching at the computer, that she had no idea I was right behind her.

'Jeez! What's the matter?' She looks all around, hand to thumping chest, alarmed at my stern tone, concluding that something must be terribly awry.

'Why didn't you tell me about your plan to adopt Basil?'

Kitty flushes from the neck up, and probably down as well, a sure sign of guilt.

'Basil?' I don't think she's connecting my solemnity with something as small as a mouse. I suddenly realise how childish I'm being and decide to try to make light of it, one of my more successful coping strategies.

'Yes. You and Amelia are leaving me out of the pet planning. What's happening?'

'Oh, that! It's just a bit of fun really. We thought if we managed to catch Basil we could make him a cosy little home. I left you a note about it in the diary. Did you not see it?'

She rummages around the cluttered admin area, suboptimally located right beside the stained stainless-steel sink, shifts a teetering pile of books waiting to go out on the shelves and flips open the diary to today's date. There's a cartoon of an adorable little creature, tiny paws gripping a piece of holey cheese, along with a note saying: 'Eloise! We need you! Join the Basil fan club!'

I feel several things at once, or in quick succession: really stupid, pathetically thankful, full of love and camaraderie, irritated at the overuse of exclamation marks and quite bonkers for letting the weirder, bruised parts of my mind dominate the robust, clear-thinking bits. I wasn't left out at all. Let me just pop Mr Paranoia back where he belongs, somewhere in the limbic system of my overwrought brain.

'Whaddaya reckon? Can we keep him?' Kitty presses home her perceived advantage. 'I'll clean his cage out and feed him and everything.' She looks about twelve years old — so hopeful, her smile sweet and her tone a bit wheedling.

'I vote yes for Club Basil. If we can catch him.'

'Ah, well, I have a plan for that—'

There's a loud bang followed by several screams. We both spook until I see the Sherlock Tomes sign dangling over the footpath, swinging as if in a strong wind, one side having come unfixed. The screams have turned to laughter. Wandering through the shop, past an elderly couple looking at the cards who haven't noticed a thing, I can see what's happened. It's school kick-out time and some delightful children have jumped up and smacked the sign so hard that it's hanging all lopsided. They're still to be seen, scooting and hollering towards the dairy.

'Little buggers,' mutters Kitty darkly, once I've trudged back up to the counter.

But I can top that prank. 'When I was a kid we used to put dog poo in a paper bag, put it on someone's front doorstep, set it on fire and ring the doorbell before running off to watch from afar.'

Kitty stares at me in horror. 'You psychotic little hoons!'

'Yes, that's what children are. What did you get up to?'

'Nothing like that!'

I raise an eyebrow to display my scepticism. She laughs, shakes her head and ventures out to greet a couple of ladies who have wandered in, necks swivelling, fingers pointing in alarm at the dangling sign. I go out the back to fetch the stepladder. This involves a hazardous trip through the stock room to the Alcove of Abandoned Things, where I must fight my way through empty boxes, Christmas decorations and Amelia's collection of 'items that might come in handy one day'. The situation has escalated somewhat since my last visit and I can't face it. I decide to put 'hanging sign repair' on Garth's to-do list.

I need to get to the supermarket. Having purged myself of debilitatingly irrational paranoid notions, I am feeling much more enthused about the fact that Tama and Chloe are coming for dinner and I am 'cooking'. Garth is currently doing an industrial clean of the public areas of the house and, judging by the frustrated text messages I've received throughout the day, it's not going well.

> **11.06am.** Garth: Where is the bleach? Garth.

> **11.47am.** Garth: Why do we not own a toilet brush? Garth.

> **1.05pm.** Garth: It would be quite nice to invest in some matching cutlery, don't you think? Garth.

I arrive home laden with bags of groceries to be greeted by Stevie, who clatters down the stairs to 'help' by pushing his snoot into each of the bags with some force, as I attempt to drag them up. Mr Sherlock is nowhere to be seen. I dump the shopping on the kitchen bench and go in search of my husband.

'What are you up to?' I find him in his office, headphones on, staring at his computer screen.

'What?' The manner in which he scowls as he removes his headgear gives me a clue to his mood.

'What are you up to?'

'Hiding.'

'From what?'

'The house. Nothing in it works as it should. The vacuum cleaner only has three of its four wheels and everything smells of dog.'

'I'd forgotten how massive the living room is when Stevie's toys are all put away. And tidy now too!'

'It's all right?'

'Yes, love, you've done a great job. Tama and Chloe are our friends — they're coming to see us, not judge how tidy we are.'

He sags with relief, clearly scarred from his attempts to impose order on our lovely, canine-scented old home. I tell him to stay put and recover, and potter off to begin dinner preparation. The first step of course is to open a bottle of wine, the second to pour a glass, and the third to switch the radio on and tune in to *Checkpoint*.

I have stumbled upon a pasta sauce recipe that makes me seem like someone who knows what they're doing in the kitchen, its two successful outings so far proving that it's not a fluke. I mince garlic, glug a great deal of olive oil into a pan and cast a couple of anchovy fillets into the mix. The smell is exquisite. I take a bountiful swig of Chianti and rough up more olives than you would think should go into a sauce. A slug of passata, a few twigs of fresh oregano, some capers, salt and pepper, and I am living and breathing in a Florentine *cucina*, recreating the dishes of my ancestors. I've no idea who my ancestors actually are but this image will do nicely.

Stevie has been lying right behind me so as not to miss any inadvertent spills. All vegetarian offerings have been so far rejected but he's in luck with the clumsy opening of a can of tuna. Oily spillage expertly dealt with, his attention is taken by a door slam and a booming laugh; I didn't hear the doorbell but Garth must have. Stevie skitters out to investigate and gallops back within seconds, beside himself with joy. He loves visitors in the safety of his sanctuary.

'Kia ora, little Stevie! Who's a crazy pupsqueak?' Peripherally, I see a large form careening around the sofa in pursuit of the silver blur of Stevieness. A golden head pokes around the kitchen door, followed by Garth, who grabs a beer for Tama from the fridge.

'Oh my god, that smells amazing.' Chloe retrieves a glass from a cupboard and pours herself a wine. 'Can I do anything?'

'You can tell me the goriest thing that happened to you today.'

'It was a bit of a toughy, actually.' She drinks deeply. 'Older dude came off a dirt bike. No helmet, and travelling at speed. Shall I go on?'

'Yes please.'

'Well, he lived, but he has multiple thoracic injuries, several rib fractures, a collapsed lung, and a head injury with extra-axial hematoma. He's in ICU awaiting further scans.'

'No helmet, huh?'

'Nope.'

There's a crashing sound from the living room and we poke our heads through the doorway to see a collapsed heap of bear-like man and a triumphant ball of canine muscle turning in circles and grinning his crocodile grin.

'Boys,' Chloe says to me, aiming an affectionate smile at her husband.

I dish up my simple yet amazing dinner, showing off about the pecorino I cleverly sourced that came from Pienza, allegedly the best place in the world for such *formaggio*. We're pretty casual tonight, slouched on the sofas; Tama's even wearing his woolly slipper boots, left one draped comfortably over right jeans-clad thigh.

'What's the carbon footprint on that pecorino, do you think?' asks Garth, bursting my hubris bubble. 'Don't they make one in Waikato?'

'It's made of yum! Totally worth it,' says darling Tama, cramming an unfeasibly large amount of pasta into his mouth. I make a decision to feel no guilt about well-travelled cheese and just enjoy my evening. The anchovies have melted into the sauce beautifully, there's a saltfish piquancy on my tongue and Garth is radiating cheek and charm after a single swig of *il vino rosso*. He pats my arm to signal he's only teasing and I shove him to show I know.

'Oh yeah, I meant to say, Lily's out of ICU,' says Chloe.

'That's great news. How is she?' I ask.

'Pretty frail still. Don't think she'll be up to Battle of the Book Clubs, which is a minor tragedy as she's the one on our team who actually reads.'

'Lily's on your team?' asks Garth.

'You know she is,' I snip. 'She's in Chloe's other book club that she cheats on our book club with.'

'I did not know that.'

Chloe can see that this is about to descend into what she calls 'The Garth and Eloise Show', which is where she and Tama watch us bicker until it goes from amusing to uncomfortable, so she interrupts.

'So anyway, turns out it was a bad case of food poisoning. Not sure—'

'Food poisoning, you say. Hmm,' says Garth, holding a hand to his chin. Tama lets out a high-pitched giggle, incongruous in a man of his stature, and points at Garth with his wine glass.

'Ah, look at him, Captain Dubious. He'll be saying it was attempted murder any . . . second . . .'

'Well, we've had two such incidents. Miss Mooney was taken ill in a similar fashion to Lily, and she died. What if something is amiss?' Garth's pulling his bottom lip, this gesture a sign of vexed cogitation.

'There's no chatter at the station about foul play with Miss Mooney,' says Tama. 'We don't get that many murders around here, especially of little old ladies, eh.'

'It will be referred to the coroner though, right? Seeing as it was a sudden death? And they'll look into the mushroom link with Lily?' I ask.

'Yeah, the coroner will look at it. Dying from food poisoning is pretty rare but at her age she could have had any number of underlying health conditions.'

'It is a bit weird that there were two food poisoning incidents in quick succession, both possibly involving mushrooms,' I say.

'That might be a connection but we need a bit more information first.' Tama leans forward, elbows conspiratorially upon knees. 'But I'll tell you a well dodgy thing I saw today.'

Garth mirrors Tama's posture, distracted from poisonings as was intended.

'I've never seen this woman before, and then today I see her three times, in three unrelated places. Weird, huh?' He flops back onto the sofa, having dropped his conversational mic, wine sloshing from his glass onto his cable-knit sweater. Chloe tuts and dabs at him.

'What woman?' asks Garth.

'Yeah nah, she's quite distinctive looking, actually. Blonde shortish hair, one of those Art Deco hats, sprayed-on jeans—'

'Jeggings,' says Chloe. Tama frowns at her in incomprehension.

'And these bright red lips that are . . . I don't even know . . . but just really big.'

'Could be a lip flip,' says Chloe. 'That's when—'

'Where was she?' asks Garth, no doubt eager to divert Chloe's description of injectables.

'Um, first time was outside the station, then I popped into Clean Kai for a coffee and she was sitting in there, and then I'm pretty sure I saw her getting into a car when we were coming over here.'

'Huh,' says Garth. 'I saw a woman like that in the pub, and then

I'm pretty certain she was following me when I drove into town the other day.'

'Following you?' asks Tama.

'She might just have been going in the same direction I suppose.' Garth taps his lip.

'Well, you were obviously taken with her charms to have noticed her three times, hmm?' Chloe shuffles away from her husband in a fake huff. Tama rumbles a laugh and throws a paw around her shoulders.

'There's only one girl for me,' he says, eliciting a mocking 'awww' from the rest of us.

'Hey, I think I saw her too, just near the cemetery. She was walking a little dog.' I get a spike of anxiety. Do we now have a stalker on top of everything else?

'She's probably just new to the area,' says Tama. 'You know what it's like around here — you see the same people everywhere. Now,' he untangles himself from Chloe and claps his hands in a friendly but final gesture. 'What's for pudding?'

'Tiramisu.'

'Flown in from Venice?' Tama ducks as if expecting me to swipe him, then shakes his empty wine glass at Chloe, who rolls her eyes before emptying the last of the Chianti into it. I stick my tongue out at him and snatch up the pasta bowls. A thought occurs as I head to the kitchen.

'So with Lily out of action, who's the sixth person on your Battle quiz team?' I ask Chloe.

'Tama,' she says, laying a hand on his arm.

At which he sits bolt upright to stare at her, slack jawed. I have never seen a man this mischievous, this bold, and this tipsy, look so terrified, and it is absolutely delicious.

CHAPTER 19

Garth: 21 days until Battle of the Book Clubs

The microfiche spins on the transport shuttle and newspaper pages from days gone by flash up on the screen. I scroll through years, months, weeks, days, heading back towards 2016.

An online search of Kiri Wereta turned up a couple of articles about her restaurant but nothing about her death. On the one hand, that's not surprising because her death was not ruled suspicious; on the other hand, Restaurant Owner Accidentally Poisons Herself has clickbait written all over it. That's why I'm going old school. Maybe someone's deleted the digital copies but the microfiche articles are there in perpetuity — uneditable, undeletable.

Given the latest revelation suggesting a connection between Pinter and Faith Saxon, Kiri Wereta's cold case is perhaps not our top priority, but we owe Tama, and my gut tells me it's all somehow connected. Too many mushrooms.

Suddenly there's a loud flapping sound and the centre of the computer screen goes white; the microfiche has broken and is spinning on the spool, the loose end slapping against the machine. I click the stop icon and that's when I see it — the film isn't broken, it's been cut. I slide the two ends under the magnifier in turn and my suspicions are confirmed. I was wrong about microfiche being undeletable. A month's worth of newspapers are missing, right around the time of Kiri's death.

'Is everything okay?' A voice behind me makes me start. 'Not broken it, have you?'

I spin on my chair. The librarian facing me wears a poppy-patterned dress and cat's eye spectacles. She smiles, ensuring I know that I'm not in any real trouble.

'Hi, Agatha.' I take a deep breath, calming my nerves. 'Just doing a bit of research and the film seems to have broken,' I lie. Agatha is exceptionally inquisitive, a trait that is a boon for a research librarian, and less desirable for me under the current circumstances.

'More murders to solve?' She eases onto the seat next to me and waits expectantly.

'Hopefully not.'

'But possibly.' She leans to one side, clearly hoping to get a glimpse of something gossip-worthy on the screen.

'No, not at all. I just got sidetracked — I'm supposed to be doing research for Battle of the Book Clubs.'

Agatha sits back in her chair. Then, checking that no one is nearby, she whispers, 'Is it true Faith Saxon is going to be the guest speaker?'

I pause for perhaps a little too long and Agatha takes this as confirmation. She smiles.

'Where did you hear that?'

'I can't reveal my sources.' She takes her glasses off and gives them a polish.

'I'm not sure anything's confirmed yet,' I lie. It's not really a secret but we are hoping to get some publicity mileage by doing a big reveal across our social media channels. Eloise will spit the dummy if she thinks I've given it away.

'Well, you just want to be careful,' she says enigmatically.

I find it hard to interpret the look Agatha gives me. In the past she's provided me with several golden nuggets of information, but they came not from the spools of microfiche or dusty tomes of Hawke's Bay history but from Agatha herself. Even if I can't decipher her look it tells me I have to keep her talking.

'Really? I loved her last novel . . .' I leave the sentence hanging and thankfully Agatha takes the bait.

'Oh, she can certainly write, no doubt about that. It's her personal skills that perhaps need attention.'

'How so? I've only ever heard good things about Faith,' I say, choosing to ignore the fact that if we are correct in our deciphering of Pinter's message, Faith is working with a cruel and twisted serial killer.

Agatha folds her arms, defensive. Have I dashed my chances?

I throw more bait into the water. 'Some of our book club went to her session at the Auckland Writers Festival when she still lived here and said she was a great speaker.'

'Ha! She obviously deems the AWF important enough to bother attending.'

'Well, it is the biggest literary festival in the country. I'd love to go but Eloise and I have never been able to get away from the shop.'

There's definitely bad blood between Agatha and Faith. I keep picking at the scab. 'She must have spoken at events in Hawke's Bay, though. I'm sure I remember something a few years back.'

'That would be the one I arranged. I spent months working on the publicity, the staffing, the venue, the refreshments — it was going to be a real coup for the library.'

I know how much effort goes into running such an event. It's the behind-the-scenes stuff that nobody sees and the mental stress of coordinating everything to run without a hitch that are the real hard work. I'm guessing Agatha's event didn't go smoothly. 'What happened?'

'She didn't turn up, that's what happened. I'd booked and paid for accommodation, organised Cristina Sanders to chair, and then on the morning of the event I get a text message from Faith. She's about to board a plane to return to the US and is sorry but she won't be able to make it.'

'Wow!'

'Exactly. So you may want to have a back-up plan for Battle of the Book Clubs.'

I'm aware that I'm only hearing one side of the story, and it seems at odds with other things I've heard. 'Did she explain why?'

'No explanation, no apology. Just me left with egg on my face, having to cancel the event and try to let everyone know.'

'When was that?'

'In 2016. September or October. Why do you ask?'

'Ah, well . . .' I lose my words, my brain side-tracked by that date, thoughts travelling along several paths simultaneously: Kiri's death, the missing chunk of microfiche, Faith's sudden departure . . . all happened that year.

'Ah well . . .' Agatha prompts me.

'You know. Just trying to gauge things.'

She gives me a suspicious look, which, to be fair, I totally deserve. Attempting to smooth over the awkward moment, I say, 'So you won't be coming to Battle of the Book Clubs to hear her speak?'

'Oh, I'll be coming all right, but not to hear her. In fact she might get to hear a few choice words from me.'

I've never seen Agatha so riled; she's always given off the archetypal mild-mannered librarian vibe. It appears that inviting Faith may not have been such a brilliant idea after all, and not just because of the whole working-for-our-arch-nemesis thing. 'I hope you're not going to cause us any trouble on the night,' I joke.

Agatha toys with her glasses. 'I'm not the one you need to worry about.'

CHAPTER 20

Eloise: 20 days until Battle of the Book Clubs

I feel a bit overwhelmed by poison at the moment. Dodgy mushrooms, a dead old lady, another in ICU, and a rogue mouse. My head's revving like the engine of this old clunker of a car as I yank the door open. Stevie hops in — he loves the car, the back seat being one of his approved safe spaces. Our destination is irrelevant to him; our Zen dog is only here for the glory of the ride. I envy him.

At the back of the shop Stevie hops out of the car, turning in circles by the door, impatient to get inside while I'm still grabbing my bag. We enter the shop to be confronted by none other than the Admiral, standing ramrod straight beside the comfy chair, an air of patience about him as if he's been waiting a while. Phyllis is behind the counter, duster and furniture polish in hand. I can smell the woody, vanilla scent of a freshly spruced bookshop. She catches my eye and shrugs in the universal language for 'I don't have a clue what's going on'.

'Tardiness is not a desirable quality in a shipmate, Eloise, but I shall overlook it this once.' Bearded chin in the air and a glint in his eye, the Admiral points his silver-topped cane accusatorily in my direction.

'Apologies, sir, did we—'

'No, no, you may stand down. I'm joshing. Popped in on the off-chance.'

When no further information is forthcoming, I grab one of the upright chairs from behind the Tardis door and gesture towards it. The Admiral takes the seat gratefully. I ditch my bag in the stock room for Stevie to keep an eye on and dump myself in the comfy chair.

The Admiral leans forward.

'In the course of my storied career I forged bonds with many honourable — and no small number of dishonourable — men and women. One such person has furnished me with information that may be of use to you.' He leans back and retrieves a small envelope from the inside pocket of his blazer. I've never seen this Admiral before. His gaze is steely. I see the man who scuttled a thousand ships during his time in naval intelligence.

'I'm not one to call in favours, Eloise, not unless something, or someone, I care about is under threat. I'm hoping this might help to resolve your current situation.'

I open my mouth to thank him, or try to formulate a question, but he holds a hand up and shakes his head. He passes me the envelope, with as much ceremony and solemnity as if it contained his last will and testament.

'I haven't seen you this morning. And I haven't seen Phyllis either.' He looks up to my wild-haired comrade, who gives a nod and a quiet 'Understood, sir', then back to me.

'Of course, Admiral. Thank you.'

'Don't thank me yet, lassie. This may well be the calm before the storm.'

With no little effort, he places both hands atop his cane and hauls himself upright. He gives two sharp raps of farewell and turns to make his way down the ramp.

'As you were.'

Phyllis and I watch him, speechless, as he leaves the shop. Stevie pokes his head around the corner of the stock room, his habitually concerned gaze mirroring ours.

'What was that all about?' asks Phyllis.

The envelope is glued down so I untuck the seal flap and give it a shake. Into my hand falls a weighty metal USB drive of a type I've never seen before.

⁂

A quick text to the ever-amazing Amelia and she's dropped her plans and scooted to the shop so I can go home and investigate the Admiral's gift.

We are in the incident room. Garth is staring at the brushed-steel USB drive in his palm and Stevie is pacing up and down the landing, not quite sure where to put himself after his morning's plans were changed at short notice.

'And he didn't say anything else? Like where he got it from?'

'Nope. I get the impression he wants to maintain plausible deniability.'

Garth raises an eyebrow at this. 'You didn't ask him, did you.'

'No, I didn't. I was a bit taken aback, to be fair.' It hadn't seemed right to question the Admiral when he was so thoroughly enjoying being a spy again. 'He said we hadn't seen him today, all sneaky beaky.'

'I would like a little more information as to its provenance before we dive in.'

'Oh, come on. Stick it in the laptop. What have we got to lose?'

'All of our documents, and everything else connected to the laptop, such as our website. Essentially, our entire livelihood.'

'Oh. Right.'

'Give me a minute to scan it.'

I go and make coffee, and by the time I return Garth is sitting in front of the laptop wearing an expression of incredulity and excitement.

'It's an audio file. I clicked on it' — he sees my face — 'I'm sorry, I just wanted to know what it was and . . . well, it's Pinter.'

I'm hit by a wave of nausea so overwhelming that I run to the bathroom. I grip the basin, staring at my reflection in the mirror. A pink-haired white woman, middle-aged and looking it, bags under her eyes from stress. Pinter wouldn't recognise me as PC 60 Sherlock if I slapped him in the face with my pocket book.

There's a low hum in my ears — maybe a neighbour's leaf blower — and it's conjuring images that do nothing for my nausea.

I'm back there, in the bright room, bare skin sticking to a film-wrapped bench. There's a light, clean smell that comes and goes with the movements of the man who is now adjusting his stool. It's his hair, black and slick with some kind of product.

I feel a quick cold sensation as something is wiped across my ribs and I inhale sharply.

'Now, now, constable, it's not as if it's your first time.' The voice is gentle, reassuring. 'And anyway, I'm here. You're fine. You're just fine. Breathe in . . . and breathe out.'

Then there's the buzzing and, as it hits my skin, I know I'm not fine. I know this is the first step in a macabre game that he's played before. I can't stop him. Maybe soon, if I can get my head straight and think. For now, I'll do as he says. Just breathe.

Back in my bathroom, the urge to vomit subsides, replaced by a strong desire to do serious harm. I rub my left side below my ribs, lift my tee-shirt and crane to see the scar, the war wound. 'AY, LET HER ROT' is tattooed on a stylised scroll in Times New Roman. It's Shakespeare, from Othello's rant of betrayal and revenge.

'Are you all right?' calls Garth.

I am all right. I'm at home, with Garth.

I splash my face with cold water and head back to the incident room. Garth looks up, concerned.

'Can you do this?' he asks, and I nod.

'I can.'

He clicks the play arrow and a rather nasal upper-class voice emanates from the speakers:

> Unidentified male: . . . considerable amount of primary and forensic evidence so we may need to consider your plea . . .

Garth reaches to grab my hand. And there he is. The honeyed, righteous tones of literary agent and killer Arthur Pinter. The voice is so familiar, even after all this time, it takes me right back there.

> Pinter: Terrence, I've already instructed you to serve a Basis of Plea. I acknowledge that a crime has occurred.
>
> Terrence: Yes, Arthur, but I can't see the prosecution accepting it, can you? They have enough evidence to convict. My advice is to enter a guilty plea, then we can negotiate your sentence.
>
> Pinter: We both know I'm not going anywhere, Terrence. We might as well have a little fun with it.

There's the sound of a sigh, and something landing with a rolling clatter.

Pinter: I don't appreciate the attitude, Terrence. You do work for me, after all. Here, this'll cheer you up. Did I tell you how I foiled my own murder?

Terrence: No, Arthur, I don't believe you did.

Pinter: I was in the middle of arranging to rid the world of a crime against literature — not a particularly terrible one, but my tolerance was at an all-time low. Just as I was about to instigate my plan, the tables were turned and the predator became the prey. It was unexpectedly beautiful.

Terrence: What happened?

Pinter: Oh, I have your attention with this little plot twist, don't I, Terrence? Well, they didn't get it quite right, but I could see the potential. So I recruited them. I'm a natural mentor, and my mentee needed some considerable writing advice but has turned out to be a rather skilled accomplice. Very useful, given my current circumstances.

And that's it. The audio stops as suddenly as it started.

'What the hell?' I'm stunned. 'There's no way the police would have recorded a conversation between the accused and their counsel. So who did?'

'Highly illegal. And to what purpose?' Garth lets go of my hand in order to tap his fingers on the desk, drumming some organisation into his thoughts.

'That's some favour the Admiral pulled. How on earth did he get it?'

'That's hardly the point here, Eloise.'

'I think there are a few points, actually, Garth. If you stop that godawful noise for a minute I might be able to clarify them.'

His fingers still.

'There's only one point we need to worry about,' he says.

'And that is?'

'Pinter's not a lone wolf. He's been working with someone for a long time. Someone who turned the tables on him.'

A writer, and a hunter.

CHAPTER 21

Garth: 19 days until Battle of the Book Clubs

Although I am still undecided about the merits of the Loan Ranger over our much-maligned Tomato, I'll say this for the vehicle: it has excellent boot space and, with its drop tailgate, is a damn sight less backbreaking to unload.

'This is the last one,' I say. While Eloise locks up, I carry the final carton of books into the Eco-Hub building where we are the bookseller for the launch of a new book by William Pickett, a local foraging expert. It'll be a relief to do something so normal.

A quick catch-up with Tama at unit 39 has him up to date on the missing newspaper files. He was considerably calmer than DI Paula Taylor upon hearing the USB-drive revelations. I've rarely seen her so agitated — shocked not only at the content, but at the massive breach of protocol in recording the conversation.

Negotiating my way past the rows of chairs, a soft-plastic recycling receptacle and an indoor worm farm, I reach the trestle table that is to serve as our sales counter. I deposit the box onto a wooden surface stained with several interesting hues, unidentifiable substances and suspiciously oily patches, making it entirely inappropriate for the placement of pristine books. As usual, we have forgotten to bring a tablecloth, so I'm going to have to scrounge one.

I approach a woman in rainbow dungarees and a fluffy jumper. 'Hi, we're the booksellers. Who's in charge, please?'

'No one's in charge.' The woman looks me up and down, taking in my jeans, Sherlock Tomes hoodie and leather shoes. 'We're a collective.'

'Who would I ask about borrowing a tablecloth?'

'You could try Fern.' She nods towards a squat woman with tight grey curls and sun-rouged cheeks.

'Thanks.' I wander over to Fern, who is shouting instructions at two others.

'No, Greta, not those ones — they need a wash after Flora's goat got to them. And Bean, you know this is a smoke-free environment.'

Bean appears to have modelled himself on Shaggy from *Scooby-Doo* and has what is clearly a joint hanging from his mouth. 'It's medicinal. I need it for my anxiety,' he shouts back to her.

'Well, it's doing nothing for my anxiety,' says Fern, 'so take it outside.'

'Whatever.'

Fern fixes him with a decidedly un-eco-friendly look that is worthy of Eloise when I have said something inappropriate to the staff.

In the police we weren't really bothered about cannabis at the street level. Sure, if it was brazen we'd have to act, but it was more often seen as a way to get leverage on crims who might spill the beans on suppliers. Prosecuting dope smokers with a small personal stash would have been a waste of my time, the custody sergeant's time and taxpayers' money when it would only result in a caution anyway.

I approach Fern. 'Hi, we're—'

'The booksellers, yes. Your table's over there.'

'We found it, thanks. I was just wondering if you had a tablecloth we could borrow?'

'Thanks to Flora's goat, we don't at the moment.' Fern turns away from me, our conversation apparently over. 'Not those either, Greta. They're for the rag-rug challenge.'

I return to the table where Eloise waits.

'No tablecloth,' I say.

Eloise looks at the table and rubs a hand over it. 'Don't worry, I've got an idea.'

I instantly worry. The last time I recall her saying that was moments before she smashed the Tomato into a statue to reveal the murdered remains of a missing drug dealer.

As she heads towards the Loan Ranger my pulse quickens. Thankfully, she doesn't climb into the driver's seat but opens the rear passenger door and tugs out a large piece of turquoise velvet. It's Stevie's blanket, which we've been using to protect the seats.

'Voilà.' Eloise gives the blanket a vigorous shake to remove dog detritus and spreads it out on the table. 'No one will know.'

I pick off some dog hair. 'I'll know.'

'It's either that or lay out the books on patches of mystery origin,' says Eloise. After ten years running the bookshop together she knows I can't abide grubby marks on my pristine books.

Eloise boots up her MacBook and the mobile Eftpos machine while I open the cartons of books, cutting through the parcel tape with a key because, yes, we've forgotten the boxcutter also. I arrange the books on the table in symmetrical piles and place single copies on stands so that the cover, a quite glorious woodland scene, is visible.

Finally I unpack and erect our Sherlock Tomes banner.

'Good to go?' I ask.

'Good to go,' confirms Eloise.

I check my phone. 'Six forty-five.'

'Fifteen minutes to spare! We are top-quality professionals.'

I run my hand over the dog blanket, which actually looks pretty darn good. Top-quality professionals indeed.

Punters are starting to arrive. They'll be a mixed bunch of Eco-Hub clientele, people who've read Eloise's article about the event in the paper, the author's friends and family, and loyal bookshop regulars. I spot Beth and the Admiral hobbling in together, followed by Prudence and Matty Trindle.

'What, no Stevie?' says Prudence.

'We thought we'd leave him at home for this one,' I say.

'You'd better not leave him at home for the next Death Café.' Prudence picks a stray dog hair from our tablecloth. 'I'm making a special treat for him.'

They take their seats, and I lean closer to whisper to Eloise. 'Don't look now but that weird bloke I told you about from the shop who was talking about poisoning cats has just come in.'

Eloise immediately spins around to look. 'Which one?'

'I said don't look!'

'No one noticed.' Eloise smiles and pretends to wave to someone. 'Which one is he?'

'Narrow face, straggly beard. Carrying a plate of food. Shit, he's coming over here.'

'Of course he is, you muppet.' Eloise shakes her head in despair. 'That's Will Pickett, the author of tonight's book!'

'Are you sure?'

'Look at the back of the cover, you dork.'

'A dork and a muppet. You're showering me with compliments this evening.'

'All of which you have well and truly earned.'

The author photo is of a younger man with a tidier beard, but it's still recognisably him, so I suppose perhaps my darling wife's assessment of me is justified. Not that I'll ever tell her that.

'Hi, Will,' says Eloise, greeting him with a smile. 'Garth tells me you were in the shop last week.'

'Oh really? I didn't think he recognised me.' Will tilts his head to one side.

'How could I not?' I say, smiling. 'Your photo's on the back of the book.' Pain shoots through my left toes as Eloise's sturdy boot crushes them beneath the table.

'Have you travelled all the way down from Northland today?' Eloise asks him.

'No, I live in the rural metropolis of Waipukurau these days.'

'I'm sure I read in the AI you were up north.'

The AI is nothing to do with ChatGPT but refers to the advance information sheet that publishers send through for new books. They range in quality from interesting and informative to a desperation-level sales pitch for a book that clearly isn't on point for the New Zealand market. When they start talking about how the book has been a bestseller in rural Kentucky you know it's probably not one for Havelock North.

Will picks at a loose piece of yarn in his jumper that has formed a fluffy twisted loop like a furry caterpillar. 'I was in Northland when I wrote the manuscript but I had to come to the Bay for some of the foraging chapters and it rekindled my love for the place. So I've moved back.'

'To Waipuk?'

'Yes, Pikitea Street. Do you know it?'

CHAPTER 22

Eloise: 18 days until Battle of the Book Clubs

We sold thirty-seven copies of *Pick it with Will* at the launch: not at all shabby. It was a lovely bunch of people; once the stress of getting ready for the event was over, Fern was as smilingly calm as Bean. Perhaps he persuaded her to step outside for 'a breath of air'.

'I'm so sad I missed it,' says Kitty. 'There's a stream near my house and I'm pretty sure it's got watercress, but you know . . . it's a bit risky.'

'You only have to get it wrong once.'

'What? I'm pretty sure I could get it wrong several . . . oh, I see.' Kitty laughs, then shudders at the thought.

I enter last night's sales into the system. Today will be a good day whatever happens from here on in. It's only 9.45am but already my thoughts are turning to sushi, and to the new bakery that's nearly ready for its grand opening two doors down. Kitty says it will be our undoing but I'm very excited about it.

'Brought any snacks for Basil today?' I ask casually.

'I don't bring him snacks! Who told you that?'

'Garth.' Kitty goes a bit red and manoeuvres herself around Stevie, who has plonked himself in the stock-room doorway and is refusing to shift. Rummaging in her bag, she retrieves a small plastic box, holds it up and rattles it at me, blowing a stray piece of tawny hair from her mouth.

'Is that cheese?'

'Yes. Basil zipped between the card stands last night just after I closed up and I thought he was looking a bit thin.'

'Do you think he'll like vegan cheese, though?'

'Oh, it's not . . .' Kitty peters out as she gets busy putting the cheese in the fridge and filling the kettle, humming along with the Bach concerto floating through the shop.

'You bought real cheese, didn't you? Specially for Basil.'

'No! Mum had some that was going to waste.'

I laugh and make up a song about Basil being a lucky mouse. Stevie looks longingly at the fridge.

A familiar rumbling squeak heralds the arrival of Meryl, it being TV magazine day. She's hurtling up the accessibility ramp at speed, shopping trolley rolling merrily along, ash-blonde dreadlocks bouncing behind her.

'I sold another one!' She throws her joy right at us and we catch it.

'Bet it was the peonies. I wanted that one,' says Kitty.

Ever since Meryl's success at the guerrilla art exposition, 'Pilfered Petals', she's been painting up a storm, receiving commissions and buying new, increasingly outrageous leggings. Today's pair are crocheted in a glorious shade of blue (cerulean, we stand corrected) and only slightly bagging about the knee. I'd quite like a pink pair but I'm not sure they'd really suit me, Meryl and I being pretty dissimilar in the leg department. She's a ballerina and I'm more of a footballer.

'That's awesome, Meryl,' I say, and we all look up at the work that was the art expo's crowning glory. A riot of vibrant flowers, stolen by Meryl from Kitty's window boxes, lacquered and arranged to shoot forth from a black background, now graces the wall above the door that leads to the shop loo.

Meryl is so back on the horse now that she's practically bow-legged. Years of crippling anxiety following a promisingly artistic youth are falling from this sweet woman as her muse returns. She still loses her car keys and her bank card — not to mention her car — on a regular basis but is generally much less of a stress-head.

'Are you really, really busy, Meryl? 'Cos I've been meaning to ask if you'd like to create a picture round for Battle of the—'

'Yes! Yes please! We could do a Pictionary round! Just imagine *Boy Swallows Universe* and—'

'Shhhh, Meryl!' I say conspiratorially. 'This is fabulous but the questions have to be kept under wraps. Not even Kitty gets to see them.'

'Oh right, yes of course. Shhh. How exciting!' Meryl is nodding and grinning, bouncing on her baggy knees, gleeful to be in the thick of it, a keeper of secrets, part of something special. I take a good look at her. She appears much younger these days, brighter since the old mystery surrounding Oddbean was resolved. That reminds me.

'Have you seen Dafydd?' I ask Meryl. 'I know the police tried to interview him after the . . . um . . . the *crash*, but my copper mate says they didn't get anything out of him.'

'Yes, I went to see him. He was in the acute bit at the hospital but he's moved to the open ward now. He's not talking but I did get a lovely smile. He's quite calm, probably drugged up to the eyeballs, lucky sod. Haha.'

She's joking but not joking, full of Merylly mischief. Then she looks out the window and crumples a little. 'He always knew, didn't he? He had what happened to Oddbean trapped in his mind for all that time.' Her face sags with an old sadness. The grand reveal of Oddbean's second-to-final resting place might be the start of healing for Dafydd but it will still be a rocky, if not impassable, road.

'Anyway.' Meryl brightens. 'I'll take two *TV Guides* this week, please. Betty Next Door needs one so she knows when *The Brokenwood Mysteries* is on. I want her to watch it so we can talk about it.'

Off she goes, a skinny ray of sunshine, with promises of secret book 'Pictionary' sketches to come soon. She's left behind a freshness, a hopeful atmosphere that even Stevie is feeling as Kitty goes to the fridge. He is rewarded with a nugget of mouse cheese.

Today's emails include two from school librarians with lists of books to track down and order. One list is so long that eco-Kitty lets me print it out so I can annotate it with the results of my investigations. I pull the stool up to the stock computer and get stuck in, searching through the New Zealand suppliers, then on to the international suppliers for some of the titles not being brought in by our major players. One self-published New Zealand title is, frustratingly, only available through the US, it being cheaper for the author to have it printed on demand there rather than stored with a Kiwi distributor.

I'm about halfway done and have smiled vaguely through my reading glasses at a blur of glossy brown hair at the counter when I tune in to the conversation.

'Clients love *Freeze Frame*. It's always the most well-thumbed mag at the end of the month. Oh, and I brought you this candle for the Battle raffle.'

'Oh, Courtney. How are you?' Courtney is a beauty therapist in one of Havelock North's salons, the only one I trust with the minute amount of grooming I can tolerate.

'Hi, Eloise. Haven't seen you in a while.' I'm sure she's peering disapprovingly at my eyebrows, neglected for several months now. I'm starting to look like my grandad.

'No, and as you can see, I need to book in for a tidy.' She nods, squinting as she scrutinises the rest of me. Courtney's eyebrows are textbook: symmetrical and smooth, black against her flawless bronze skin. She catches herself staring.

'Sorry. Occupational hazard. I'm forever studying eyebrow shapes.' Kitty's hand unconsciously wanders to smooth her own youthful, well-behaved brows. 'Come and have a sniff of this, Eloise. It's English Pear and Freesia.'

I scrape back my stool and join them, glad of a break from playing book detective.

'Oh, it's divine.' She's holding a very classy-looking candle and I go in for a second whiff before Courtney fluffs the tissue back around the rim and pops it in its bag. 'That's really kind of you.'

'Well, we all have to chip in to help those families. There but for the grace and all that.'

I look at the bag properly now, emblazoned with Le Studio du Nord and their stylised female face logo and it prompts a memory.

'Courtney, I saw a woman with one of those bags recently. She's at least my age, I reckon, maybe a bit older. Blonde, wears a fedora and is beautifully made up. I've seen her a couple of times in the last few days but she must be new in town, I think. She always wears red lipstick — I swear it's Rouge Dior.'

Courtney laughs good-naturedly. 'I didn't have you down for a Dior girl, Eloise.'

'Hey, I read a lot. You get to know all sorts.' Like cooking, I love to read about fashion, interiors, things of beauty and style. It doesn't mean I apply any of it in my real life.

'I think I know who you mean. She came in for some moisturiser.

Distinctive style, certainly. She mentioned that she was here for a couple of weeks for work.' She looks at me curiously. 'Why are you interested?'

'Just being nosy, really. I was wondering if we had someone famous among us. Havelock can be a bit of a star magnet, eh.' She accepts this — it's a small place and those of us with businesses in the CBD tend to notice the comings and goings.

'Maybe you're right! I'll have to look up if there's any filming going on. How exciting!'

We chat about other things — Battle of the Book Clubs, in which Courtney's clinic staff enter a team; the new salon that's opened up on Joll Road — then she grabs her pile of slippery magazines and turns to go. She takes a few steps and comes to a halt.

'What was that?' Courtney is creeping forward, eyes scanning the worn carpet in the direction of the cookbook section.

'What? What did you see?' Kitty scoots out from behind the counter. Courtney points, but it's half-hearted.

'It was a blur.' She blinks a few times. 'I must be seeing things. I'd better grab a coffee before my next client.'

CHAPTER 23

Garth: 18 days until Battle of the Book Clubs

Eloise's ridiculing of me for not recognising Will Pickett has given me a great idea for a Battle of the Book Clubs round. We've done author photo rounds before, but people generally only guess the most famous authors, which means everyone gets David Walliams and no one identifies the current New Zealand Poet Laureate.

My cunning plan is to take the famous authors we all know and Photoshop them as if they were in disguise. I say Photoshop but I'm actually going to use a very old version of Paintshop Pro because I can't afford an Adobe licence and I don't approve of pirating media of any description.

Stevie joins me in my home office, snuggling beneath my desk and sitting on my feet, which we both enjoy.

After about an hour I no longer care whether the concept works as a quiz round because I'm having great fun. So far I have given Tina Shaw a great big ginger beard and masquerade mask, added a stripy shirt, beret and a string of onions to Monty Soutar; and made Roald Dahl look like the McDonald's clown in protest at the number of people asking if we have the Ronald Dahl books.

Stevie's ears prick up, tail flicking against my legs before he dashes from under the desk. His claws clatter on the rimu stairs and he issues a half bark, the one he uses when he is caught between wanting to woof a welcome while also wanting to go unnoticed. I glance at the clock on the computer — 4.27pm. I don't expect Eloise back for another hour and a bit, but the rattle of the garage door and the roar of a diesel engine over-revving confirm that she's home early. My pulse rate rises. Why?

'There's another one,' she shouts, charging up the stairs, Stevie at her heels.

As is often the case, a significant part of this conversation has already taken place in Eloise's head and I am left playing catch-up. My thoughts go to the shop and Basil. Do we now have an infestation, a veritable plague?

'Another mouse?' I ask.

'Another message.'

This doesn't clarify matters greatly and the confusion must show on my face.

'From Pinter,' snaps Eloise. 'Paula just sent it through.'

'Oh.'

'Is that all you've got to say?' Eloise storms into the lounge. 'We get a message from a serial killer and your only response is "oh".'

I'm momentarily silent, filtering through possible responses. Ruling out 'Calm down', 'Would you like a cup of tea?' and 'The message wasn't actually for us', I plump for 'Sit down and tell me about it'. This is apparently an acceptable response, as Eloise drops onto the sofa and pulls her MacBook from her bag. I join her and after a long pause while our wireless network thinks about whether we are in range, even though I can practically reach out and touch the router, the texts appear on screen, sent in an email by Paula.

> Unknown: Mendelsund all good for you, Mendelsund for me with Priestley's Goole.

> Pinter: Do not disappoint me, my Merovingian.

I read the messages a second and a third time, hoping for a spark of understanding that doesn't arrive. 'Well, that's as clear as Chinese self-assembly furniture instructions.'

'I was hoping you'd make more sense of it. Your brain works differently from mine.' Eloise pats me on the leg. 'Differently from everyone's.'

'What was the first message again?' I ask, ignoring the backhanded compliment.

Eloise pulls it onto the screen, and the one after it too.

> Pinter: It's been a while. I trust Mendelsund was as anticipated?

> Pinter: I am delighted to hear that the gears are finally in motion and that my Faith appears to be well placed.

I scribble the messages onto a sheet of paper, both because I work better with hard copy and because we think differently when interacting in a non-digital form; that's true for everybody's brain, not just mine.

'There are three uses of the word Mendelsund across the four messages so that has to be the place to start.'

'You said you thought it referred to me — "the Girl with the Dragon Tattoo".'

'Yes, but that doesn't really makes sense now, so I'm prepared to admit I may have been wrong.'

Eloise leans back, folding her arms. 'Who are you and what have you done with Garth Sherlock?'

'Harsh.' I stick out my bottom lip.

'Okay.' Eloise uncrosses her arms. 'I accept that you're the real you. No one else can look that sulky.'

'Also harsh.'

'Also true.'

Childishly, I grab the MacBook, turn it so Eloise can't see the screen, then google Peter Mendelsund. On top of all the book cover designs, I find something else. He has another string to his bow.

'That's the ticket!' I tap a finger against the screen, knowing that because Eloise can't see what I've discovered, it will vex her excessively.

'Stop being a cock or I'll set fire to your Ben Aaronovitch collection.'

'Book burning! You wouldn't dare.'

'You're right, but I'd put your signed copy of *Winter's Gifts* up as a raffle prize.'

She probably would, so I spin the MacBook around. The screen shows another book cover, with a bicycle made from typed letters as the centrepiece.

'Peter Mendelsund — *The Delivery*,' reads Eloise. 'He's written a novel.'

'It would seem so.' I rub my goatee, the rough whiskers tickling my hand. 'Although I'm not yet sure how that revelation helps us.'

'*The Delivery,*' repeats Eloise. '*It's been a while. I trust "the delivery" was as anticipated?*'

'What?'

'That's how Pinter's first message reads if you replace *Mendelsund* with *the delivery*.'

I bounce excitedly on the sofa, applying the same logic to the second message, the reply from his New Zealand counterpart. '*The delivery* all good for you, *the delivery* for me with Priestley's Goole. What the hell is Priestley's Goole? Something to do with a flesh-eating grave robber? That sort of sounds like Pinter, although he decorated flesh rather than eating it.'

'It's G-o-o-l-e not G-h-o-u-l, and it does make sense.'

'How?'

'J.B. Priestley, *An Inspector Calls*,' says Eloise.

'I read it in school but can't remember much. Some rich sod did the dirty on a younger woman.' I sit back, a thought striking me. 'Is it a reference to Franklin White? What he did to Tracey, and countless others by all accounts?'

'No, no, no. Goole was the inspector in the play.' Eloise grabs a pencil and scribbles down: 'The delivery all good for you, the delivery for me with the inspector.'

'Bloody hell! They're talking about the books. The one delivered to the bookshop, *Betrayal*, was delivered successfully. But *The Cause of Death*, delivered to the house in Waipuk, is now with Tama, our friendly detective inspector.'

'Maybe. But we shouldn't jump to conclusions again. We might be wrong.' Eloise draws a ring around the message. 'It does makes sense.'

'And the bit about the Merovingian?'

'Wasn't he a character in *The Matrix*?'

'*The Matrix Reloaded*, actually.' Not that I was obsessed with the films when they came out.

'Do you think it's the codename for his connection in New

Zealand? Faith Saxon or whoever it is?'

'Could be. Pinter was a literary agent, so he could be Agent Smith, which would make you Trinity.'

'And who would you be?'

'Well, Neo, obviously.'

Eloise snorts. Then, seeing that I wasn't joking, she pats my knee. 'Of course, love.'

CHAPTER 24

Eloise: 17 days until Battle of the Book Clubs

Kitty and I are suffering from 2pm ennui, trying hard to resist the emergency chocolate. We've done all the stock, Kitty is chasing up customer orders, Garth has dropped Stevie in on his way to 'do something' and I'm mooching around the shop in search of the worst patches of dust. One of our favourite customers, Bernard, is following me, trying to get inside info on Battle of the Book Clubs.

'Have you got a special guest lined up, Eloise?'

'We did have Fiona Kidman but she can't come, so we're in the middle of sorting out a replacement.'

'Who's that, then?'

'I couldn't possibly say.'

The savvier of Battle teams keep a close eye on happenings in the run-up to the event. They do their homework on the special guest as soon as the name is revealed, on which authors are doing talks at the bookshop or appearing at the local Readers and Writers Festival, on who's won recent major literary prizes. Bernard is on the Sci-fi and Fantasy Book Club team and they're very competitive.

'Hurgh.' Bernard bats his thigh thoughtfully with a copy of *Jack Scratch*. It's a hardback graphic novel and gives out a violent thwack at odds with the good-natured grin on his face.

I move around to the Māori language section, noting patent fingerprints in the dust, the whorls clearly visible to the naked eye. They're quite small and high up, so it was probably a child being carried, patting things and tracing their fingers along the shelving. A quick squirt of furniture polish and they're gone. I feel fleetingly sad, as if I destroyed something precious.

Bernard's huge frame darkens my peripheral vision. He's following me closely, murmuring his way through the *Jack Scratch* blurb. 'Cap'n Catnip. Ka mau te wehi.' There's a low, rumbling laugh. He's choosing a book for the boy he mentors, who has become captivated by graphic novels.

'Are you doing a quiz round on Māori writers?' he asks, picking up a copy of Tīhema Baker's *Turncoat*.

'Bernard. Mate. I'm not telling you anything about Battle of the Book Clubs. To be honest, we've only written about two rounds of questions so far, so there's not much to tell anyway.' I should be writing questions right now, but the dusting won't do itself.

I continue on to the dumpbin containing Amelia's current top Young Adult picks. Vampires are back, and there's a beautiful cover swarming with butterflies which, on closer inspection, have incisors to match those of Predator. I wave it at Bernard, who squints and says, 'Cool!' He grabs it but I snatch it back. It's too scary for his wee boy.

'It's just that our team need all the help we can get this year. The new guy's gone to Rarotonga for three months with work, and we're having trouble getting a full crew.'

'That's a shame,' I offer vaguely.

I'm deconstructing the Dalek now, removing the books that bear the brunt of whatever wafts through our door from the road. There's a fresh layer of fine yellow pollen from the nearby trees and I carefully wipe each book, placing them in a pile before spraying and polishing the shelves. The pollen will be back tomorrow but I'll know I did it, and so will the persistent Bernard, who is still talking until—

'Aaaaaaargh!' A sound at a pitch much higher than anything I've heard from Bernard before squeezes its way from him as he bolts towards the door. 'A rat!' He points to the floor around the card stand. I can see neither tail nor whisker but I can guess the identity of the vanishing vermin.

'It's not a rat, Bernard, it's just Basil.'

'Who the hell is Basil?' Bernard's usual baritone is still hovering around tenor but he's tentatively approaching again.

'Kitty's mouse. Or he will be if she can ever catch him.'

Kitty appears, tiptoeing through biographies, armed with mouse cheese, Stevie creeping warily behind her, sniffing hopefully.

'Did you see him?' whispers Kitty. 'Which way did he go?'

Bernard points, in the manner of a silent cinematic ghost. Kitty and I crouch to peer under the shelving, Stevie between us, eyes fearful, whiskers a-quiver. We wait in unaccustomed silence. Nearly a minute passes.

There's a small commotion in the doorway and a strident voice calls from behind Bernard.

'Permission to come aboard?'

'Oh! Granted, Admiral,' I call as I haul myself up from the carpet. Bernard steps aside and the elderly gent limps on deck, confusion clouding his brow.

'What's all this? Why are the crew keeled over?'

Kitty has unboxed a few squares of cheese and is lying flat on her stomach, cooing to the gap between the shelving and the floor. She's also fiddling with some kind of translucent green tube, apparently a humane mouse catcher. Stevie's eyes flit between the cubed treats and the Admiral, for whom he has a grudging affection.

'We've got a mouse, sir. Kitty's trying to catch it.'

'Invaders, you say? Remove the food, Kitty. You'll never get rid of the blighters that way. You can borrow the ship's cat overnight if you like. Excellent mouser.'

A horrified Kitty clambers upright, face flushed, green eyes blazing. She opens her mouth to speak but the Admiral gets in first, expounding as he marches up the steps to the counter.

'Has my *Navy Today* docked? I've finished last month's and there's the second part of an article on Exercise Bersama Lima I'm keen to catch up on.'

Kitty, trailed by Stevie, follows the pounding of his cane on the fake wooden floor.

'Also, Kitty, I really do not recommend poison in this instance,' the Admiral continues. 'No stink worse than a fallen rodent you can't find.'

'That's something we agree on then,' mutters Kitty as she bends to riffle through the special magazine orders behind the counter.

I look over to Bernard, who has cautiously moved over to the picture books. I can still see him clearly over the intervening military history stand because he's 6 foot 5 of mouse-fearing muscle.

Kitty hands the Admiral his *Navy Today*, and as he flicks through to his article I take the opportunity to study him. He's been a part of our bookshop whānau since the beginning, thrilled to find a place that will order his esoteric books and magazines, and people (well, Garth) who understand his military mores and terminology. I imagine the man he was fifty years ago. He's formidable enough now, despite the dotty elderly gent persona, so must have cut quite a figure in his youth.

He meets my gaze with his own, firm and kind. Something in his eyes calms me.

'Admiral, the information you—'

He claps the magazine closed and slaps it on the counter, startling Kitty, who is monitoring the CCTV screen, presumably for any further evidence of our tiny guest.

'This contains the report I've been waiting for, thank you, Kitty.'

As Kitty puts through the sale, the Admiral turns to me.

'I'll see you at Battle of the Book Clubs, Eloise. I'm sure you'll get it all sewn up. Good day.'

Although it takes a moment to shuffle the one-eighty degrees required to leave, he has decisively shut down any further conversation. Even so, I feel bolstered. I dash off an email to Tama and Paula, informing them of the Admiral's inclusion in our tactical support team, and giving them a roundup of the latest evidence. There'll be raised eyebrows and busted brain cells occurring in both hemispheres as we all strive to keep up.

I'm about to go and check on Bernard when Stevie, who has been pacing behind the counter, stops stock still. He drops into a crouch and begins a slow stalk out onto the shop floor. Nudging Kitty, I follow at a safe, 'don't spook the Stevo' distance. An expectant hush has fallen over the shop; even the traffic outside seems to still in anticipation. Silently, Stevie makes his way down the ramp until he comes to a halt between the cookbooks and a card stand. He lowers himself to the floor, concentrating fully on a tiny creature that is frozen in place, valiantly pretending not to be there.

Mirroring Stevie's stealth, Kitty appears from behind the Dalek, commando crawling towards the fugitive. Bernard watches from the other side of the picture books. Nobody appears to be breathing.

Stevie's gaze never wavers, pinning his prey in place. In slow motion, Kitty cups her hands around the timorous beastie.

Sir Basil is in custody.

CHAPTER 25

Garth: 17 days until Battle of the Book Clubs

'It's Franklin White, it has to be.' I point accusingly at the screen on the aged stock computer where glows a Wikipedia page. It's heading towards closing time, and I've dropped in to the shop to cover Kitty, who has had to shoot out on some urgent business. The school rush is over, and as I don't want to do the dusting I'm back into trying to decrypt Pinter's messages.

'Have some tea.' Eloise passes me a steaming red and white mug.

Taking a sip, I stare longingly at the goodies cupboard under the sink. 'Emergency Hobnobs too?'

'If I let you have a biscuit every time you went off on one, you'd be . . .' Her voice trails off.

'I'd be what?'

'Fatter than you are.' Eloise gives my arm a gentle stroke. 'Sorry, I tried to think of a nicer way to put it.'

'You think I'm fat?'

'I think you'll make a great Father Christmas if we do a grotto again this year.' Eloise tilts her head. 'Well, physically at least.'

'That wasn't my fault. Nobody told me that as a Santa impersonator I had to actually lie to the children.'

'It's not lying, it's called pretending. And all you had to say was yes, you would be visiting with your reindeer and sleigh on Christmas Eve, and not that you'd sub-contracted the job to their parents.'

I take another sip of tea and try to steer my thoughts back on track. The Merovingian. Not just a rude, salacious character in *The Matrix*, as I'd thought, but apparently an entire dynasty in the Dark Ages. That's not the part that has provoked my outburst about Franklin White, though. I point at the screen again. 'Look. The Merovingian dynasty was the ruling family of the Franks. It couldn't be clearer. Franks . . . Franklin White. How much more evidence do you need?'

'Oh wow. You've just found a word on a Wikipedia page that is similar to another word.' Eloise folds her arms.

'I'll grant you it might be circumstantial but it can't be discounted because of that.'

'You'd be happy to stand in the witness box and submit that as evidence, would you?'

I don't answer.

'Didn't think so.' Eloise takes a sip from her own mug, the one that's 'handmade' — glazed pottery that cost a fortune because apparently producing a mug that looks like it was a five-year-old's craft project is an expensive process.

'You don't reckon it's worth considering?'

I'm so wound up in the case that I'm aware I may be losing objectivity, not that Eloise is any less invested. In fact with all that she suffered she's likely to be more conflicted. Even so, as always, I value her opinion.

'Sure, we should look into it.' Eloise tucks a strand of pink hair behind her ear. 'I mean, Franklin is certainly as sleazy as the *Matrix* Merovingian, only I don't see how he'd have any connection with Pinter. I'm sure he doesn't have a literary bone in his body. And how would White do anything from prison anyway?'

'Pinter's in prison, and a bloody secure one too. Nobody's ever escaped from Belmarsh but he's still managed to finagle his way back into our lives.'

'Pinter's a psychopathic criminal mastermind.' Eloise makes a 'maybe' gesture with her free hand. 'Franklin, not so much.'

'He got away with a murder for twenty-plus years, and according to Tama he still might get off the hook.'

'That doesn't make him competent. Sometimes it's better to be lucky than good.'

I peer into the stock room, where Stevie is making whimpering sounds. He's lying with his head on his paws, nudging his nose against a pile of empty boxes that seems to have appeared from nowhere. 'It's all good, boy, I'll get rid of them later.'

'Forget the stock room,' snaps Eloise, dragging me back to the computer. 'What does the rest of the article say?'

'I only got as far as the Franks.'

Eloise scrolls down the page, reading. 'The Merovingian wasn't just the Franks, it was the Saxons too.'

'Damn!' I look up guiltily, my hand over my mouth. To my relief, the shop is still empty. 'We're back to Faith Saxon!'

'It looks that way.'

'Is it too late to cancel her and get someone else?' We thought we'd struck gold when Faith said yes.

Eloise clutches her misshapen mug tight in both hands. 'I think it is. Keep your enemies close and all that.'

An unusual scrabbling of claws and whining emanates from the stock room. What's got into Stevie? For thirty-odd kilos of muscle he's normally as quiet as a mouse. 'If it is Faith, what's her endgame?'

'Aha, caught you,' comes a voice from the counter.

We both look around, startled.

'Faith Saxon *is* coming to Battle of the Book Clubs!' says Matty, who I would bloody well swear wasn't in the shop ten seconds ago.

'We can neither confirm nor deny.' I try to keep my face blank.

'So, that's a yes, then, Garth.'

There's the sound of tumbling boxes followed by a yelp from the stock room. Eloise pushes me towards the counter. 'You help Matty. I'll deal with Stevie.'

'Oh, is Stevie all right?' Matty clasps his hands together. 'It sounded as if he might have been hurt.'

'He's fine.' There's a sharpness to Eloise's words as she disappears to check on our fur baby in the stock room. Why is she leaving me to deal with Matty when it'll be her that he's come to see? I feel like I'm missing something.

'Other than refusing to confirm who our guest speaker may or may not be, how can I help you?' I ask.

'It's more of a social enquiry, really. Do you know of anyone who might want to join our Battle team? Damian was taken ill after the event at the Eco-Hub. He's actually in hospital.' Matty places his hands on the counter, lips pursed. 'I'm not saying that Mr Pickett's food was to blame but you can never be quite sure what you're eating, can you?'

I'm often uncertain of what to say when customers share bad news about friends or relatives, and doubly so when it involves anything medical. However, today my delayed response is not down to social awkwardness but the revelation that another Battle team member has been struck down. Eventually I manage to say, 'That's awful.'

'It is.' Matty smooths his hair. 'On the bright side, he's terrible at quizzing and only turns up for the wine, so if you can suggest someone better we might be in with a chance of winning this year.'

CHAPTER 26

Eloise: 17 days until Battle of the Book Clubs

Matty's unintended bombshell having just exploded in our faces, we do the only reasonable thing after closing. We pack Stevo in the car and head to the pub.

The Shamrock is pleasantly busy this early evening. The landlord has just sparked up the heaters in the garden bar and vape steam is wafting inside, clinging to my Sherlock Tomes hoodie.

'Shall we sit outside?' I am in possession of one pint of delicious hazy IPA and one pint of Very Tasteless Lager. Garth is in possession of Stevie, who is becoming agitated at the dithering over seating, darting back and forth on the short bit of lead Garth's allowed him, scanning for a safe place to settle.

'No.'

'Why not?'

'It's outside. Chilly. Smoky. Noisy. I won't be able to hear anything.'

Fair enough. Garth struggles when there are multiple conversations occurring around him, only hearing snatches of many rather than all of one. I lead us over to an alcove table in the quieter part of the lounge area. Stevie hops up onto the upholstery and shoves his face towards Garth's capacious, treat-filled coat pocket. I take a sip of beer as I ease myself into the seat opposite.

'Good grief, Eloise. Bit parched, are we?' I look at my glass as I place it on the table. It's nearly half empty.

'Well, it has been a strange afternoon.'

'If you drank that fast every time we had a strange afternoon you'd be permanently pissed.'

'Winning at life.'

We allow ourselves a chuckle, and Stevie gets a dried duck tender that's destroyed in seconds. By the unspoken understanding of a couple married since dinosaurs roamed, we give ourselves a moment, a brief respite from the difficult conversation ahead of us.

It's work kick-out time and regulars swing through the door, some coming over to pat Stevie and ask how the bookshop's going, some heading straight to the bar with a look of thirsty relief. The noise level's gone up and I hear a delighted screech of laughter that makes me smile. A glorious Motown remix is playing and I'm glad I chose to be situated away from the speakers: distracting for me, discombobulating for his nibs.

'Did you order food?' asks Garth.

"Course.'

'What is it?'

'It's a surprise.'

He frowns, perturbed. He always has the same thing and I always order it for him. My unease makes me irritable and I don't put him out of his misery.

'So. Damian,' says Garth.

'Yes. Unfortunate.'

'It's a little more than unfortunate. Someone's picking off Battle team members, I'm certain of it.'

'It could still be coincidence.'

'You know it isn't. And there's the whole Faith Saxon thing. Is she in on it or not?'

The waiter chooses this moment to deliver a very large pizza.

'What is that?' asks Garth, disapproval creasing his brow.

'It's a pizza,' says the waiter, confused, gently placing it on the table before returning to the service hatch.

'But what's that red stuff on it? Is it' — he leans in closer — *'beetroot?'* His face is a picture of disgust and I feel the momentary lightness of gentle amusement before a second pizza arrives, layered in mortadella. Garth's relief is palpable.

'The Battle team members could all have been at the same party or something,' I say. 'That kind of thing happens all the time around here. Look how many people have stopped for a chat this evening.'

Garth waves a slice of pizza in time with his shaking head before shoving it into his chops. 'Ahh! Hot! Burn!' he huffs, mouth wide open, trying to keep nuclear-hot cheese from the roof of his mouth.

'Okay. Let's inventory the victims,' I suggest.

Garth nods, still huffing blistering cheese heat.

'Lily. Lovely old lady. Possibly poisoned by breakfast mushrooms, or by a dubious brownie at the Grey Folks meeting. Star member of Chloe's Battle of the Book Clubs team.'

Garth nods. 'Tama's not happy about that,' he says from a mozzarella-seared soft palate.

'Next up is Miss Mooney. Permanently removed from her Battle team by the Grim Reaper armed not with a scythe but with an imaginative bit of mushroom-embellished baking.'

'You're getting a bit dramatic. Is Prudence rubbing off on you?'

'Nah, this beer's six per cent.'

'Oh, right.'

Garth takes a dainty sip of his boring beverage, mulling. 'It's Battle that connects the two. I know we're a small community but not *everyone* is in a book club. Look how many people come by the shop and ask how long we've been open, even though the shop's been there for years.'

'Okay. So next up is Damian from the *Pick it with Will* launch. He's in Matty's team.'

'Well, that one could have been an accident — with foraged food on offer it's hardly a surprise he got sick.' As far as Garth's concerned, vegetables should all come wrapped in plastic.

'All three were at different events and locations. The only thing that seems to link them—'

'—is that all were going to be in Battle teams.' Garth's shoulders sag.

'Oh dear.'

'Yup.'

'Oh dear, oh dear, oh dear.'

We stop talking for a contemplative pizza break. My beetroot and bean paste topping is divine. Garth eyes it warily as if I might force-feed it to him. I waggle a piece in his face and he throws a piece of sausage at me.

The moment of levity is over too soon. Stevie profits from the sausage hurling, I finish my beer and Garth and I stare at one another, each daring the other to say what needs to be said. Inevitably, it's me who bites the bullet.

'I think someone is trying to sabotage our quiz by picking off team members.'

'Do you really think it's Pinter? Ferreting about with his cryptic texts? What the hell is he up to?' Garth frowns, squeezing his brain in an effort to understand.

'Continuing his mission to ruin our lives in as drawn-out and cruel a way as possible.'

'If it carries on, our reputation and our business will suffer, that's for sure. God knows where it will end, especially if more people die. But why is he doing it now, after all this time?'

'Argh. I'm so tired and this beer's doing its job beautifully. My brain can't link anything together.' I hurl myself back in my chair and pull my legs up after a cursory boot cleanliness check.

'Should we call it off? Cancel Battle?' says Garth.

'Hang on a minute. There are consequences to that. The Oaks really need the money, for a start. We could perhaps just . . . I dunno . . . warn people that something fishy might be going on.'

The waiter returns to clear our plates, catches my eye, points at our empty glasses and raises his eyebrows. He can see the conversation is tense.

'Yes please.'

'Just a Coke, mate, thanks,' says Garth.

A post-work posse crashes through the door sounding like they've pre-loaded. That or the anticipation of being in the pub has made them giddy. Stevie's forehead creases at the racket and Garth instinctively rubs our pup's lovely ears. He clears his throat, thinking through an idea as he speaks.

'If we send out an email we could cause mass panic. And if it gets into the news it would alert the perpetrator that we're on to them.'

'So our choices are what — carry on as if nothing is amiss or come up with an excuse to cancel and see what happens?'

'Or catch our poisoner. I think we need to chat with Tama again.'

CHAPTER 27

Garth: 16 days until Battle of the Book Clubs

The aroma of coffee fills the air and I inhale deeply while I wait for Kim to deliver my own delicious fix.

Eloise's dark eyebrows rise, a look of disdain on her face. 'Do you have to?'

'I do. It just smells so good.'

'But the sniffing. You're worse than a hard-core cocaine addict.'

'I can't help that I cherish the roasted bean. We all have our poisons.'

'Not the best choice of words under the circumstances.'

'Fair point.' I bottom-shuffle on my stool to get more comfortable. I've managed to nab us my favourite corner table where I can sit with my back to the wall and observe the rest of the café. There are the obligatory estate agents sitting by the counter looking at their phones while ignoring each other and their coffees. Then up near the doors there are a couple of young mums with buggies. A baby in one buggy gums a board book. Even from this distance I recognise the unique style and colourful drawings of the wonderful Donovan Bixley. I think it's *The Great Kiwi ABC Book* and from the happy smile on the baby's face it tastes as good as it looks.

As I stare past the mums and out through the glass doors my gaze comes to rest on the remnants of the statue wrecked by Eloise and the Tomato. Twisted rebar pokes from the ground, lumps of concrete clinging to it like overcooked chicken to a kebab stick. Yellow caution tape flutters in the wind; the police tape has been removed, the crime scene having given up its secrets.

My hand drifts to my left shoulder, fingers massaging the muscle that still pains me where the seatbelt bit in. I hope solving our present cases proves less violent.

'Where were you?' asks Eloise as my attention returns to her.

'Crashing into a statue.'

Nodding, she smiles. 'Kind of fun, wasn't it?'

'No.'

She holds her thumb and index finger close together. 'Just a teensy bit fun, maybe?'

'Still no.' I reach across and take her hand, giving it a squeeze. 'Necessary and instrumental in solving the case, I'll give you that. Fun, no.'

'I must admit I was worried about coming back here.'

'Why? We did what we had to do.'

'It doesn't always work like that though, does it?'

'I suppose not.' I drum my fingers on the table, then stop when Eloise gives me the look. 'Do you think Tama will be on board?'

'On board with what?'

'If we go ahead with Battle we might be letting a murderer murder.' The chrome machine on the coffee counter hisses as if a pantomime villain has just come on stage. I really hope it's my drink they're making; maybe it's being back at the scene of the crash or maybe it's the stress of Pinter and the poisonings but my nerves are shot.

'We're not letting them, we're catching them.'

'If we get it right.'

'We will get it right. We're good at this.'

We are good at this, but sometimes the cards don't fall your way. I remember a job back in the day when I was an incident response driver. We'd had an informant tip-off about a ram raid that was to take place on an electrical appliance shop and we were loitering nearby, ready to swoop in and nick the offenders. Unfortunately, a 10:9 shout came across the radio — an officer in serious trouble needing assistance, the one call where you drop everything to get there. Blues and twos blaring, we raced to assist, rescued a colleague from a serious beating and in the process totally missed the ram raiders.

And that's my concern: Eloise and I can plan and prep and do everything possible to apprehend our culprit, but if things don't go our way it'll be a damn sight more serious than a few nicked VCRs.

Kim heads towards the table, a large pottery cup in each hand, and I offer a silent prayer of thanks to the gods of caffeine because surely there has to be more than one god for something so miraculous.

'We've got a green Popular Penguin in the shop for you,' says Eloise, taking one of the cups.

Kim sets the other cup in front of me. 'Brilliant. Which one? I've ordered a few; I'm on a bit of a crime spree.'

'Us too,' I say.

Eloise kicks me under the table. 'Erle Stanley Gardner, *The Case of the Postponed Murder*.'

'I'll pop in after my shift today. I can't wait to be embroiled in another murder.' Kim holds a hand to her mouth and glances at the statue remains. 'Oh! Not that I meant . . . you know . . . it's just . . .'

'It's fine, Kim,' says Eloise, smiling at her. 'We get it.'

As Kim hurries away Tama joins us, sliding onto a stool. 'What was that all about?'

'You know how it is,' says Eloise. 'You solve one murder by smashing a car into a statue and suddenly you're a celebrity.'

'Okay, superstar,' says Tama, grinning. 'What's so urgent?'

'Do you want a coffee?'

'I don't have time. I've got the quarterly Crime Statistics and Performance Management meeting at HQ, which is absolutely as interesting as it sounds.'

'We'll try and keep it quick.' Eloise leans in and lowers her voice as she outlines our fears that Pinter has orchestrated the poisoning of Battle team members. At the news about Damian, Tama frowns and folds his arms.

'So that's three people taken ill—'

'Poisoned,' I correct him.

'—at events you were involved in. Why wouldn't he just poison you two and be done with it?' asks Tama.

'Pinter's complicated,' I say, twisting my fingers together. 'Killing us would be too quick. That may be his goal but he wants to take his time, to enjoy it. He wants to make us suffer, like he made—'

Eloise holds up a hand. 'We don't need to go there.'

Tama's forehead crinkles. 'And ruining a book quiz makes you suffer? Gets him even for you ending his killing spree and putting him in the choky?'

Hearing him say it out loud does make it sound pretty thin. Unlike Eloise and me, Tama isn't blinded by Pinter and is able to apply a more rational copper's brain.

'Obviously it doesn't get him even. It's probably just the start of some far more demonic plan,' says Eloise.

We all sit in silence for a moment and my gaze returns to the fluttering caution tape around the remnants of the statue. A blue hatchback in the car park draws my attention. It's the same model as the one driven by Fedora Fatale.

'Do you have any actual evidence of deliberate poisoning?' Tama asks, clearly still sceptical.

'We were hoping you might help us get the evidence,' I say. 'Are you able to pull the toxicology report for Erma Mooney?'

'And maybe ask Chloe to check the hospital system to find out what ailed Lily and Damian?' Eloise adds. 'All three were admitted to hospital.'

'You're asking a lot.' Tama exhales puffing out his cheeks. 'I'm not sure that I want Chloe mixed up in this.'

He's right — we *are* asking a lot. If Tama gets caught he'll lose his job and his pension; if we involve Chloe the same would most likely happen to her. I feel guilty that we're even asking, only it was Tama who sort of got us started on all this, and with the ever-present spectre of Pinter we can't really do this without his police resources. 'It could solve a murder, and potentially more if the current victims don't recover.'

'And maybe prevent some additional poisonings,' adds Eloise.

Tama frowns. 'Prevent more murders?'

You don't have to be an expert in body language to know he's doubtful. Hell, I'm doubtful too, but there's that annoying itch at the back of my brain, that thought just out of reach, that feeling I can't shake that we're on to something, we just don't understand what.

Eloise cups her hands around her coffee. 'Battle of the Book Clubs is a great quiz but it's hardly worth committing murder just to get your name on the trophy.'

'That leaves us with a bigger plan,' I say. 'Pinter.'

'Or coincidence,' says Tama.

'Don't forget Pinter sent that book to Belinda. And maybe had something to do with her death too.' My fingers ball into a fist.

'And where Pinter's involved the body count will continue to climb,' warns Eloise.

'Does any of this link to the Kiri Wereta cold case? And if it does, how was her death part of Pinter's plan to hurt you guys?'

Eloise straightens, a look of determination in her eyes that I last witnessed not thirty metres from where we now sit. 'That's what we're going to find out.'

CHAPTER 28

Eloise: 15 days until Battle of the Book Clubs

Garth and I are sitting in the Loan Ranger looking at a photograph on my phone of a photogenic young woman: big smile, black pixie haircut, nose ring, skinny jeans. You can feel the energy busting out of her. It's the hero image of an old article in the *Omnom Magazine* archives.

'Can you read it out? I don't think I've got my glasses,' says Garth, patting himself down optimistically.

'Yup. Here we go:

'*Kiri Wereta is an up-and-coming star in the culinary firmament. Her brand-new café, Found Food, is taking on more staff to meet demand for her cuisine, billed as 'take away that gives back'. Kiri says the combination of fresh ingredients, herbs, spices and tantalising colours is the key to their success. 'We use as much foraged food as the season allows. Working with Mother Nature enables us to get creative with our textures and flavours.'*

'Sounds amazing,' I say.

'Hmm,' offers Garth.

We stare out of the car at a neat weatherboard home: white picket fence, roses, the lot. This is where Kiri lived, in a unit at the bottom of the garden of the property belonging to her parents. We've phoned ahead and spoken with her mum, under the pretence of writing an article on the dangers of amateur foraging. Garth has Tama's copy of the coroner's report on his lap. The cause of death is listed as accidental:

> **Circumstances of Death**
> On the last day of her life, Ms Wereta had returned home after closing her café, calling in to see her mother with some chocolate and beetroot cake, several of which she had taken to a 'cake off' at the food bank in Hastings for a charity auction.
>
> Mrs Wereta reported: 'Kiri was cheerful enough when she called in but was clearly unwell and said she was feeling shivery and dizzy and had a headache. She said she was going to bed. About an hour later I went to check in on her and she'd vomited and wasn't responding. I called the ambulance straight away.'

The pathologist goes on to state that liver and renal tests were abnormal and that death was most likely due to organ failure brought about by accidental mushroom poisoning.

'Come on, then,' I say. Neither of us moves. A face appears at the window, a hand is raised in greeting, then beckons. I wave back and we get out of the car.

The front door opens as we head up the path. The lawn either side is lush, dark green and pampered. Mrs Wereta sees me looking, folds her slim arms and chuckles.

'That lawn is like a fourth child to Sid. He never stops mucking about with it. Drives me nuts.' She's proud rather than truly irritated. She ushers us into a neat living room.

'I saw you dithering in the car. Not easy, is it, visiting bereaved parents, but I like talking about my girl. So I made the tea while you got your courage up.'

She's physically very much like her daughter, exuding vitality. The only real difference is her long, plaited hair, silver glinting through the black. Garth perches on the two-seater sofa and accepts a cup of tea, catching my eye. We rarely accepted food or drink when we were police but this woman's hospitality is irresistible. Mrs Wereta sizes Garth up, then hands him a scone with jam.

I sit on a wingback chair, the sage fabric worn and soft. There are family photographs everywhere: on the walls, standing on an occasional table, on the dark wood dresser. It's cluttered and cosy.

'Yep, we got five moko and another on the way. Another girl.' Mrs Wereta sips her tea, then proudly points and names the framed chubby faces. 'Nothing if not fertile, my boys!' She sniffs and raises her eyebrows.

I laugh and she meets my eye and smiles.

'You have a lovely family, Mrs Wereta. We're so sorry about what happened to Kiri.'

She puts her tea down and looks thoughtful. Then she points at the wall to the left of the fireplace. Kiri's wall.

'Look at that one. She could barely walk and she's putting little flowers on that cake for her brother. "Pink and green" she said, over and over. She knew it would look good and she was right. We made that cake for Shaun every year after that. Still do. Pink and green.'

Nearly every photo of Kiri shows her in the kitchen or at a picnic, the growing girl in her element, feeding her whānau.

'She obviously got it from her mum. These scones are delicious, Mrs Wereta.' Garth, when fed, can be quite charming.

'Ah maybe, maybe. It was her passion, her vocation as they say. That café was a dream come true for my girl. Amazing. Even after how it ended. She got her dream.'

I sip my tea, eyes roaming the evolution of Kiri from batter-smeared toddler to rangy teen, to confident, successful woman. Mrs Wereta watches me, bobs her head to affirm that her child had a good life. Short, but lived well. Then she sits up, her face business-like and determined.

'She didn't even like mushrooms, that's what I find so hard to get my head around. Bloody pathologist found mushrooms in her vomit and said they were the poisonous kind. But right from when she was little she wouldn't eat them. She spat them out, saying they were all wrong and rubbery. She was all about textures, right from the get-go. That horrible word "mouthfeel". She was always on about stuff like that.'

Mrs Wereta is calm enough but there's clearly a sense of doubt, a mystification over why Kiri died the way she did.

'And she knew what she was doing. She did her homework, had pictures of all the stuff you should steer clear of — the bad mushrooms, yes, but also other stuff like karaka kernels and some of the ferns that aren't so good. She was nobody's fool.'

'So you don't believe she would have willingly eaten the mushrooms?' asks Garth, cutting to the chase as usual.

'Nope. She wouldn't.'

'Do you have a theory?' Mrs Wereta looks at Garth, then at the ceiling, as if Kiri's spirit hovers there, waiting to enlighten us.

'Well, I've been thinking about it for all these years. I can't fathom why she'd have eaten mushrooms unless someone made her do it.'

Emboldened by his witness's candour, Garth goes straight for it.

'Do you think someone might have wanted to harm her?'

Mrs Wereta's face is stunned for a second, then it falls into the shape of an old sadness.

'She was a well-loved, successful girl, Mr Sherlock. There are some jealous types out there. But there were no threats, no arguments. The police didn't find anything like that. I can't work it out.'

'Tell us about Kiri, Mrs Wereta,' I chip in. 'What was she like? What did she get up to?'

'Hoho, anything and everything. The twenty-eight years that girl lived were packed with adventure, I can tell you. She worked and travelled soon as she left school and went all over: Mexico, Peru, places like that. When she came home we had a right old kitchen shake-up. We were her guinea pigs!' She laughs at the memory. 'She never poisoned us with anything although I nearly expired from the chilli in the beans one time. She wrote this crazy story about it, from the chilli's point of view no less.'

'I'd heard she was a writer,' Garth sits up, interested.

'Yes, she was always making things up — recipes, stories, all sorts. There was a publisher interested in doing a cookbook based on what she did in the café. She'd started writing the recipes for it and they were just haggling over the details. Hang on.'

Mrs Wereta goes to the sideboard and rummages around in a drawer, bringing out some papers. They're recipes written in a beautiful curling hand, illustrated with pen drawings: what looks like salmon wrapped in kawakawa, wild fennel feathering up the side of the page.

'They were going with that kind of old-fashioned look — handwritten and illustrated. Not like all those celebrity glossy ones these days, eh.'

'It's stunning. The instructions almost read like a poem,' I say in genuine admiration. It's clear Kiri loved the process, and respected the need for foraging to be sustainable, venturing out for kawakawa in the morning, taking just a few leaves from several plants to maintain their vitality and abundance. The content is similar to Will Pickett's book, but the format and style a fresh take.

'Big imagination, Kiri. She liked to scribble in her spare time.'

I can feel Garth eyeing me.

'Do you have any of her writing?' he asks.

'I can probably find something. It'll be out in her unit. Most of her stuff is still in there, although I'll have to do something about it soon as her little brother's moving in with his missus and the twins.' This thought lightens her face from wistful to hopeful.

'I'd love to read the chilli story, Mrs Wereta.' I look over to see Garth licking his sticky fingers appreciatively.

'Āe. I'll drop a copy into the bookshop for you.'

Our meeting seems to have come to a natural end and I stand to help Mrs Wereta tidy the cups and plates away to the kitchen. She boxes up a couple of scones for Garth, 'seeing as he enjoyed them so much'.

'What are you really up to?' Mrs Wereta calls, leaning against the doorframe as we head down the path. Like her daughter, she's nobody's fool. We turn and I can't quite fathom the look on her face: suspicious, intrigued, keen maybe. I decide to 'fess up, but only a little.

'We've heard about some food poisoning incidents recently that don't have solid explanations. We're just trying to see if there's anything, past or present, that might connect them.'

'Why? What's it got to do with you?'

It's a good question, and one she has every right to ask.

'When we work that out, Mrs Wereta, we'll let you know.'

CHAPTER 29

Garth: 14 days until Battle of the Book Clubs

Agatha greets me at the door as it's after hours and the library is only open to those attending a writing workshop. She's wearing a brightly coloured dress that matches her rainbow cat's eye spectacles. 'Welcome, Garth, here for the workshop? I didn't know that you wrote.'

'I try. I think that there's a frustrated wannabe author inside most booksellers.'

'Librarians too,' admits Agatha.

I've spent years scratching in notebooks trying to write the next great fantasy novel, hoping that being surrounded by the books of so many wonderful authors, their genius would seep into me by some sort of literary osmosis. After yet another round of rejections from publishers and agents, I've decided that perhaps some actual training in the craft might be a more pragmatic approach.

I head up the stairs to the events area where three rows of eleven chairs have been arranged facing a large TV display and a lectern equipped with microphone, water bottle and laser pointer. I am immediately vexed by the fact that the central access aisle has unevenly divided the odd number of chairs and have to fight to stop myself from rectifying the abomination.

Taking a seat by the aisle, I try to distract myself by focusing on the first slide of a PowerPoint that glows from the screen. It shows three brightly coloured children's building blocks embossed with the letters ABC, alongside which is the presentation's title 'The Building Blocks of a Novel — a workshop by Adele Broadbent'.

Having come straight from the shop after closing, I am the first to arrive. Normally I will do anything to avoid getting to an event early because making small-talk is one of my biggest fears, ranking just below snakes and just above the zombie apocalypse. Today I've put on my big-boy pants in the hope of catching Matty Trindle, who, as the current chair of the local branch of the New Zealand Writers' Association, is organising the event.

'Hi, Garth,' says a voice behind me.

'Hi, Adelios.' I turn in my chair, not needing to stand, as even in her platform shoes Adele is knee high to a grasshopper. Only when I see the puzzled look on her face do I realise what I've done. In the shop we have pet names for many of our most beloved authors and because I was on a Netflix *Narcos* binge at the time of the release of Adele's latest novel, *If Only*, she became known to us as Adelios Broadbentios. The key part of that is the 'known to us' clause. It's a bookshop secret that I've just blabbed. I have no choice but to brazen it out and hope she thinks she's misheard. 'I'm really looking forward to the workshop.'

Adele twiddles nervously with a green earring in the shape of a question mark, her gaze passing over the rows of empty chairs. 'I hope people turn up.'

'They absolutely will, you're a brilliant writer.'

Adele grows just a little bit taller at my well-deserved praise; the additional height will prove useful if she's to see over the lectern.

'You're too kind.'

'Not something I'm often accused of.'

She gives me another perplexed look and I hear Eloise's voice in my head: 'Weirdo.'

'Is it true that you've got Faith Saxon for Battle of the Book Clubs?' Adele asks, probably trying to steer the conversation back to normality. 'I loved *The Weed Killer*.'

'It was great. Gruesome though. She's giving Paul Cleave a run for his money!'

'So that's a yes?'

'Destroyers of the Universe don't need any help — you've won it for the last six years!' Diversion accomplished.

A battered box file under one arm, Matty Trindle saunters up to join us. 'Oh, I see how it is. Sneaking some clues. Did I just see money change hands?'

'You most certainly did *not* see money change hands.' I stand and put on my best affronted face. 'It's very clear in the rules that all bribes must be concealed in brown paper envelopes.'

'I'll leave you to it — I need to get my notes in order.' Adele retreats to the lectern, presenting me with a perfect opportunity to quiz Matty.

'You've come prepared, I see.' I gesture to the box under his arm, which has NZWA written in thick letters on the side.

'Always trying to recruit new members. Are you any good?'

'I'm more of a dabbler, really. Not a proper writer.'

'All the novels in your shop are written by people who started out as dabblers. Don't be coy, send me something,' says Matty. I will never send him anything.

Eloise invariably laughs at the emails I draft, saying I just barrel into a subject without any preliminary chit-chat or what she calls 'niceties'. To be fair, she's correct; if I'm sending an email it's for a reason. Eloise would say the same rule applies here — I should preface my questions with some 'niceties'. But there's not much time, so, hoping that my scribbling confession has done the warm-up job, I launch straight in. 'I'm interested in finding some information about a couple of possible former NZWA members and I'm wondering if you'd remember them or have any records?'

Matty pats the box file. 'Well, I'm not sure how much I'd be allowed to tell you. Data protection and all that.'

'Data protection is unlikely to be an issue. They're both dead.'

'Oh.'

From the expression on Matty's face I realise that I probably could have done with some niceties there as well. But it's too late to backtrack so I blunder on. 'Kiri Wereta. Do you happen to remember her?'

Matty's eyes move up and to his left, a sign that he's trying to recall a memory. 'No, sorry. Not ringing any bells.'

'What about a Belinda Henare?'

'Maybe. That name seems familiar.' Matty fiddles with an ornate silver cufflink in the shape of a book. 'I can't recall the details, though.'

'Is there any way you could check back in the records?'

'Check for what, dear boy?'

'Whether they were members, what connections they had to the literary scene, that sort of thing.'

'That's not going to be easy.' Matty looks dolefully down at the battered box file. 'The NZWA records could best be described as an explosion in a filing cabinet and we lost a plethora of information when we transitioned to a new web platform in 2020.'

'Well, anything you can find out would be useful.'

His immediate duties calling, Matty heads away as a gaggle of writers ascend the stairs, among them a few faces I recognise. I'm not sure 'gaggle' is the collective noun for writers — from my experience I feel it should be a procrastination of writers or possibly an indecision of writers. No, that's unfair, it should be something positive — an editorial of writers, an anthology of writers. A creativity of writers.

Feeling like an impostor, I take a seat.

At the half-time break the room is buzzing with excited writers, discussing the building blocks of character, plot and setting and how they interlink. The workshop has been inspirational and I can't wait to get stuck into the second half. Adele appears buoyed by the progress so far and is chatting enthusiastically with Matty and Will Pickett by the lectern as Agatha wheels over a trolley of drinks and nibbles.

Feeling suddenly peckish, I make my way to the refreshments the library has kindly laid on.

'It's a surprise to see you here,' says Beth, placing a jug of orange juice on the table. 'I didn't know you wrote.'

'Enthusiastic amateur. You?' A nagging feeling scratches at my mind, something's out of place, only I can't grasp what.

'Oh, no. I'm a reader through and through.' She gestures to the plates of food. 'I'm just here as a Friend of the Library.'

'Your moonboot is gone!' I say a little too aggressively, having suddenly realised the source of my angst.

'What? Oh yes. Got rid of it yesterday.'

'That must be a relief.'

'Life changing.' Beth hands me a plate. 'You should try the caramel slice.'

'Seeing as there's no Eloise here to monitor my diet, I might just do that.'

I pick up a plate and select a golden-brown sausage roll and a piece of the caramel slice, then as an afterthought I add a mini potato-top pie, because potato is a vegetable and I don't want to be entirely unhealthy.

I'm debating whether to start with the caramel slice, because I'm technically an adult and therefore allowed to eat pudding first, when there's a commotion over by the lectern. I take a huge bite of slice just in case it's an emergency and I need the energy, then hurry over.

Adele is slumped on the floor, bent over double clutching her abdomen, trying to scream quietly. Alongside her lies a wine glass, a slick of merlot staining the carpet.

Swallowing down caramel slice, I dial 111.

CHAPTER 30

Eloise: 13 days until Battle of the Book Clubs

'Adelios, I'm so glad you're okay!' The welcoming smile on the patient's face freezes as she tries to parse the words she just heard.

We're visiting Adele Broadbent in hospital and I realise I've just called her by the Very Secret pet name Garth and I use for her. She elbows herself up in the bed, grimacing at the effort, and frowns at me. The guilty flush starts in my armpits and bleeds upward.

'Once could be a mistake, but twice? Why are you guys calling me Adelios?'

Garth takes the seat by the window and I pull out the chair beside the bed. It makes a god-awful scraunch.

'All our very favourite authors have nicknames.' Garth is attempting to be charming, smiling at Adele in a way he seems to think is endearing.

'But that's not my nickname,' she says, exposing the flaw in Garth's claim.

'Ah, not to you it isn't, but it is to us.'

'I must still be quite sick, possibly hallucinating,' says the tiny pale figure, flopping back against the pillow.

I'm keen to move this conversation on from confusion and embarrassment, so I present Adele with our thoughtful gift — a couple of easy-read magazines. Garth wanted to bring grapes 'because that's what you take people in hospital', but I explained that nice eating grapes have a high carbon footprint (seeing as he was so worried about the pecorino) because they are not commonly grown in New Zealand, and, more importantly, the poor woman has only just ceased vomiting and is probably on dry toast, if that.

'What's the prognosis?' asks Garth, launching straight in, as per.

'Well, I'll live, but they're keeping me in until they're happy with my kidneys. Some kind of poisoning but they're doing blood tests and stuff. I'm conscious now, and not throwing up, so I'm happy.' She picks up one of the magazines, an old-school music one I thought she might like, and holds it at arm's length, squinting. 'Nik Kershaw. Nice.'

'Poison?' Garth scrapes his chair forward, interested. The noise on the rubber floor is atrocious. Adele is starting to look as if she'd rather not have visitors this afternoon.

'Was it something you ate, or . . .' I wave in the general vicinity of the world, where dangerous things lurk waiting to poison people. More often around here than you'd think.

'I didn't eat anything before or at the workshop. Never do. I don't know if I touched something or inhaled something.'

'What were you doing before the workshop?' Garth drums his fingers on the arm of the chair. I try not to be irritated but I can't concentrate, so I glare at him until he notices and stops, folding his arms against his chest.

'I was in the garden, clearing the weeds out of the veggie patch ready for planting.' Adele addresses an itch on her wrist and I notice a blistery rash. 'Just thinking about it makes my skin prickle. I should wear gloves.'

'Could it be something in the garden that got you?' I ask.

'Dunno. Could be.' She huffs back onto her pillow and closes her eyes, patting Nik Kershaw's face. Garth is inhaling to release another question but I get in first.

'Come on, husband, let's leave Adele in peace. She looks knackered.'

'That's Adelios to you,' she says.

⁂

'Let's pop in on Lily while we're here,' I suggest as we head down the corridor, glancing at Garth to gauge his reaction. As anticipated, his face is that of a person trying to come up with a socially acceptable excuse for not visiting our treasured customer. He tries. He fails.

'Nope. I can't do any more sick people today. This place is depressing.' Lots of people hate hospitals but Garth's aversion extends to doctor's surgeries, the vet, televised medical dramas and conversations involving illness or injury of any sort, unless it concerns his own knees, in which case he'll chat. 'I'll wait in the car.' He's already pulling his phone and earbuds from his pocket and I know he'll be immersed in geopolitics within moments of arse hitting seat.

I get the information I need from the front desk and trip the yellow brick road of hospital navigation, a line leading to what I still think of as the geriatric ward but which is now known as the older persons ward. I wander in and a nurse looks up from his computer as I approach the desk. He smiles, inviting enquiry.

'Kia ora. I'm looking for Lily Ross.'

'Bed 26.' He points and off I pop.

Lily is upright and knitting as I approach, trying to politely acknowledge the curious stares of several older persons and not invade the privacy of those who are snoozing. There are some visitors fussing around with water jugs and pillows, and one bloke with his size tens up on the bed regaling an older man so physically similar it has to be his dad with a story about Jock and a large amount of beer.

Lily looks up and I am struck in the heart by how pleased she is to see me.

'Eloise! How lovely. I'm very bored.' She chucks what might be the arm of a jumper on the bed, knits her fingers together and plops them on her lap, fully expecting to be entertained.

'You look great, Lily. Will you be allowed home soon?'

'You've just caught me, I think. I'm waiting on the doctor to do the final sign-off. I'm flippin' desperate to get home for good. Puss will have missed me. Our Joanna doesn't give her treats when she pops in to feed her.'

The sun is scattering in, lighting up the glossy floor and stroking our skin. It's cosy in here, oddly full of life as Jock's mates chuckle about his hangover. Lily nods in their direction.

'That's Tom. Stroke. His lad comes in every afternoon. This is one of his cleaner stories.' She looks over her glasses at them. 'Highlight of my day.' I follow her gaze and see the 'lad' holding on to his dad's arm, tears of laughter streaking his face, shaking Tom a bit to emphasise a detail of the story. It seems Jock may be redecorating his bedroom after a particularly virulent bout of beer-related nausea. Tom's face is lopsided, clearly amused.

'Speaking of vomit, Lily . . .'

'Awwmigod, don't remind me.' She fidgets and pretend pukes.

'Do they know what caused it yet?'

'I've lost about a stone, you know. Can't afford to do that at my age.' She picks at her nightie, presumably to demonstrate a lack of Lily within it.

'Just think how much cake you'll be able to eat to put it back on though,' I quip, and am surprised to see her face wrinkle in disgust.

'Oh no, not for me. That's the last thing I remember before I conked out. Matty handed me a plate of brownie and I was so looking forward to it. It had cream and everything. Next thing I knew, I woke in here feeling like death. I still feel sick just thinking about it. No, I think I'll have to develop a Guinness habit to get my weight up.' The anticipation closes her eyes and relaxes her cheeks, but my ears have pricked up.

'Matty gave you the brownie?' I ask.

'Yes. He was telling me how he researches his books. Probably looking for more material among us oldies. We've been around the block a few times.'

'And how does he do his research?'

'I can't remember a word he said. But it was very interesting.' Lily starts to giggle and I catch the bug. We have a lovely few moments where she gets herself under control before catching my eye and cracking off again. Tom's lad looks over and calls, 'What's the joke?' This sets Lily off again and she waves him away. I scurry to gather my thoughts as something feels important here.

'Did Matty make the brownie?'

'Not sure.'

'He often bakes for Grey Folk, doesn't he?'

'He does. Nearly as good as his mum was, too. There's a roster but I don't look at it anymore. I can't be bothered baking these days.' I can't either, and nod in sympathy. Turns out Lily can't be bothered with knitting but her daughter-in-law requested a jumper, assuming that knitting was something one became good at over the age of sixty-five.

'I'm looking forward to eating good food again. They try in here but . . . I don't know . . . budget cuts or something.' She sighs, remembering something. 'I hope they've changed my home help. The temporary one keeps cooking what she wants to eat. I can't face a full English first thing in the morning and I bloody hate tinned tomatoes — and mushrooms.' She scrunches up her face at the thought. 'Oh, thank god, here comes a doctor.'

A woman in a doctor-ish coat whose hair is so red it appears to be on fire is striding towards Lily's bed. She comes to a halt and turns her icy blue eyes in my direction.

'Are you family?'

'No, no, I was just visiting and . . . err . . . I'll be off then.' I peck Lily's cool, divoted cheek and make my escape to think about mushrooms, and cake, again.

CHAPTER 31

Garth: 13 days until Battle of the Book Clubs

The hospital doors slide open and I make my way past the smokers gathered outside. I'm not a fan of cigarettes but I do commend the commitment of the hospital-gowned and wheelchair-bound nicotine addicts, some of whom appear to be plugged into oxygen cylinders and other medical paraphernalia. And give them their due, at least they're not vaping, polluting the air with sickly-sweet-smelling clouds.

Making my way across the car park I admire a dark, metallic blue Ford Falcon parked next to the Loan Ranger. It's tricked out with tinted windows, a set of snazzy alloys, lowered suspension and a spoiler the size of a blue whale's flukes.

The car shudders, the doors opening in unison as four burly Black Dogs unfold themselves from inside. I should turn and retreat to the relative safety of the hospital but my brain is bizarrely sidetracked by the realisation that the Falcon's suspension isn't lowered at all: it was just struggling with the combined weight of its occupants.

'Boss wants to see you,' the largest of the four says to me, folding his thick forearms across his muscled chest. His long black hair is tied up in a knot that pulls the skin on his prominent forehead tight. I am not a fan of the man-bun, tending to associate it with pretentious hipsters, but there is nothing hip about the man stood before me and I keep my feelings on the issue to myself.

'We're visiting a friend in hospital,' I venture, even though I suspect that these gangsters aren't the types for bleeding-heart stories. 'I'm just waiting for my wife.'

'The only person you're visiting is the boss.' Man-bun pulls a black cloth sack from the rear pocket of his jeans. 'You can be bagged and punched in the guts or you can walk with me over to the doughnut shop.' He gestures to Don's Doughnuts in the middle of a parade of shops across the road, sandwiched between a dairy and a florist.

I glance back towards the hospital.

One of man-bun's associates growls. 'I'll fuck you up if you make me run.'

'Time to choose.' Man-bun brandishes the bag.

It's not much of a choice, and it's not like I'm going to come to any harm in a doughnut shop — well, not if you discount my pre-diabetes.

The shop has only one occupant, other customers being temporarily dissuaded by the gang presence outside. He's wiry and a little younger than me, with greying shoulder-length hair and a face I might consider kind if I didn't know better. Smoke trails from a cigarette in his fingers. He taps ash on the floor and points to the seat opposite. 'I ordered you a latte.'

The word seems incongruous coming from this man. I sit opposite and place my hands around the plastic-lidded paper cup. Drawing some comfort from its warmth, I meet the boss's eyes. With calloused fingers that seem better suited to stripping an engine or delivering a beating, the boss opens a white cake box in which nestle a selection of doughnuts ranging from the traditional to colourfully iced with a variety of extravagant toppings. 'Help yourself.'

It would be rude to decline; under these circumstances even Eloise couldn't chastise me. I reach for a salted caramel ring. The boss's hand shoots out and grabs my wrist. 'Only fair to warn you. Don's Doughnuts are more addictive than meth.'

I scrutinise the sugary fried confection at my fingertips. 'They don't actually contain meth though, do they?'

The boss smiles. 'No need. These are for a different type of addict.' He relaxes his grip and I take a bite. The sweet-salty sugar melts in my mouth and I understand the warning — it tastes phenomenally good. I swallow, washing down the dough with a glug of coffee.

'Good, eh?' says the boss.

'Exceptional.' I lick my fingers. 'Although I don't suppose you brought me here for my culinary opinions.'

'Sharing kai is important.'

My tongue runs over my teeth. Is this like in some fantasy story where accepting food from the fae somehow binds you to do their bidding? There is very little that is fairy-like about my current company, so perhaps I'm over-thinking. 'To be honest, I was kind of hoping we were done.'

'We are done.' The boss selects a custard-filled doughnut and rips into it. 'For now.' A frosting of sugar clings to his upper lip and the tip of his nose, which, were I not mildly in fear of my life, might be considered comical. I fret over whether to tell him. I've never understood the etiquette for this sort of thing. How well do you have to know someone to tell them they've got spinach in their teeth or a low-hanging booger? And how does the fact that they could end your life with a click of their fingers play into the equation?

I decide not to mention it, and instead try to work out why I'm eating doughnuts and drinking a latte with probably the most dangerous man in Hawke's Bay. 'And you brought me here because . . .'

'This time, I'm doing you a favour.' He says it like it was community-mindedness that had motivated me to find out who had ripped off the Black Dogs for a hundred grand, and not the fact that they'd threatened to beat me to a pulp if I didn't. 'Got some information about your cop friend.'

He must mean Tama; I can't imagine a situation where he'd be in contact with Paula from the UK. 'The DI?'

The boss nods. 'Knew him when he was on the beat. One of the good ones.'

Tama has always struck me as a decent bloke, and in the job you do get to know criminals, even becoming friendly with some. But there's a line, one that I just can't see Tama stepping over.

'What's the information?'

'He's being followed.' The boss takes a phone from his patched leather waistcoat and pulls up a photo. I immediately recognise the blonde-bobbed Fedora Fatale, photographed outside the Shamrock.

'Who is she?'

'A private investigator.'

'Why is she investigating Tama?'

'We've dealt with her before. She's hard case. Our barrister hired her and she got a few cases tossed, threw doubt on the cops' evidence.'

I've seen this done by defence counsels when we were in the job, and it's usually a last resort. If the evidence in court is good then the only hope is to make the officers look bad by digging up dirt in their personal lives. I had a colleague who was in court giving evidence in an 'assault on police' case who was presented with a list of his last five video hires from Blockbuster: *The Terminator, Lethal Weapon, The*

Predator, *Demolition Man* and *Reservoir Dogs*. 'These are all violent movies, are they not, PC Birnam? Do you enjoy violence?'

'She's working for your lawyers?'

The boss shakes his head, dislodging a small shower of sugar dust from his face. 'Not this time. She's been hired by Franklin White.'

So that's why he's passing on this information. It's not about helping Tama, it's about thwarting Franklin White. The man who, thanks to me, they believe stole their money. And he may well have done. I mean it wasn't like I specifically told them it was Franklin. They sort of jumped to that conclusion and I was happy to let them run with it, Franklin being the most deserving candidate.

'You want me to tell Tama so he can make sure his ducks are in a row?'

'No. That's where it gets complicated.' He fixes me with the dark eyes of a killer. 'I'm going to tell you something else, and it doesn't go beyond you and me.'

'Okay . . .' I agree, feeling that I have no choice.

'We have a player in deep with the cops. If you tell Tama he's being watched he'll go to his bosses and they'll go to their bosses and someone's going to figure out they've got a leak.' He looks into the doughnut box. 'So the way this is going to work is, I keep you informed, you keep Tama out of trouble.'

I shuffle uneasily on my chair. 'How am I supposed to do that if I can't tell him?'

'That sounds like a you problem.' He picks out another doughnut. 'As long as Franklin White goes down, and the cops don't rumble our man, we're sweet as these doughnuts.'

'I can't control what the courts do.'

'And I can't control my temper, so you'd better hope that Franklin fucking White gets banged up.'

He crushes the doughnut, jam oozing over his fist like blood.

CHAPTER 32

Eloise: 12 days until Battle of the Book Clubs

I'm glad to be in the peaceful sanctum of Sherlock Tomes. Today's email load is light, and lovely Kitty is fossicking happily around the poetry section. I might even get a chance to write some quiz questions. I decide to check in on Garth, at home levelling up his D&D character. A nice, normal activity to get him back on an even keel. Normal for him, anyway.

> Me: You ok after your brush with the underworld?

> Garth: 10 extra hit points. Strength +1.
> An extra attack and now a crit on a 19 and a 20.
> Improves saving throws too. Garth.

It's possibly the longest text I've ever had from my husband, so I'm taking it that he's okay, though I don't understand a word of it.

> Garth: Thanks. Be down soon for the raffle prize delivery to Chrissy. Coffee? Garth.

I'm a little incredulous that we're now on speaking terms with the Black Dogs. I mean, what is this? Better the devil you know? If you can't beat 'em, join 'em? When life gives you lemons, hang out with gangsters? I'm all for interacting with members of our community, but Garth popping off for a natter and a doughnut with a gang boss while Pinter is dripping poison down the phone wire is disconcerting to say the least. Also troubling is making sure Tama is up to date with developments, the latest of which is the poisoning of Adele, while keeping mum about Fedora Fatale. This secrecy makes me uncomfortable. Thankfully, he's already noticed her so will be a little more careful in the environs of unit 39.

Clambering through the chaos of the stock room I poke my head around into the furthest recess to check on Stevie. He's snuggled next to his new best mate, who, if I'm being honest, is starting to niff a bit. Clearing and stacking as I go, I make my way back into the shop.

'Kitty?'

'Hmm?' She's reading the blurb of a new book on freshwater ecology, away with the eels.

'Kitty. I need to talk to you about Basil.' That gets her attention.

'Is he okay? You haven't let him out, have you?' She inhales sharply. 'Oh my god, has Stevie eaten him?'

'Of course he bloody well hasn't. Basil needs his nappy changed, that's all. I can smell him and if you want to keep Garth off his scent then you need to get him freshened up.'

'Oh. Right. Okay.' She bustles purposefully up the steps and heads for the low cupboard next to the fridge. Its awkward inaccessibility and clusters of old mouse droppings make it the ideal home for Kitty's secret stash of rodent-care items. She shoves the mini-fridge slightly aside in order to open the door and fishes out the humane trap, hands it to me, then goes out the back to retrieve the mouse himself.

She reappears with what can only be described as a mouse mansion, closely flanked by Stevie, who is not letting his new BFF out of his sight. The rodent dwelling has two storeys connected by a staircase on which Basil has been seen to do complex acrobatics. His bedding is plush, his diet that of a mouse king.

'Here, you can hold him while I do the things,' Kitty says to me. She opens the hatch and deftly scoops up Sir Baz, popping him in the tube. 'Don't let him go, though.' She squints at me and I choose not to be offended by the suspicion in those eye wrinkles.

'After this epic adventure? The Odyssey of the Basil? Not on your nelly.'

I place the trap on the bench. It's Perspex, which is great because I can see him, but why is it green? Are mice attracted to green? He's quite a handsome boy, I have to say. Ears the shape of pāua shells, huge black eyes, the most quivery of quivery whiskers. He nibbles at a piece of Whittaker's Creamy Milk, then sits back on his bum, tiny mouse feet splaying to the sides, waving the lump in his surprisingly human front paws before chewing through it at the rate of a quick-cut saw. Then he looks at me as if to say, 'Is there any more?'

I leave Kitty to the housekeeping and pop Basil-in-Perspex under the counter to attend to a customer after some birthday cards. I close the till and retrieve our VIP guest.

'Are you sure Garth doesn't know?' Kitty asks.

'Well, I haven't told him. I think Stevie would if he could though. He's in love.'

'I know! It's so cute how he just wants to hang with Basil.' Stevie receives a cube of Basil's cheese for being a wonderful guardian of the mouse, then Kitty holds her hands out for her baby.

She carefully unhinges one end of the trap and holds it over the enclosure, allowing Basil to catch a whiff of freshly chopped apple and plop himself into his newly laundered home. She places the lid on top and we take a moment to gaze lovingly at our new family member. So mesmerised are we that we don't hear Amelia come in through the back door.

There's a gasp and we look up to see her frozen for a moment before she does a little dance of excitement and joins us in reverence of the rodent.

'I thought you were getting him one of those wire cages, Kitty. Wouldn't that have been cheaper?' asks Amelia.

Kitty straightens, reddening slightly.

'Well, apparently you have to be quite careful with those because of their little feet. We don't want him getting bumblefoot from a wire floor.'

We all nod wisely, Amelia and I with vastly different ideas of what the hell bumblefoot is, I suspect.

'Shit!' I suddenly remember. 'Garth's coming down soon. We'd better hide the fugitive.'

There's a scramble to secrete Basil and his accoutrements. I am wrenched away by actual bookshop work as a white-haired lady approaches with a piece of notepaper clenched in her hand. She hesitates upon seeing the mouse-related tableau but decides her questions about John Boyne are more important.

'Is *Earth* as good as *Water*?' she asks, peering over my shoulder enquiringly. I decide to stick to the elemental conversation, it being easier than explaining the shifty behaviour of the staff.

'Oh yes, it's incredible. But I do worry about what's happened to John Boyne for him to write such traumatic things so heartbreakingly well.'

She nods, makes her purchase and leaves, passing Kitty on her way back from disposing of Basil's soiled materials in the public bin outside of the front of the shop. The back door slams just as Kitty's making her way to the counter.

Garth appears through the Tardis door to find three faces smiling innocently up at him.

'What's going on here?' he asks, immediately suspicious. 'Where's Stevie?'

'Good morning to you too, Garth,' says Amelia, all sniffy innocence.

'Huh,' says Garth and heads for the kettle.

'I thought we were going out for coffee, love,' I say, starting the pat-down for phone, wallet and keys that is the precursor to me leaving anywhere, while body-blocking him from venturing towards the stock room. He takes a step back from me, right hand to left elbow, left hand stroking his chin. He looks at each of us in turn, three grown women who are awkwardly frozen in the suspicion of his gaze. Shit. He's definitely on to us.

'What are you doing here? It's not your day, is it?' he asks Amelia.

'Oh, I just popped in to . . . um . . . to ask Kitty about the Sci-fi and Fantasy Battle team because, you see, well, I might go on that team because . . . well, because I might. So anyway, I'll, um . . .'

Garth narrows his eyes at her as she makes to leave. 'Not so fast.'

Amelia freezes.

Garth eyes his next suspect. 'What is that on the sleeve of your cardigan, Kitty?'

We all look. Dammit! A curly bit of woodchip has attached itself to Kitty's cardy. How the hell did he spot that? Kitty turns the colour of Garth's least favourite vegetable.

'Oh, you know bloody Bateman and their packaging experiments. Must be a bit of that,' she says, picking it off and chucking it in the sink. 'Right. Coffee, Garth? I think there are a couple of Tim Tams left.'

First I've heard, but I'm impressed with her distraction techniques as she bends to rummage in the under-sink goodies cupboard. It's working, too. Garth's shoulders relax and he swings his arms to his sides, craning to see if the cupboard does indeed hold treats. Then there's a whine from the stock room.

'Stevo? Hello, my little Steve-a-woo, what's the problem?'

'Oh, he's—'

'Found them, Garth!'

'Oddbeans Special Roast, love?'

But it's too late. A very special kind of silence is emanating from the stock room. It is broken by the excited moan-whelps Stevie uses to try to communicate something.

Garth reappears, a look of disbelief on his face.

'And when were you going to tell me about this?'

Three booksellers and a dog form a speechless tableau, staring at Garth.

'Is this a good time?' All eyes turn to the counter, on the other side of which stands Mrs Wereta, Kiri's mum. She's holding a manila folder.

'Mrs Wereta!' What epic timing. 'Yes, yes, of course. Lovely to see you. We're just having an impromptu staff meeting.'

'It would appear we have one more staff member than I thought,' says Garth grimly.

Mrs Wereta looks between us, puzzled.

'Right. Anyway, you said you'd like to read some of my Kiri's writing and I found quite a bit of stuff in the sleepout.'

'Oh that's wonderful. Thank you.' She rummages in the folder and retrieves a stiff piece of A4. 'And look here. I forgot about this, what with everything that happened soon after.'

She hands it over. I stare at it, computing the implications, then hold it up to Garth. He squints and makes an 'I don't have my specs' gesture so I read it out.

'NZWA Tall Tales Competition 2016. Winner: Kiri Wereta. Judge: Faith Saxon.'

CHAPTER 33

Garth: 12 days until Battle of the Book Clubs

The Loan Ranger wallows over a speed bump like a stagecoach over a wagon rut. Eloise floors the accelerator and, powered by considerably more than four horses, we surge towards Hastings.

With one hand I grab the door handle for support, physical and emotional, while trying to balance a cardboard tray containing three takeaway coffees on my lap. 'Are you trying to frighten me into not talking about the mouse in the room?'

'You should be happy that we caught him.' Eloise swerves around a cyclist. 'I thought that's what you wanted.'

'It is. And then I wanted him disposed of in an ecologically friendly way, not kept to stink up my stock room.'

'*Our* stock room.'

'You knew about this, didn't you?'

'I don't really think Basil is the most pressing matter. Kiri Wereta died the same year that she won the local Tall Tales competition in

2016. The competition that Faith judged. That's what we need to talk about.'

Eloise is right of course. 'Don't think we're done with Basil; there's still a discussion to be had.'

'And we'll have it. Just not in the middle of a poisoning spree.'

Gripping the door handle tighter as we slingshot around the St Georges Road roundabout, I refocus my thoughts. 'Do you reckon Kiri's death was linked to the competition?'

'It's got to be, surely. Only who murders someone over a short story?'

It does seem rather far-fetched, but so does poisoning people involved in a fundraising literary quiz and we're entertaining that possibility. 'Someone who loses their publishing contract over it, perhaps?'

'Or a man who would maim and murder over the Oxford comma.'

We screech to a halt outside a run-down two-storey office complex that may have looked quite swish in the late 1980s. Above the door, next to a sign for a pest control business, is the Mighty Oaks logo.

'Come on.' Eloise shoulders her door open. 'I'll grab the raffle prizes from the boot.'

'So, how's it going, Chrissy?' I place the coffees on the Formica table, which is a horrible pale blue colour and reminds me of my childhood. Like most of the items of furniture in the three rooms that house the charity, I suspect it has been scrounged. When your job is supporting families dealing with cancer there are far better uses for your meagre resources than a state-of-the-art desk or a fancy lounge suite.

Chrissy inhales deeply, then suddenly bursts into tears. Not just the trickle-down-the-cheek kind; it's full-blown waterworks with snot and wailing. I'm stunned. I've never seen her cry before. Despite her job and the awful situations she deals with every day she always has a smile on her face. I feel like we've just kicked a puppy (which Eloise and I would never do), or stolen a biscuit from a toddler (which, for me, is a possibility if the biscuit in question was a Toffee Pop).

'Oh Chrissy, what is it?' Eloise shoves the box of raffle prizes onto a bench, then drapes an arm around her shoulder.

'I'm sorry, I'm sorry,' says Chrissy through her tears. 'I shouldn't put this on you.'

I want to add my comfort too, only I'm not very good with hugging — Eloise never cries — so I'm at a bit of a loss. 'We're friends,' I say, 'of course you can put it on us. What can we do to help?' I fish in my pocket for a clean handkerchief. I always carry a spare because Eloise never has one and invariably steals mine. I'm unsure of the protocol for handkerchief sharing but Chrissy gratefully takes it.

She wipes her eyes and sucks in a deep breath, regaining a degree of her legendary poise. 'Reagan has taken a turn for the worse and the hospice won't admit him.'

'Why not?' I ask.

'They're stretched and he's "not close enough to death". I've just spent the last of our funds on hiring a hospital bed to make him more comfortable at home.'

'You're out of funds?'

'We've got a bit of petty cash and an overdraft that I was hoping would tide us over until Battle of the Book Clubs.'

'Oh no,' says Eloise. 'That's awful.'

I look at Eloise and raise my eyebrows, hoping she'll interpret my gesture as a query about whether we have the funds to help out. I'm never sure how much money the bookshop has in the bank because Eloise handles that side of things, although I do know that we're pretty much hand to mouth.

Eloise misses my cue. 'In that case we'll make damn sure this is the best Battle of the Book Clubs ever,' she says. 'Isn't that right, Garth?'

'Err. Of course. We'll just . . .' I don't know what we'll just, and I certainly don't want to embroil a beleaguered Chrissy in issues of serial killers and poisonings.

'We'll just pull out all the stops. It'll be fine.' Eloise shoots me a smile, which I can't return, because actually nothing is fine.

'Oh, thank you.' Chrissy hugs Eloise. 'You're a lifesaver.'

Eloise takes a lengthy gulp of her Guinness, trying to drink exactly the right amount so that the line between the stout and the head falls between the bottom of the harp and the top of the word 'Guinness' printed on the glass. Apparently it's what 'the young people' do these days. My suggestion that we are not young people and that we don't need to follow trends on TikTok or Instagram or Myspace is met with derision, partly because everyone calls it Insta now and what even is Myspace?

I take a modest sip of my Coke, not feeling the need to partake in any imbibing games. The Shamrock is in mid-afternoon lull and we are far enough from the handful of other occupants to keep our discussion discreet.

'I feel for Chrissy and the kids, I really do,' I say, 'but more people are going to get poisoned if we go ahead with Battle.'

'You heard Chrissy. What choice do we have?'

'People might die.'

'That's not on us.'

'It kind of is.' I place my Coke dead centre of a circular beer mat. 'And they'll be customers, friends, maybe our staff. Maybe one of us.'

'That's why we're going to find Pinter's pawn and knock them off the board.' Eloise bangs her glass into a salt cellar, which fortunately doesn't fall off the table, as we don't need to encourage any more bad luck.

'And we do that how? Battle is less than two weeks away.' I place the salt cellar back next to the pepper.

'Same as always — good detective work and a lot of shoe leather.'

'My knees aren't so keen on the shoe leather these days.'

'They've never been keen on the shoe leather. Front thumpers and blues and twos all the way with you.'

'No guts, no glory.'

'No investigation, no paperwork, more like.'

I shrug. 'No one ever complained when we rocked up to a fight, or an RTA with body parts all over the road.'

Eloise bats her eyelashes sarcastically. 'My hero.'

'Well, if the cap fits.' I raise my glass and Eloise clinks her pint against it. 'And putting on my detective cap, I feel that we're missing something important.'

'Obvs. Otherwise, the case would be solved and the culprit banged up behind bars.'

'No.' My forehead crinkles and I bite my bottom lip, trying to make sense of my thoughts. 'I mean, of the things we know, I feel like there's some key point we've overlooked.'

'Okay, so let's go back to basics.' Eloise holds up three fingers and counts them off. 'Means, opportunity and motive.'

'Which cases are we looking at? The cold case or now?'

'Let's start with now. We're up to four victims: Lily, Miss Mooney, Damian and Adele.'

I down another mouthful. 'Means: Poisoning. So, we're looking for someone with a knowledge of and access to poison.'

'Without knowing what poison was used that's not much help, so let's make that an action — get a look at the toxicology reports. Hopefully Tama will come through soon. That might also help us understand how only a single victim was targeted in each case.'

'Opportunity: they've all been at public meetings where food and drinks were being consumed. It looks as if mushrooms might be out of the frame for Lily because she said she didn't eat any.'

'And Adele said she didn't eat anything at her event. We don't know about Damian.'

I cast my mind back to the food at the writing workshop, ruing the fact that I didn't get to finish my salted caramel slice before Adele collapsed. 'She didn't eat but she had a drink. There was red wine all over the floor when she fell.'

'So it had to be somebody who had an opportunity to poison her drink — hers and no one else's.' Eloise looks over at the bar where two shiny black hemispheres are set into the ceiling. 'Do they have CCTV at the library?'

'I don't know. That can be action two — get a copy of library CCTV if it's available.'

'Action three: get an attendance list for the writing workshop, the Pickett launch and the two meetings where people keeled over and do some cross-referencing.'

'That leaves us with the motive: ruin Battle of the Book Clubs to get back at us.'

'Pinter is that petty, but . . .' Eloise takes another long drink, although this time it's not part of a silly game; it's just that she really enjoys Guinness. 'Perhaps the motive is more complex.'

'I thought you were convinced it was Pinter.'

'He's definitely pulling the strings, no doubt about it, but could his person on the ground have their own motive too?'

'Like what?'

'The people targeted are all on the best Battle teams. Four of them have their names on the trophy, and Quill and Ink consistently place second or third.'

'So it's not just about ruining the event. Someone is so desperate to win Battle of the Book Clubs that they're prepared to kill for it?'

'No. The killing is for Pinter. The winning is about something else.'

'Like meeting Faith Saxon?'

'Oh yeah, the world's worst-kept secret. Maybe, but Lily and Miss Mooney were nobbled before Faith came on board.' Necking the remains of her pint, Eloise holds up four fingers. 'And that just leaves action four.'

'What's that?'

She hands me her empty glass. 'Get me another pint of Guinness.'

CHAPTER 34

Eloise: 11 days until Battle of the Book Clubs

'Maaaate, you shoulda been there.'

Clearly I didn't need to be, because Annabelle, our book rep du jour, is performing a full re-enactment of the winning goal at the recent Wellington Phoenix versus the inaccurately named Melbourne Victory match. I'll have to let her do the whole thing or she won't settle.

The meeting/event space in the shop is small, but big enough for a short, athletic woman to use as an imaginary football field. Scene I is the chap from the opposition: Annabelle performs a sprint on the spot, looks up for the pass, dribbles a bit then shoots, eyes following the invisible ball, hands scrunching the hair at her temples from its ponytail as she clutches in mock horror, mouth agape in the deep disappointment of a striker who has been robbed. Annabelle cackles with glee.

'Rippled right down the side of the net. What an opportunity lost.' She is clearly thrilled. 'But not to worry, right? 'Cos only two minutes later — if that, my friend — here comes a free kick.'

Scene II: She shuffles into position, huffing and wiping ghost sweat from her eyes. Small run-up, sweeping right-footed boot and I can practically see the ball arcing towards the penalty box. 'Then the big lad, Finn Surman, heads it and . . . *gooooooooal!*'

There's a bit of running in circles now to represent the Phoenix's celebrations. Then Annabelle stands still, locked in a silent reverie, before lowering herself into the comfy chair, a small smile on her lips, shaking her head at the joy of the memory.

'*Brilliant* goal.' She comes to, back in the room, and focuses on where I've taken the seat opposite. 'Want to look at some books?'

'Yes please.' I'm still coming down from the secondary high caused by all this excitement. I used to love going to see Nottingham Forest with my dad, back in the days of Brian Clough. I think Annabelle should come up with a one-woman show of condensed football matches. I'd pay to see it.

We turn to the task in hand, the December list from one of the major publishers, along with a few agencies. December lists are usually quite short, sometimes sweet, the bulk of the Christmas heavy lifting having been done by the October and November titles. There are several mid-list books I don't take, and some from romance authors who are making it big on TikTok with stories involving ice hockey and Formula One drivers.

'Is that young adult?' I ask, looking at the pastel illustration on the cover, a drawing of a young woman with big hair and a young man with a hockey stick over his shoulder and a salacious grin.

'No. No, no, no, no, *no*. It's healthy sex and a lot of it . . . and it's quite, umm, imaginative. Adult, definitely not YA.'

That won't stop them trying to buy it, and who can blame them? It's probably a lot healthier than what they'll find online otherwise.

Phyllis is covering the shop while I'm in the sales meeting and I'm distracted by her description of a book she's recommending to a customer.

'. . . an allegory for death. Swirling mists and trapped spirits. Gothic, ghastly and gorgeous.' I can't think of the title — another book I ordered months ago and have no memory of, but I want to read it. Well done, past me.

A Baker Boy cap bobs behind Phyllis as she makes her way up the steps to the counter. It's Matty, carrying said item of gothic gorgeousness, which has an enticing billow of grey and phosphorescent green on the cover.

He holds it up and waves it at me. 'Exciting! Can't wait to get home and start reading.'

Matty. How fortuitous. I look to Annabelle, who is riffling through her paperwork but seems relaxed. Reps can have appointments stacked closely throughout the day and I don't like to waste their time. I'm going to, though.

'Annabelle, do you mind if I just have a quick word . . .' I point at Matty.

'Nah, you go ahead. I need a wee and a stretch anyway.' She proceeds to haul herself from the comfy chair. I head towards Matty.

'Sure, if you're going to Dublin the Ha'Penny Bridge is the one they all go ga-ga for, but it's the Rosie Hackett Bridge I love. What a woman. Just get me started on her.'

'Reeeeally?' says Matty. 'I spent quite a bit of time in the UK a few years back but never made it to Ireland. Phyllis, might we arrange a coffee so I can pick your brains about that?'

'Oh. Well, I don't know, I'm quite busy with the bookshop so . . .'

'Or a whiskey maybe?' He leans in. 'I know a place that's stocking a Redbreast Single Pot Still.' Phyllis straightens up at this, shades of the revolutionary Rosie.

'You're on.'

I smile at Matty. 'May I borrow you once you've bought your creepy book and mined my staff for information?'

'He's all yours.' Phyllis proffers a till receipt towards Matty, who waves it away. 'File thirteen it is, then,' she says, scrunching and chucking it at the little cardboard box we keep by the till. It sails into its centre as if hurled by a camogie champion, which it was.

Annabelle has disappeared through the Tardis door to the loo and Phyllis goes to look through the spare stock, so we're reasonably private but I still lower my voice.

'I just wondered if you'd had a chance to look up those writers Garth asked you about.' Matty looks blank for a second.

'Belinda Henare and Kiri Wereta?' I say.

'Oh, yes! I couldn't find anything in the disaster zone we call the NZWA records,' he says, then, seeing me sag into a sulk, adds, 'but it's not over yet, Eloise. I know a man with the memory of an elephant. If anyone has that kind of information in his mental rolodex it'll be Duncan Beaton. He was the secretary before he moved to Canada. I haven't kept in touch,' Matty lowers his voice further. 'He's a terrible bore, but I'm sure someone will have his email.'

'Thank you, Matty. And also, sorry to be a pain, but would you have an attendance list for Adele's workshop? Garth promised to email some notes around.'

Matty rolls his eyes. 'You two are so demanding! I think you owe me more coffee and cake.'

Annabelle chooses this moment to bounce back through time and space.

'That's better. I can have more coffee now.' She wanders behind the counter and Phyllis fills the kettle.

'I must go and see dear Lily,' says Matty. 'She's back home now.'

And I really must get back to dear Annabelle, who is being very patient with me, but I'm filled with alarm and an urge to ring Lily to tell her not to eat any treats brought by visitors. It's tricky. Matty could be a suspect, but we only have the vaguest circumstantial evidence — he handed Lily a plate of food that he had previously warned me off. I might just phone her for a chat and make a joke about it.

Matty leaves, his choice of book not enhancing his innocence in my eyes. I finish my book-buying mission with Annabelle and thread around to the stock computer to look up Lily's number. Going into the customer database boots something else to the front of my brain. Beaton. Canada. What are the odds that Dorothy Beaton, with whom I've had a years-long email conversation about providing book vouchers for her Hawke's Bay grandchildren, is connected to the aforementioned Duncan Beaton? I might not need to wait for Matty, especially if he's deliberately procrastinating.

I pull up Dorothy's email address.

CHAPTER 35

Garth: 11 days until Battle of the Book Clubs

The library's automatic doors shoosh apart in a manner that pleasantly reminds me of *Star Trek* — the Shatner classic obviously. A discreetly positioned camera records my entry, which answers the CCTV question; whether I'll be able to blag a copy is less clear. My pulse quickening, I make a beeline for the circular service desk.

'Hi, Agatha, how's it going?'

'Good, I think. Still processing the events of the other night, really.'

'It was a bit of a shocker, that's for sure.'

Agatha clutches a Vincent O'Malley history book like a teddy or a comfort blanket. 'I hear Adele's going to be all right though, so that's good.'

'Yes, we visited her in hospital,' I say, prefacing my upcoming big lie with a truth in the hope that they will cancel each other out. 'That's why I'm here. Adele needs a copy of the CCTV footage of that night for an insurance claim. Would you mind popping it on this USB drive? Also, do you have a pen and paper I could borrow?'

I don't need a pen and paper but the inclusion of a second question, to which the answer will be positive, makes it far less likely my first request will be declined.

'Oh, yes. Is a Post-it note okay?'

'Fantastic, thanks.' Taking the pen and block of Post-its, I hand over the USB drive.

'I won't be a minute,' says Agatha, a slightly befuddled look on her face as she disappears into the back office.

I pace the speculative fiction stacks while I wait, pushing down the incredible guilt I feel for lying to Agatha. It's an unfamiliar burden. I'm a small-town bookseller, not a cop, and I never felt guilty in the police; not that I ever lied, but it was not uncommon to be economical with the truth. 'You might as well tell us exactly what happened because we've got DNA and hair samples' isn't a lie, even if it omits the fact that the DNA and hair belong to the victim's cat.

Sure, the CCTV evidence may help us catch a murderer and possibly even prevent more murders, but is that justification enough for my deceit? 'The end justifies the means' is a dangerous path to go down . . . I've seen good coppers turn bad that way. In fact I was one of them, and that was down to Pinter.

'Here you go, Garth.' Agatha hands me back the USB drive, interrupting my spiralling thoughts.

'Great. Thanks.' I rip off the top Post-it note, hiding the fact that I haven't written anything, and place the remaining block and the pen on the counter. 'See you at Battle of the Book Clubs if not before.'

'You will,' says Agatha. 'And this year we're damn well going to win!'

Chloe messages as I'm leaving the library and asks me to visit her in the Emergency Department. With any luck it'll be to do with the toxicology results we asked for.

In the police, visits to ED were a frequent occurrence. Mostly it was on Friday and Saturday nights to deal with drunken idiots who had injured themselves and then got violent towards the nurses. It was another glorious opportunity to see the very worst of humanity. One occasion in particular sticks in my mind, although this one at least has a degree of levity to it. I got the shout that David Diamond, an individual well known to the police, was causing problems. We arrived to find David wandering about holding a half-full urostomy bag with various tubes snaking beneath his jumper. He was gesticulating and shouting, not making much sense. It was obvious he was either on something, or hadn't been taking his meds, or most likely both.

I had a generally good rapport with David and approached him without too much concern for my safety. 'Hey, David, let's just keep it calm, mate, and then you can tell me what the problem is.'

Waving one arm in the direction of the nurses, he said, 'It's them! They're just taking the piss out of me.'

'They are, David.' I looked down at his urostomy bag. 'But that's kind of what you're here for, isn't it?'

At that point one of the nurses disappeared behind a cubicle curtain, holding back snorts of laughter. The joke was somewhat lost on David, but his anger was punctured.

The hospital smell, lighting and décor send a shiver through me as I enter the ED. Thrusting my hands into the front pocket of my Sherlock Tomes hoodie, I self-hug as I approach the reception desk.

'I'm here to see Chloe McGregor,' I say. 'She's expecting me.'

The receptionist pulls a note from where it's stuck behind the counter. 'Garth Sherlock?'

'That's right.'

'Chloe's with a patient at the moment but you can wait in the office.' She lets me through a security door and ushers me into a small room that is clearly not big enough for the files, paperwork, computer terminals and other miscellany of a busy ED. The room is even less than ideal for a meeting.

I've been waiting for about ten minutes, the hospital malaise making me increasingly fractious, when Chloe hurries in. 'Sorry, Garth. I'm going to be a bit longer. There's a kid with half a jelly snake stuck up his nose.'

I squirm. The Kiwi icon of jelly jet planes I get, but why on earth would you want to immortalise a vile serpent as a sweet? Also, why would you shove it up your nose?

She leans across me and logs into the computer terminal I'm sitting in front of. I'm not good with people in my personal space and I wonder why she didn't use the computer right next to her.

'I'll just open this search box here and enter the patient's name,' she says. 'Then, when their record comes up on screen, I'll go into Reports and check their medical history, looking for any tests that may have been run recently.'

What is she doing?

'Now, I've got to finish dealing with jelly-snake boy, and then we can talk. Will you be all right on your own for, say, fifteen minutes?'

She smiles, glances at the computer, then leaves.

Oh my hat. She's left it logged in with the patient details on screen. Good on ya, Chloe!

I scooch my chair closer to the keyboard and type 'Erma Mooney' into the search box. It comes up with a couple of options. One of the DOBs is far too young, so I select the other one. Huzzah! It's her. I pull up various reports, skim reading them while I photograph the screen. From the doctor's notes it appears that her CT scan, blood sugar, blood count, electrolytes and renal function were all normal, or normal for someone of Miss Mooney's age. It's in her liver where things started to go haywire: she had raised ALT and AST — whatever that means — and prolonged APTT and INR, which also means nothing to me but I'm guessing isn't good. I take more photos then start another search, for Lily Ross.

CHAPTER 36

Eloise: 10 days until Battle of the Book Clubs

I can't quite believe how dodgy we've all become. Chloe, she of the immaculate strawberry blonde ponytail and gourmet cuisine, has joined the rest of us on the dark side: her husband with his illegal lock-up and her bookselling mates — us — all deviating from our safe, prescribed course by oxygenating things that should be left in their airless, dark holes.

Then there's the corruption of an innocent librarian, tricked into handing over CCTV footage; Garth's going straight to hell for that one.

I decide to alleviate the guilt I feel by making a conscious decision to not give a shit. Lives are at stake here and the official channels have done no good so far.

We've excused ourselves from the bookshop for a day of admin and investigation. Phyllis has been recruited as Kitty's second in command, armed with several books on the bridges of Dublin and the promise of an after-work drink with the persuasive Matty Trimble.

Battle is looming and planning is proceeding apace: we have eighteen teams registered, six of the eight rounds written, volunteer scorers booked in, and the food and drinks pre-order form drafted. With that under some kind of control, our focus for the day is to find something to pin our suspected poisoning investigation on. To that end, Garth has begun analysing the library CCTV footage.

'Come and look at this,' he calls from the incident room. I press 'send' on an email to the Battle venue and join him.

I peer at the grainy CCTV footage, glasses on and the screen close to my face, then glasses off and holding the laptop further away. I can feel Garth getting more and more irritable. He pulls the screen from my hands.

'There's a lot going on there,' I offer. Agatha is fussing with the chair arrangement, a few members of the Friends of the Library are setting up the refreshments, Adele is chatting with Matty.

'Yes, but do you see it?'

'I see a lot of things.'

'Here, look. So this is right at the beginning of the evening, before the punters have arrived. Adele takes a drink just . . . about . . . now.'

I peer closer. 'Did she bring that water bottle with her?' It's a plastic one, like you'd pick up at the service station or dairy.

'And she continues to sip from the bottle for the five and a half minutes Matty has her cornered after he's finished with me.'

'So it wasn't until half-time that she had a glass of wine,' I say.

'I'm getting to that bit.' He could have summarised all this for me and then shown me the footage but I can see he has to go through this process, so I bite my tongue.

'It wasn't Adele's wine that got chucked all over the carpet.' He slides the bar at the bottom of the screen forward to the half-time break. Adele is leaning against the podium, talking to an unknown woman.

'Look.'

Suddenly Adele slumps, reaching out for support. The woman gets a knock that sends her glass into her chest, spilling wine onto her clothing and the floor.

'So the poison wasn't in the wine. It was in her water bottle.' I look at Garth.

It's awful to watch. Poor Adele.

'Stevie, car,' I say, attempting to exude alpha pheromones and confidence as I clatter down the stairs and retrieve the key from the box. Stevie stands on the landing, statuesque and unmoving, and looks at me with suspicion.

'Car, Steve. Come on.' I open the door and aggressively unlock the car, as if the force with which I press the button on the key will amplify the volume of the unclunk noise Stevie associates with an imminent journey. No Steve. Back inside I go.

He doesn't move a buff canine muscle until my foot hits the bottom step, then, with a speedy circular flourish, his haunches disappear up the second set of stairs and I hear the scuffle of our sometimes scared, sometimes mischievous dog as he digs his way under the bed. Garth emerges from the bathroom, toothbrush in face, laughing.

'Garth, car.' I glare at him and he retreats with speed.

After a small struggle during which Stevie plays dead and doubles his bodyweight, I wrest him from his hiding place and soon have a perfectly happy dog and a minty husband in the car.

'I'm really looking forward to this,' says Garth, clicking his seatbelt. 'You are too, Steve, aren't you? Look at him, all smiley and sitting up like a person. What a good boy.'

'He's a little shit-bag.'

Garth looks startled. Usually the Steveburger can do no wrong in my eyes.

'We're twenty minutes late and it's all his fault.'

'No, Eloise, it's 9.58am. We're two minutes ahead of schedule.'

'I only told you 10am to stop you nagging me. We should have been on the road by twenty to at the latest to be in good time for the meeting. Cyril only gets a short lunch break.' Garth gapes at me, so visibly scandalised by my admission of subterfuge that he can't speak. This cheers me up immeasurably and I'm dimly aware that this is not the response of a loving wife and fur mother.

'Have you done this before?' he asks, then raises his voice a little. 'Flat out lying to me? Is this something you do often?'

'I wouldn't say *often*.' The lip is out. He is betrayed. 'Come on. You do little things to make your life easier, don't you? What sorts of things do you trick me with?' This elicits a wily smile.

'I couldn't possibly say.' I decide that we are even and have reconciled.

'Coffee and pie to go in Dannevirke then?' He flashes a proper grin now and we are back on course.

A short time post pie, we are cruising serenely over the Saddle Road, weaving through the giant turbines of the Te Āpiti wind farm. I love this route; the eerie, powerful triffids standing sentinel, the wind howling through the Manawatū Gorge. It's so very sci-fi and the temporary escape from the Bay is doing me the world of good already.

'I wonder how high those towers are?'

'Seventy metres. Can you . . . can you please keep your eyes on the road?' asks Garth.

'How do you know that? What about the blade length?'

'Thirty-five metres. Can you please slow down?'

'Wow. They're monsters! Can't go much more slowly, love. We're on a schedule as tight as these corners.'

He makes an oddly feral sound. I glance over and he does look a little green. I take my foot off the gas a fraction.

We gain considerable ground on the straight bits of road, and before long Garth has regained his colour and we are enjoying our second coffee of the journey, sitting outside Café Camp on Ruahine Street in Palmerston North. Across from us sits an upright gentleman, obviously tall even when seated, who is feeding Stevie forbidden carrot cake crumbs. This is Cyril Church, forensic pathologist and friend of Tama's. Apparently they've worked a few gritty cases together over the years and since Tama can't get us the toxicology results, he says this is the next best thing.

'Obviously I can't discuss the details of individual toxicology reports.' Cyril lowers his voice. 'I haven't diaried this meeting and I'd rather you kept my name out of anything that becomes official.' He stirs sugar into his flat white with his left hand; I count ten stirs. His right hand rests on Stevie's content head, which is leaning on his thigh absorbing the calm of the quietly authoritative presence that occasionally conjures sweet treats.

I start in gently. 'Of course we don't want to do anything that would put you in jeopardy, Dr—'

'Someone has died, Cyril.' Garth has decided on a more forthright approach. 'We don't think these cases are coincidence and we don't think they're accidents. We'd like to know what you know.' Garth sits back in his chair and drains his coffee as Cyril's focus snaps towards him.

'I see.' Cyril fights the urge to assert his authority and wins. He relaxes, mirroring Garth's posture.

'Well, a recent case that may be pertinent to your . . . ah . . . investigation did show a rather unusual toxicology result.' Cyril looks down at Stevie and strokes the satin of his ears. His eyes meet mine. 'You have to understand that I ran these tests as a favour to DI McGregor. The official results will come from ESR in Wellington and that will take several months.'

'Understood,' I say. 'What did you find?'

'Thallium. Thallium sulphate, to be precise. It's a metal used in optical lenses, imitation jewellery — all sorts of items.'

I'm not quite sure what 'all sorts of items' might be.

'How does it get inside or on a person to poison them?' I ask.

'I was getting to that. It was indeed "inside the person", as you say. It must have been ingested deliberately or hidden in food. It was used in rat poison back in the day but after a few notorious murders in Australia it became far more regulated, so I'd be surprised if the ingestion was accidental.'

We all take a moment. Even Stevie senses the disquiet, huffing and turning to lie on my feet. Cyril is momentarily crestfallen at the abandonment.

'So you'll be recommending that the police investigate?' says Garth.

'Well, yes, inasmuch as I will produce a report for the coroner and a witness statement for the police when the test results are officially returned.'

'The coroner,' I say. 'So this is a poisoning that resulted in death. Are we talking about Erma Mooney?' Cyril blinks at me, his silence maintaining plausible deniability.

'Well, as lovely as this has been,' he looks at Stevie, 'I really must be getting back to work.'

'Can I just quickly get your take on this, please?' Garth opens the gallery on his phone and shows Cyril the images of Lily's records.

'Ah, yes, interesting. Without further tests I can't be certain, but I would say in all likelihood it's thallium again.' He taps the screen. 'See here. They've administered Prussian blue — that's the antidote.'

'Why didn't they do that for poor Miss Mooney?' asks Garth.

Cyril leans in to look again at the phone. 'Lily was poisoned first, yes?'

'A few days before.'

'In that case I might suggest that, having failed on their first attempt, your poisoner perhaps upped the dose to allow no chance of recovery.' Cyril stands. 'Nasty stuff, thallium.'

'Oh! Please don't go,' I say. 'There are other—'

'I know what you're going to ask, Eloise, but not all the incidents you're looking at have been referred to me. Unless it's obviously suspicious or the person died suddenly, I may never hear about it.'

Cyril bends down to give me an awkward pat on the shoulder, as if I were Stevie's sister.

'You have my number. If you have any questions around procedures or specific poisons, rather than specific people, give me a bell.'

It's all I can do to not grab him as he starts to walk away.

'Cyril, do you think thallium in her water bottle could have poisoned Adele?' He's familiar with this 'case' from our preliminary emails.

'Ah, no. Thallium doesn't dissolve like that. It's a soft heavy metal. She would have noticed. I suggest you look into something like, um, let's say ethylene glycol.' He all but winks.

'Antifreeze?' asks Garth, and I'm impressed he has that knowledge in his temporal lobe.

'Yes. Even tiny amounts in a drink or food can cause a good deal of trouble. Right, I really have to go. Keep in touch.'

He casts a regretful glance Stevie's way and does a quick turn, waving behind him as he goes. We both wave back, even though his back can't see us.

'Well,' I say.

'Indeed,' Garth replies. 'Two different poisons? Someone's going to quite a bit of trouble to knock off star team members. How horribly disconcerting.'

'I'll say. Where would you even get thallium from? And how do you target someone with your thallium home baking so that no one else gets done in?'

'No idea. My brain hurts.' He scratches his head as if he can let some of the pressure out. 'Tell me what you've planned for the rest of our day in Palmy.'

'Okay, so I thought we'd check out the dog park with the agility stuff in it, and we can visit Bruce at the bookshop.'

'Then lunch?'

'Then lunch.'

'It's a deal.'

CHAPTER 37

Garth: 9 days until Battle of the Book Clubs

'Ahhhh!' I fling the pricing gun across the stock counter and wipe my inky fingers on my jeans. The mechanical monster is being as temperamental as a lovelorn teenager this morning. For every sticker that it inks and prints correctly it spits out two more partially printed, then jams and rips the sticker roll or loses a sticker inside itself, which then requires winkling out with a pair of scissors.

'We should just get a new one,' says Amelia, hands on hips.

In principle she is correct, although like many aspects of running a small business it's not quite that simple. I looked into the price of new models a few months back and they are ridiculously expensive. Yes, if we calculated the cost of time wasted and stickers ruined it would probably make sense, but we have to balance that against the fact that we also need a new mobile phone for the shop, which is actually cheaper than a pricing gun, and are about due to place a wrapping paper order, which is more expensive than a pricing gun.

'I think what is required is more caffeine.' I flick the kettle on and then immediately flick it off again, because the shop phone rings and the kettle at full boil makes a noise like a jet engine on afterburner.

'Sherlock Tomes, Amelia speaking, how can I help?'

With my coffee fix on hold until Amelia is finished on the phone, I pick up the few books I have managed to price and wander onto the shop floor to home them. There's a new Stacy Gregg that's got 'award winner' written all over it and a Tania Roxborogh that I'm keen to read.

'Garth, can you grab a copy of the Juliette MacIver — the one with the three wolves on the cover?' yells Amelia.

'If you make the coffee, yes.' I shelve the remaining books and find *Odd Wolf Out* in entirely the wrong place. I suspect a child has rehomed it, as our staff are all admirably pedantic about putting the right book in the right place, even if there is sometimes dissent about what the right place might be. For example, I wanted the vegan cookbooks placed in the horror section, Kitty vehemently disagreed and Eloise punched me, so that was the end of that discussion.

A muted woofing echoes from the stock room, followed by the clatter of plastic.

'Oh no! Stevie, you didn't!' Amelia abandons her coffee-making duties as I race by her, coming to a halt at the stock-room door.

'He did.' The pooch who can do no wrong lies resting with his head on his paws, his eyes fixed on the chaotic, tumbled mess that was previously Basil's home. Sawdust is scattered across the floor, along with a container of gourmet mouse food. Basil is nowhere to be seen. 'Did you just help Basil escape?' I look sternly at Steve.

His remorseless golden gaze turns to me. 'Ruff,' he answers quietly.

'And I suppose you want us to clean up this mess?'

Whining softly, Stevie retreats.

'It's not his fault,' says Amelia, behind me. 'Stevie and Basil have bonded.'

I rein in my anger. It's not Stevie fault, it's mine for capitulating to the pressure to let them keep the blasted mouse. He's not a pet, he's a rodent. 'I'm sorry, Stevie, I didn't mean to shout at you.' Kneeling, I let him settle, then slowly approach. He stoically accepts my consoling pats on his flank.

The kettle flicks off and I hear the unpopping of a jar. I've just picked up the mouse house when Amelia brings me a cup of coffee. 'Here you go, boss.'

Immediately I am on alert. Rarely am I acknowledged as the boss, that title being reserved for Eloise. I wait until the coffee is firmly in my hands before subtly airing my suspicions. 'Thanks. What do you want?'

'Can a valued member of staff not simply be trying to look after their hard-working and animal-friendly employer?'

'This is about Basil, isn't it?'

'Basil? No, not at all.' Amelia waves a packet of biscuits at me. 'Chocolate Hobnob?'

I take a biscuit. 'He has to go. He's not a pet, he's a wild animal.'

'You don't mean . . .' Amelia makes a mousetrap action with her hands.

'No. We'll catch him with the humane trap again, then release him somewhere. Okay?'

'We could have a release party. Cake and such!' Amelia claps her hands together, which startles Stevie just a little. 'Oh, and while I was making the coffee an email came through for you and Eloise. Someone from Canada by the looks of it.'

My mellow moment of carefree caffeination is broken. It has to be a response from Duncan Beaton, NZWA secretary at the time of Kiri Wereta's death.

'Okay. I'll look at it on the stock computer so I'm not in the way.' I think I do a reasonable job of hiding my trepidation.

The stock computer is a heap of junk that, like the pricing gun and the phone, needs replacing. We were going to do it last January when we had some funds after Christmas but the cyclone the previous year hit most local businesses badly, so we're nursing it through another twelve months and hoping that the never-ending Windows updates don't kill it before then.

After an inordinate wait and words of encouragement to the ailing PC, the email finally displays on screen.

> Hello wonderful Sherlocks,
>
> Duncan here, and yes, I was indeed secretary of the NZWA in 2016. There was a lot of paperwork but I'm afraid I was forced to dispose of most of it when we emigrated here. The old grey matter, which is thankfully still functioning to a moderate degree of effectiveness, despite my advancing years, tells me that Kiri Wereta was not an NZWA member. However, the name sent a flag up the old flagpole and prompted me to delve into the depths of my old computer files, which I never quite get around to tidying up, and I found out something that might be interesting.

Bloody hell, Duncan, get to the point. I'm assuming that as secretary of the NZWA he was a writer, and I deeply suspect that his stories would have benefitted from a considerable amount of red editorial ink. The thought draws me uncomfortably back to Pinter and his savaging of authors' manuscripts — and, indeed, of authors.

Hoping that Duncan's verbiage does eventually offer some clue, I continue reading.

> As she wasn't a member but her name rang a bell, I wondered if she had entered one of our writing competitions. I have a penchant for Excel spreadsheets, which I found to be the most efficacious method of storing and scoring competition entries, so I looked back through the files and discovered something most unusual that I had completely forgotten. One of the shortlisted writers in our 2016 Tall Tales competition was called out by the judge for plagiarism! Goodness me, I remember now we had to keep that quiet.

Thanks, Duncan, I already know that.

> This discovery sparked something in long-dormant neurons, so I delved a bit deeper and lo and behold, what should I discover but . . . wait for it . . .

I *am* sodding well waiting for it, Duncan . . .

> The winner of the 2016 competition was Kiri Wereta.

And yes, I know that too.

> But this is where matters get most interesting because Faith Saxon, who was our most esteemed judge that year in case you didn't know . . .

Yep.

> . . . couldn't decide on a single winner, so there was a joint winner that year: a local author who was better known for her children's picture books, Belinda Henare.

CHAPTER 38

Eloise: 9 days until Battle of the Book Clubs

It's a beautiful evening, just beginning to cool as Garth, Stevie and I reach the summit of Te Mata Peak and stop to take in the valleys, scarps and spurs that play out to Napier to the north and Waimārama in the south. There are a few cars in the car park containing couples waiting for the glory of a Hawke's Bay sunset, and a detective inspector who emerges from an SUV armed with a flask and a paper handle bag.

Three of us settle on a bench looking out to the Māhia Peninsula and one crawls underneath it, glad of a rest after the climb. Stevie huffs and groans as he settles himself, accepting the dried duck tender Garth wafts at him. I untie a merino top from my waist and put it on before the sweat of the climb cools enough to chill me through.

'So the offender is on the run again, I hear?' Tama, unpacking pea snaps and chocolate, grins a highly amused grin.

'Hmm. I intend to deal with the situation this evening,' says

Garth. 'The recapture may involve the Admiral's mouser after all.'

'It bloody well won't, Garth. Kitty has a plan involving—'

'Yes, yes, I know about Kitty's cunning plan but—'

'Soooo, hot chocolate anyone?' intercedes Tama, handing me the flask in a diversionary move while he rummages for cups. I turn my attention from Garthy McSulkface to the ever generous and thoughtful DI McGregor, gladly accepting a steaming cup and passing one to Garth. Drinks in hand, we get down to business.

'Paula's been in touch. There's been another text intercepted from Pinter, to the burner phone in New Zealand.' I hold my phone out and Tama reads aloud.

'*I trust the Eau de Toilette is fragrant?* What the heck does that mean?' He looks from me to Garth and back again. No one responds. Tama unwraps a block of chocolate.

'Did Paula say anything else?'

'No. She's in the middle of a double homicide and hasn't replied to my last two messages.'

The occupants of one of the cars, a man and a woman, have got out to stretch their legs and look around. They move to the front of the vehicle and lean on the bonnet. The man lifts his phone to snap the sun as it touches the ocean.

'Double chocolate,' says Garth, snapping off a row of creamy milk. 'Excellent. Chocolate helps me think.'

As the sun begins to sink into the sea, we mull over this fresh communication. Why would Pinter and his partner in crime want something smelling nice, literally or metaphorically? Does it have to do with freshening something up or making it clean? After a few minutes of determined sugar consumption, I admit defeat.

'I've got nothing. Has he sent some perfume to the accomplice? But why?'

It appears my gentlemen friends are also unable to contribute.

Garth updates Tama on the Tall Tales competition.

Tama nods, getting his head around it, talking it through with himself. 'So Kiri Wereta had a connection to Belinda Henare.' He's slouching thoughtfully, one beefy calf resting on a beefy thigh. His smart button-down is slightly untucked, giving him the air of a truant schoolboy with a bit of a paunch.

'Yep. They were joint winners of the competition in 2016,' I say.

'I think we have enough evidence now to justify the police reopening investigations into both deaths, don't you? Especially as Faith Saxon was involved, as the judge,' Garth says to Tama.

Tama raises his eyebrows. 'Except that Kiri died in 2016 and Belinda died seven years later. Why the gap if they were both murdered?'

'We don't know yet. But surely you need to reopen the cases. It's a hell of a coincidence if both were natural causes.'

'We can't reopen them, as they were never open in the first place. Neither of them was recorded as a crime,' says Tama, out-pedanting the pedant.

'You know what I mean, Detective Inspector.'

Tama does, and is humbled. Garth's tone is sharp and I give him a nudge. We need to be more solicitous of our friend. If bloody Fedora Fatale really has been watching him and gets that lock-up exposed, Tama will be ruined. I open the pea snaps and try to focus. In the contemplative silence, I take a breath and order my thoughts aloud.

'The recent cases are clearly suspicious. I'm certain someone is trying to sabotage Battle of the Book Clubs by poisoning team members. There's already been one death. Then the police need to take into account the older cases, Kiri and Belinda. There are four links here: Pinter, poison, the literary world, and me and Garth.'

Tama looks at me, nodding, nostrils flaring a little.

'The problem is,' he says, 'we only know about the thallium and ethylene glycol because of a mate doing a favour. We can't move on anything until the results come back officially from ESR. And even then, if we widen the investigation, questions will be asked about what you two have been up to. How do you know about Kiri and Belinda if not from me?'

'Can't you just say the poisoning aspect rang a bell and you decided to dig in to the past a bit?'

'But *I* didn't, Garth, *you* did, and Kiri's family know that. It'll come up that you've visited them and been poking around, and the head-shed will want to know where you got your initial information. My career would be over.'

'Okay. So how could we have got on to it without information from you?' I ask. A harrier hawk swoops overhead looking for a bedtime snack and I briefly wonder where he's going to perch for the night, before turning my attention back to more urgent business: how to get our findings into the open without dropping Tama in it. He and his lock-up are already at risk. I open my mouth to air that concern before remembering Garth's promise to the Black Dogs. Shit. That was close.

Tama gestures and I hand over the pea snaps. At the rustle of the packet, Stevie commando-crawls from his hidey-hole, millions of sensory receptor sites in his snozzer firing up at the scent of salty goodness.

'That is, indeed, the problem,' says Garth, and sips his hot chocolate. The three of us gaze out across the Bay and I absorb the warmth of companionship. Despite everything, the wild beauty of this place lifts my heart, its ancient, storied history surely impervious to the temporary evils of the world.

CHAPTER 39

Garth: 7 days until Battle of the Book Clubs

'No, stay away, kāhu!' Kitty shakes her fist at the distant hawk that glides high on the spring thermals above the wooded green slopes of Te Mata Peak. The gesture is somewhat incongruous for someone who is the shop's environmental champion and the secretary of the local Forest & Bird group.

This afternoon, however, it's all about Basil. Now that we've finally recaptured the little bugger, we've closed the shop early for a celebratory staff picnic so we can release him into the wild. Although I appear to be the only one who will be celebrating. It was hard work persuading Kitty that Basil's quality of life would be better roaming free than in a cage at her house with the constant threat of a Noggy-related incident.

'It's okay, Basil, we won't let the nasty hawk get you.' Kitty pokes a piece of grass through one of the wire-mesh side holes in the downsized mouse house that has become Basil's temporary accommodation, a gesture I feel is more likely to terrify than reassure the tiny rodent.

We traipse in single file up the limestone path, the earthy scent of composting pine needles strong in the air. Eloise is on point as she's most familiar with the Peak's myriad trails, although the way Stevie is dragging her along, all bulged muscles and enthusiastic panting, I suspect he too has been this way before. Behind Eloise, flanked by Amelia, Kitty carries Basil as if he were some endangered species. Honestly, I've seen bomb techs carry IEDs with less care. Phyllis and I bring up the rear, carrying the bulk of the picnic. I sense that, like me, Phyllis does not regard Basil with the same reverence as the rest of the crew does.

'Shall we stop here?' Amelia puffs to a halt, hands on hips.

'Good idea.' I'm equally puffed from carrying a wicker picnic hamper in one hand and a chilly-bin in the other. Eloise was in charge of the picnic drinks, and from the weight of the container I suspect she has crammed in an entire cocktail bar.

'It's just around the next corner,' says Eloise.

'Is it really? Or is this an Eloise "just around the next corner"?' I've had many experiences of taking Stevie for a 'pleasant stroll' that involved ascents that would have made Sir Edmund Hillary reconsider his life choices.

'Fifty metres tops, honest. And it's a lovely spot. Defo worth the walk.'

I count out the paces and it's more like a hundred. Still, I don't complain. It is a lovely spot, a grass clearing surrounded by bush with a stunning view over the Heretaunga Plains and the distant Kaweka Range beyond.

'Aye, here will be grand.' Phyllis unslings her rucksack, which contains the lion's share of the catering, mostly prepared by herself, which I'm very much looking forward to. In fact it's possibly the only reason I agreed to this charade in the first place.

With his body low to the ground, Stevie drags Eloise around the clearing, checking out the smells and having a good old fossick. His tail actually wags before he settles under a bush, so the decision is made: this is the site of the inaugural, and hopefully only, Sherlock Tomes mouse-rewilding picnic.

Eloise spreads out a couple of tartan rugs and we all sit, with varying degrees of groans and grumblings.

'Is that one of the redwoods creaking?' asks Kitty.

'No, just me knees,' I answer without any hint of jest.

'You should talk to Will Pickett,' says Kitty. 'He could tell you what to forage that would be good for your joints.'

'Ha! The only foraging Garth does is in the biscuit aisle,' says Eloise.

Stevie raises his head from his paws at the 'B' word.

'I always know exactly what I want in the biscuit aisle, no foraging required. So, what's the order of events?' I'm struggling with the buckles on the hamper. I bought it ten years ago as a Christmas present for Eloise after she had dropped many, many unsubtle hints. In fairness to her, I'm not very good at subtle. Since the cries of joy on unwrapping it, and the excitement of unpacking all the contents, we've used it I think twice — more if you count its role in propping up a growing pile of books. Maybe disuse is why the leather straps in the buckles are far from pliant.

'Drinks first.' Eloise pulls out a bottle of bubbles from the chilly-bin, rips the foil away from the cork and untwizzles the metal cage.

'Try not to let it pop; it'll scare Stevie.' I abandon the hamper and put my hands over our sensitive boy's ears.

'And Basil.' Kitty has taken over the hamper and has it open in seconds, handing out plates. I push down my annoyance, both at her ease of opening the thing and the fact that she is distributing the crockery haphazardly on the rug rather than with any sort of care or precision.

'Perhaps we should let the rascal rodent go first?' I suggest.

'No, he can have some picnic crumbs,' says Amelia. 'One last feed before he has to fend for himself.' She is chopping up a block of cheese with the care of a slasher-movie serial killer with a machete. Someone far more suspicious than myself might even suspect that she is deliberately producing as many crumbs as possible for Basil's pre-release meal.

'Woohoo!' cheers Eloise. The bubbles are freed with more of a phutt than a pop, which thankfully doesn't spook Stevie, whose attention is entirely focused on the prosciutto platter being unfoiled by Phyllis.

Eloise fills the glasses — only a token amount for me — and proposes a toast. 'To bookish rodents.'

We all raise our glasses. 'To bookish rodents.'

'And bookish booksellers,' adds Kitty.

'Is there any other sort?' asks Amelia.

'In a good bookshop, no,' says Phyllis.

We again raise our glasses, then tuck into the splendid feast that Amelia, Phyllis and Kitty have prepared. Well, splendid apart from Kitty's chocolate beetroot cake, which as far as I am concerned Basil is welcome to.

***

With full puku, and the warmth fading from the late afternoon sun, it is at last time to say goodbye (or good riddance) to Basil, who is staggering with the weight of farewell crumbs. Even Phyllis brushed a tiny shard of Tim Tam through one of the holes in his box, so perhaps she does have a soft spot for the little fella. I have not participated in such nonsense, instead sneaking cheese and ham to Stevie when Eloise wasn't looking.

Carrying the plastic box as if it were a Ming Dynasty vase, Kitty paces away from us. 'Do you think here's good?' she asks.

'Significantly better than my bookshop,' I respond.

'*Our* bookshop,' says Eloise.

Kitty places the box down, lifts off the lid and slowly backs away. The bookshop whānau crane their necks to see Basil poke his inquisitive whiskery nose over the edge, and I swear we all stop breathing for a moment. Then he scrambles over the side and onto the grass.

'Be safe, little Basil,' whispers Kitty, her voice cracking.

From overhead comes a screech and a whoosh as the kāhu dives, wings swept back, hurtling towards a small but well-fed rodent that to date has had to contend with nothing more dangerous than a grumpy, middle-aged bookseller.

The release party freezes in horror, Kitty with her hand to her mouth, Amelia with her arms stretched out, Phyllis's eyes wide, Eloise with glass paused at lips and me eating a Tim Tam because it's dinner and a show.

A growl rips from beneath Stevie's bush and he's bounding across the grass, thirty-five kilos of sleek-furred, muscle-bound interceptor.

Even at his terrific turn of speed he's not going to be fast enough to catch the dive-bombing kāhu. It doesn't matter. A cacophony of ferocious warning barks emanates from deep within him and the kāhu swerves away, the morsel of Basil not worth the risk.

Collectively, the group before me sags as I reach for another Tim Tam, and a slice of prosciutto for Stevie, because I'm not a total dick.

CHAPTER 40

Eloise: 6 days until Battle of the Book Clubs

The mood of the shop is sombre this morning, the pōhutukawa-red walls seeping sadness. Something is missing, and of course it's Basil. No sooner did we (well, most of us) come to know and love him than he was gone, running free and wild, the breath of Te Mata o Rongokako tickling his whiskers. Even Stevie didn't want to come to work today, choosing to send forth a deep sigh from beneath the bed in reply to my suggestion that we get going, companion to that of his father, on the bed.

'What if that hawk got him later?' Kitty is banging at her keyboard, glum as can be.

'You mean the brave kāhu, Ms Forest and Bird? He has to eat, doesn't he?' counters Amelia, assembling the gubbins required for hot beverages.

'There's plenty to eat up there. He can have roadkill! He doesn't need to eat Basil.'

Amelia wafts her hand in my general direction; we've been shop whānau long enough for me to know that she is requesting that the milk be passed from the fridge.

'Basil took off like a hawk was after him,' she says. 'He'll have found a little family and a nest by now. It's been twenty-four hours; he's probably a father of six.'

I snort. Kitty tries to resist but the relaxation of her shoulders indicates she may be enamoured with the thought of baby Basils.

'They're swamp harriers anyway,' she says.

'Who are?' says Amelia, the milk swinging back my way as she reaches for the sugar tin.

'Kāhu. They're swamp harriers, or harrier hawks. Did you notice that beautiful burnished red on the underside of his wings?' Kitty turns around from the computer screen in order for us to receive the full benefit of her birdy knowledge. 'That's from when Māui tried to trick his grandmother into giving him fire. She chucked a burning toenail at him, so he turned into a kāhu to try and escape but the fire singed the undersides of his wings.'

This turn of events is just what we need: a legend — and a Kitty distracted from absent friends.

'A toenail? Really?' says Amelia, and bustles off to find Gavin Bishop's *Atua: Māori Gods and Heroes*. I finish making the coffee, a task that often becomes a multi-person job due to the number of distractions in a bookshop.

A tinkle comes from my back pocket and the diversions pile up as I remove my phone and unlock the screen. It's a reminder to go and meet that rapscallion Matty Trindle at our favourite haunt in the seething metropolis of Hastings. I mumble that I'm off and leave the general air of gloom with a tiny chink of daylight poking through.

I watch the chef in the Italian restaurant across the street spinning pizza dough. It's dazzlingly dexterous.

Through the whoosh of the sliding door comes the full force of Matty Trindle, a neat wee package, currently in the process of whipping off his Baker Boy cap. He accompanies this with a deep and dramatic bow, straightening to take the stool next to me.

'Sorry I'm late. Had to see a man about a cock.'

'That's way too much information for 9.30am, Matty.'

He smirks and wriggles into a more comfortable position; his legs don't quite reach the stool's footrest, so he ends up swinging them.

'I've just come from visiting Harold. Do you remember our little blue friend from last time we were here?'

'How could I forget?'

'Precisely. He's doing very well, thank you for asking. He was a bit traumatised after our SPCA adventure and was plucking his feathers out for a while, so I had to knit him a little jacket — it was the dearest thing — but he doesn't need it now. Which is a shame.' With a little shake and a purse of his lips, Matty looks across the road. Before I lose him to the shapely forearms of the pasta chef, I jump in.

'So what did you find out?'

He looks me up and down with disdain. 'I was promised coffee.'

'I've already ordered. Won't be long.'

'And pastries.'

That, I had forgotten. I know my bantamweight buddy has a penchant for mille-feuille so I get up and buy us one each, so he doesn't feel awkward about eating alone.

'I thought you were watching your figure, Eloise.'

'I am. It looks amazing. Just needs a little more cream and sugar.'

Matty loves a bit of banter but I'm getting impatient now. Elegantly shoving puff pastry in my mouth, I give him the old 'tell me what you know' eyebrow-raise and lip-scrunch combo.

'Okay. So.' Matty dabs delicately at nothing around his own mouth. 'The author who was shortlisted in the 2016 story competition but lost her publishing contract after being called out by Faith Saxon for plagiarism was . . .'

He nibbles some icing, avoiding eye contact.

I do not rise.

He caves. 'Lizzie Borden.'

I'm confused.

'Lizzie Borden?'

'Uh-huh.'

'As in, "Lizzie Borden took an axe and gave her mother forty whacks"?'

'Well, no, obviously it wasn't *that* Lizzie Borden because she died ages ago. Still creepy though, eh?' He's grinning and nibbling with straight little teeth, having a marvellous time.

'I'll say.' Perhaps the writer in question was unaware of the American woman famously tried for murdering her father and stepmother in 1892. I've heard that some people don't listen to true crime podcasts, so it is feasible. Or perhaps she doesn't care and thinks it's a cool name for a writer precisely because of who Borden was. Maybe she's actually a copycat axe-wielding murderer . . .

'So what have you found out about this Lizzie?' I ask.

Matty is exaggeratedly scandalised by this, clattering the little cake fork onto his plate. (I have eschewed mine.)

'What have *I* found out? It is you, dear Eloise, who is the detective, is it not?'

'You didn't even google her out of interest?'

He gives a deep, throaty laugh that you'd never think could fit inside such a compact person.

'Of course I did. And you should too.' He tries to play it cool but soon crumbles from sheer excitement.

'There's very little out there about this writer. The only thing that comes up is an ancient Twitter thread from a user called LBNZ123 — I know, so original — who goes on an absolute rant at the NZWA for failing to support New Zealand writers and for ruining their careers. It might well be from her. It's blistering. What the youth of today would call a "sick burn", I believe.' He looks delighted.

'How did you find that?'

'It took hours, and I had the most wonderful side quests through the bickery and feuding that goes on in certain parts of our literary community. It was delicious. Speaking of which, the next shout is yours too because I lost a whole afternoon to the internet on your behalf.'

I nod, lost in a maze of thought about LBNZ123. Who and where is she? Why have I never heard of her if she's a local writer? Matty swings himself from the stool and engulfs me in a perfumed hug. He's a mix of Parma violets and something fresh and green.

'Matty, you smell amazing.'

'I do, don't I, darling? Harold's mum gave me a bottle of scent as a thank you. I'll text you the name.'

He gathers his bits and bobs and turns to go. 'Well. Looks like you have some homework to do. I hope that helps. I'm off to plan a trip to Dublin. Your Phyllis has me all overcome with tales of the twenty-odd bridges over the Liffey. Have fun!' And away he swooshes.

I watch his fluid stride as he crosses the street. He becomes intrigued by the Italian restaurant for a few moments before flowing around the corner and out of sight.

I sit a while, chaperoned by more coffee, relaxing into the lack of husband, beloved canine and shop. My phone tings and I rummage in my tote. It's a message from Matty: a link to the Twitter thread.

> @nzwa Congrats to the joint winners of the 2016 Tall Tales Competition, Kiri Wereta and Belinda Henare!

There follow screeds of acclamations, the camaraderie and collegiality that is the flipside of Matty's bickery and feuding. And then this:

> @LBNZ123 This competition is a shameless sham, a bogus shitfest of nonsense run by talentless, anachronous has-beens with no business passing judgement on creativity. Shame on you, NZWA.

Ah, the old 'shame on you'. The classic retort of the outraged. This is a sick burn indeed, full of rage, terrible alliteration and — I look up *anachronous* — marginally contextual vocabulary.

Now I really want to know who Lizzie Borden is.

Another ting.

> Matty: Name of delicious scent is Thallium by Cyrus

CHAPTER 41

Garth: 6 days until Battle of the Book Clubs

One of the lesser-known skills of the bookseller is industrial origami. The cardboard dumpbins, which publishers use to promote their lead titles, most often arrive flat-packed and require a complex folding procedure to assemble. They invariably turn up without instructions, or, on the rare occasions an instruction sheet is included, it's the size of a postage stamp and written in hieroglyphics from some long-lost cardboard-folding civilisation.

Generally, they all follow a similar design ethos, so after ripping, tearing and entirely butchering a couple, their assembly becomes mostly instinctual. Occasionally, and for no apparent reason, some publisher's marketing division will decide that the standard dumpbin is not good enough for their latest and greatest and will introduce a never-seen-before revolutionary design whose assembly would qualify for a challenge on *The Crystal Maze*.

After Kitty and Amelia refused to touch it, I find myself battling with one such dumpbin, and, rather than Richard O'Brien capering in the background making unhelpful quips, I have Eloise. She has returned from her coffee with Matty, rather disappointingly without bearing takeaway latte or baked goods.

'I don't think that's right.' Eloise tilts her head like Stevie on hearing the rustle of a Scooby Snack packet.

'Don't you?' I place the glossy black strip of now slightly bent corrugated cardboard back on the floor. I am using the area near the till, which is the only place large enough to lay the giant cardboard pieces flat, and even then I've had to push the comfy chair back against the graphic novels.

Pain skewers my joints as I kneel up to assess my progress. I have assembled the segmented tray in which the books will fit. That's progress — feather in my cap there. My sense of achievement is somewhat reduced by the realisation that Eloise might be right: I think there are some pieces left over that should have been attached to the tray during assembly. I emit an exasperated groan.

'Just trying to help,' says Eloise unhelpfully. 'If you don't want my advice, you just have to say.'

'I don't want your advice.'

Eloise holds up her hands, all defensive. 'Okay, I'll say no more, but that's definitely wrong and it's going to be a bugger to take apart.'

I half stand, then collapse into the comfy chair, rubbing my knees. 'I think some LSD is in order.'

'Good idea.' Eloise retrieves a folding chair and plops onto it. 'I could do with a Little Sit Down too.'

'You've been sitting down all morning — and eating cake.'

'Mille-feuille.'

'Is that not cake?'

'Pastry. And custard.'

'Well, it's more than I've had.'

There is a small cough from Amelia, who's hovering at the till pricing cards.

Holding my fingers to my lips I turn to her. 'Shh!'

Eloise looks suspiciously between the two of us. 'Secrets, eh?'

'What happens in the bookshop stays in the bookshop,' I say.

'Unless we can shamelessly use it to promote the shop on TikTok.' Amelia smiles sweetly.

I turn to her. 'You didn't?'

'Maaaybe.'

My eyes widen. 'I never saw a camera?'

'You were one hundred per cent preoccupied,' says Amelia. 'What with the dancing and the music and everything.'

A sinking feeling grips me as Eloise reaches for her phone, although it could just be the chair sagging, as I haven't got around to tightening the screw I was supposed to have looked at a couple of weeks ago.

Boppy music plays from the phone and Eloise's eyebrows rise. She turns the screen towards me and there I am in full HD, a pink glazed doughnut held in front of each eye as I act out my impression of the Great Crested Garth foraging for food in the bookshop.

'While the cat's away . . .' says Eloise.

There's a snivel from Kitty, who is working on the stock computer. 'We don't have any mice to play with, now that Garth forced Basil from his home.'

I shoot Eloise a meaningful look. 'As head of HR I was just trying to boost morale.'

'Since when are you head of HR? You have the interpersonal skills of Hannibal Lecter.'

'I've just appointed myself.' I sit up straighter, trying to project an air of authority, my efforts somewhat hampered by the sagginess of the chair. 'Also, I think you'll find that Hannibal Lecter was actually quite charming.'

'Yeah, right until he ate your liver with some fava beans and a nice Chianti,' says Eloise.

Amelia makes the *sspssspssspssspsppp* sound and we all shiver.

I take a moment to settle and for the chill needles tingling my spine to subside. Pinter never ate anyone, but arguably what he did was worse. No fava beans, no Chianti, just—

'Moving from one serial killer to another, I have news,' says Eloise briskly. 'According to Matty, the name of our mystery plagiarist in the 2016 competition was Lizzie Borden.'

'What?' I'm not sure I've heard correctly.

'Oh well, that's slightly terrifying,' says Amelia.

Kitty clutches a copy of *Brave Kāhu and the Pōrangi Magpie* to her chest. 'This is all getting a bit dark. When I took this job the only serial killers I expected to encounter were between the pages of the books.'

'Lizzie Borden was actually a spree killer rather than a serial killer,' says Amelia knowledgeably. 'The axe murderer, not the author,' she adds by way of clarification.

'Wasn't she found not guilty?' I'm sure I've watched a true crime documentary about her at some point.

'Doesn't mean she didn't do it.' Amelia makes stabbing movements with the scissors.

We used to have a card in the shop with a Churchill quote on it: 'If you're going through hell, keep going.' Sometimes I have to apply the same sentiment to conversations with the staff: 'If sidetracked by random facts, inane banter and spurious comments, keep going.'

Against the odds, I try to steer the conversation back on track. 'The point is, now that we have a name, does it get us any further forward?'

'We have to assume it's a pseudonym,' says Eloise, 'so I don't see that it does. There's pretty much nothing online.'

I drum my fingers on the arm of the chair. 'The publisher that was offering her a contract will have known her real name.'

'Probably.'

'So surely they'll have a record, or someone would remember. I mean, that name doesn't exactly fly under the radar.'

'Maybe. Although it was nearly ten years ago and you know how quickly people move on in publishing. And we don't know which publisher it was, or even what country they're in.' Eloise leans over and presses my fingers flat against the chair's arm to stop the drumming. 'Also, it will be confidential, they're hardly likely to just tell us.'

'Not officially, no. But we have contacts — surely we can find someone who will do us a solid.'

Eloise scrunches her face in disgust. 'You know how much I hate that expression.'

'I lose track of the expressions and words that mortally wound you, there being a veritable *smorgasbord* to choose from.'

The grip on my hand tightens and Eloise's look hardens to one I've seen before, usually when she's about to start throwing fists.

Thankfully, Kitty intervenes. 'I don't know if this helps but I saw that email from Duncan and I looked up Belinda Henare in our database. You know that there's two of them, right?'

'What?' say Eloise and I in unison. I can't believe we didn't think to do this before. As cops, a Police National Computer check would have been the first thing we did.

'I double checked to make sure they weren't the same person — you know how that sometimes happens on a mailing list,' Kitty continues.

'How did you double check?' asks Eloise.

'Well, all the contact details were different, although weirdly they both live in Waipukurau. But one of them hasn't bought anything since 2016.'

CHAPTER 42

Eloise: 5 days until Battle of the Book Clubs

We have a Death Café meeting this evening and I'm pretty excited about it. Prudence has arranged a guest speaker, a local funeral director. I'm putting chairs in a circle to make it inclusive and cosy.

Garth lugs in more chairs. 'Anything from Tama yet?'

'Nothing.' We've told our friendly DI about the second Belinda Henare and he said he'd look into it. 'He does have an actual job as well as running around after us.'

'Fair point. Do you really need this many chairs?'

'I reckon we'll get a good turnout this time. Our speaker is going to talk about embalming and preparing the body and everything.'

'Oh god.' Garth swallows, turning a bit sickly looking. 'Is Reagan coming?'

'Yep. Chrissy's bringing him.'

'Won't it be upsetting for him? Being so close to, well, the end?'

'He's a grown man, Garth, and is facing this thing, his end, with more dignity and bravery than I ever thought possible. He wants to know everything.'

'Right. Right.' Poor Garth. He looks so uncomfortable. He prefers the denial approach when dealing with death, illness or anything adjacent. In his view, knowledge isn't always power.

'Are you going to stay for it?' I ask.

'Well, you know what, love, I thought I'd get off and, um, go to the supermarket so I can have dinner ready when you get home.' He smiles, looking somewhere to the left of me, then at the floor. I stare at him for a moment, then decide to let him off the hook.

'That sounds lovely. I'll try not to eat too much cake.' He all but collapses in relief, then claps his hands, a puppet revitalised by its master.

'Cake, you say? Hmm, tempting.' He knows he's in the clear now so can engage in a bit of banter. 'But a promise is a promise. Come on, Stevo, let's get you in the car.'

Unusually, Stevie does not bolt towards the back door at the word 'car', and I turn to see what's caught his attention. Prudence has arrived, carrying a plate draped in black netting. The smell is heavenly and our pooch is captivated, his skinny white-tipped tail swishing slowly as Prudence comes behind the counter and places her goodies by the sink. He doesn't take his eyes off her as she lifts the edge of the netting to reveal individual coffin-shaped cakes, black and red, each iced with a set of initials.

'They're *dead* cakes,' she breathes, trying to spook Garth. 'Do you want yours now, Garth, or will Eloise bring it home for you later?'

'There's one for me? What the hell is a dead cake?'

'I kind of adapted bits of folklore I found on the internet,' Prudence replies. 'A dead cake honours the dead person. You don't have to put names on them but I thought it would be nice.'

'*Nice?*' squeaks Garth, backing away. 'Come on, Steve.' But Stevie isn't budging. He is sitting nicely at Prudence's feet, being a Very Good Boy.

'There's one with your name on it, Stevie Wonder Pup, but you have to wait until the guests are all here,' Prudence tells him.

Stevie gazes at her with adoration, ignoring Garth, who huffs a farewell, disappearing out the door in a waft of complaint about weirdos and treacherous dogs.

Prudence puts the kettle on and I hoof myself up on the bench to reach the glasses and extra mugs on the very top shelf. I wouldn't let anyone else climb the furniture but where my own personal safety is concerned, I usually go a solid 'safety third'.

'Watch out, Eloise, wouldn't want you to fall! Heh heh heh.' Reagan has arrived, his attempted shout more of a hoarse stage whisper, collapsing into a rasping giggle.

Chrissy pushes his wheelchair up the ramp and Reagan biffs chairs out of the way to make room. The wheelchair is new, and strangely unexpected. I mean, how did I think his demise was going to go? I head over and lean in to kiss his cheek.

'And don't get me started on *corpse* cake,' murmurs Prudence, her eerily smooth, deep voice floating over to us. I glance nervously back to Reagan, but I shouldn't have worried.

'Corpse cake? Sounds relevant!'

'Corpse cakes are traditionally made by the woman of the house and left to rise on the chest of the corpse to absorb some of the person's virtue, which is then transmitted to the eater.'

'Ha. You'll be shit out of luck here, then. Not much virtue left in this old bag o' bones.'

'Behave yourself,' says Chrissy, manoeuvring the wheelchair into position within the circle. Group members are trickling in now, producing more cake and biscuits than ten hungry Stevies could eat.

Beth arrives, greets Reagan and offers him a biscuit with an intricate geometric icing pattern.

'Oh my god, it's the Death Star. That is completely epic.'

'I remembered you were a fan.' Beth smiles. What an absolute sweetheart.

'This is a wonderful moment in my soon-to-be-over life,' says Reagan, shoving the entire biscuit into his mouth and munching in closed-eye rapture. The Admiral stomps up the ramp, the cool of evening escaping from the folds of his clothes.

Prudence, still fluffing about with cups and the ever-mounting pile of edible offerings, slips Stevie a bit of cake she's sliced into small pieces.

'It's okay, Eloise,' she says, just ahead of my objection. 'It's a doggy recipe with liver in it.'

'Mmm. Internal organs,' says Reagan.

I'm relieved to spot our guest speaker and raise my voice in welcome, and to gather the troops. There are about fifteen people here altogether and it's a bit of a squeeze.

The funeral director is not what we were expecting. Her name is Floss, she looks about eighteen and is so slender as to almost go missing when she turns sideways. Her bright brown eyes shine with intelligence and good humour, which is just as well considering Reagan's presence.

'Can I just say, I would like this lady to be in charge of my body,' Reagan says to Chrissy. 'She has lovely hands.'

Prudence leaves the edibles — including a whopping great Death by Chocolate cake handed over by Floss — and we settle in to the talking part. It's absolutely fascinating and we all learn so much. I keep an eye on Reagan and I see Chrissy is doing the same but he seems happy as a clam, even in the face of details about embalming, preparing the body for viewing and options for eco-burials and cremations. Floss describes it all with such gentleness and care that it sounds unthreatening, even comforting.

Reagan sighs. 'To be honest, I'm getting moments where I long for this, this — I dunno — relief. For someone to just take care of it all for me. I'm getting tired of dying.' He laughs gently, but it's to try to put us at ease. Chrissy rubs his arm and he grasps for her hand.

'But first,' says Floss, 'I think you have time for a bit of cake, Reagan. Everyone should have a piece of my Death by Chocolate before they actually die.' Because of where we are and what we're doing, this statement oddly lightens the tone and Pru and I get up to clatter crockery and reboil the kettle. Chrissy and Beth have leapt up to assist and there are so many 'helpers' behind the counter now that it's becoming a bit of a bun fight so I remove myself and just watch.

Beth slices the Death by Chocolate. The fudge is shining, boulders of spongy cake rolling across the plate as it's cut.

'It's just like that Michael Rosen poem, Eloise, do you know it?' she asks. 'The one where the little kid is trying to "tidy up" the chocolate cake and ends up eating it all.'

I do know that poem and she's spot on. I've had great fun reading it aloud to pre-schoolers. '"One side doesn't match the other; I'll just even it up a bit, eh?"' I quote, and Beth carefully tidies one edge of the cake, then scoops up the crumbs and crams them into her mouth with perfect comic timing. Stevie, who has been riveted, whimpers and stamps his little white paws. I join in the laughter, feeling so at home with this disparate bunch of death nerds.

It's a lovely vibe tonight, supportive and funny. Reagan gets as many pats as Stevie and I think how nice it would be if we habitually treated people with such warmth, even when they're not dying.

Beth shimmies through the assembly, cake plate held high, dispensing Death by Chocolate. It's all warm, companionable and a bit chaotic.

'Eloise, could you please just move—'

'Jesus Christ, Eloise! Help him! Help him!' I turn at Reagan's shout to see my most precious thing convulsing, silver fur tremoring, tiger eyes rolling and flickering, and foam beginning to fleck the fur around his mouth.

No! Not my Stevie. I skid to the floor next to him, lift his head into my lap and try to open his mouth but he's rigid, teeth chattering. I can't get in there, I can't help him. I pull my phone out and ring the vet clinic, shouting instructions to the others as I listen to the out-of-hours options, stabbing to get it on speaker phone.

'Chrissy and Beth, get him in the car.'

Reagan is crying, wringing his hands. It's awful and I don't have time to reassure him, even if reassurance were to be had.

'Prudence, ring Garth and tell him to meet me there.'

The emergency vet is on the line and can meet me at the clinic in ten minutes. Within seconds my Death Café whānau have my precious boy in the car. Beth is in the back seat with Stevie's head in her lap and my legendary inattention to road rules becomes my superpower.

If I find out that someone has done this deliberately, I'll fucking kill them.

CHAPTER 43

Garth: 5 days until Battle of the Book Clubs

My knees scream and my lungs burn like I've been tear-gassed as I put one foot in front of the other in a shuffling run. Eloise has the Loan Ranger and getting a taxi would have taken too long, so I'm on Shanks' pony, and it's an out-of-shape, cronky old beast.

I can't remember the last time I ran like this. A shadow of shame envelops me; I should have tried harder to keep fit. My beautiful boy needs me and I'm a wreck. I let the emotion drive me on, adding to the guilt of having left Stevie at the shop rather than forcing him to come home.

Chest heaving, I push on along Napier Road, past the tangled remnants of the demolished statue, forcing unwelcome thoughts from my mind. Stevie is a big strong dog — he'll pull through.

A hundred metres away I clock the Loan Ranger abandoned outside the vet's. Adrenaline floods my system, making me want to puke.

Only a faint glow emanates from the large front window, the main lights in reception still switched off. I barge through the door and see Eloise standing forlorn in the semi-darkness, like a lost child. Tears streak her face and her fists are clenched tightly against her stomach. This can't be right — Eloise never cries.

'Is he—'

'I don't know.' Eloise throws her arms around me, shoving her wet snotty face into my sweat-drenched neck. 'They wouldn't let me go in with him.'

'They?'

Eloise sniffs, wiping the back of her sleeve across her nose. 'When Charlotte saw Stevie she phoned for a nurse.'

'That's probably standard procedure,' I say, trying to convince myself as much as Eloise.

'I don't think so. It was Kylie. She hardly said a word and you know how chatty she normally is.'

'What happened?' I guide Eloise to the easy-wipe plastic chairs and we both sit.

'I don't know. He ate something at Death Café. I think he's been . . . poisoned.'

My mind spins. 'Like, by accident? Chocolate or something?'

Eloise gives a tiny shake of her head and her red-rimmed eyes meet mine. 'I don't know. I was watching him most of the time. Prudence gave him some "dog friendly" cake she made for him but that was all I saw.'

'You don't think Prudence—'

'I don't bloody know, but someone at Death Café poisoned our dog.'

I can't get my head around this. Stevie's such a beautiful soul, everyone loves him. 'Why would anyone do that?'

'Maybe it wasn't meant for Stevie.'

'Fuck! Do you think it was meant for you?' I pull her closer and nestle my face into her bright pink hair.

'Or someone else there.'

Intertwined in silence we wait, contemplating, hoping, fearing . . . hating.

'Pinter's protégé. Do you think they've — I dunno — infiltrated us?' I'm trying to think of everyone who was there, how long they've been around the bookshop, how they're connected to us.

The surgery door opens and Charlotte walks through, latex gloves on her hands, plastic apron covered in something gross.

Eloise and I stand, hardly daring to breathe.

'We've given Stevie an emetic and some activated charcoal. Kylie has set him up with a fluid drip and is going to keep an eye on him overnight.'

'Is he going to be okay?' asks Eloise.

There's a long pause. Too long. Charlotte peels off the gloves. 'We've taken blood samples, which we'd normally analyse here but our machine is being repaired, so we'll send them off to the lab in the morning. The results will give us an idea whether there's permanent organ damage or if there could be further complications.'

'So he's not out of the woods yet.' Tears glaze my vision, then spill down my face.

'I'm afraid not, but he's stable for now.'

'Can we see him?' asks Eloise.

'He's asleep and it would be better to wait until he's come around.'

'I need to see him.' The tone of Eloise's voice is absolute and we follow Charlotte into the recuperation bay.

Stevie lies in a crate on his side, a blanket beneath him. He doesn't look natural — not curled up in the snuggly ball pose he likes to adopt when he's cold; or sprawled out, legs splayed, when he's content and about to do something naughty. His fur is slick where he's been sponged clean and a clinical disinfectant smell hangs over him.

Eloise kneels down and reaches through the crate's bars and strokes his muscled flank.

'It's okay Stevie, Mummy's here.'

He doesn't stir — no contented snoof or large intake of breath, no response at all. I don't touch him. I don't know why; I just know that for me it doesn't feel like the right thing to do.

'Come on, love, we should let him rest.' I ease Eloise to her feet.

'We'll call you in the morning,' says Charlotte. 'And as I said, we'll know more once we get the blood results back, but that could take a few days.'

'Would it help if we found the actual food that poisoned him?' I ask.

'Possibly.' Charlotte looks at Stevie. 'It might give us a clue to how much he's ingested and in what concentration.'

'Right,' says Eloise, clearly pleased that we have something to distract us. 'We have evidence to gather.'

⁂

The Loan Ranger lurches to a halt. The bookshop's front door is ajar, the lights are still on, and I see movement inside up near the till.

'You didn't lock up?' I ask.

'I had more pressing issues,' snaps Eloise.

'No judgement.' I hold up my hands in defence. 'I was just surprised.'

'As was I when our dog got poisoned.'

We head inside. The folding chairs have been tidied away and the plates cleared. Prudence stands at the sink washing up. On hearing us she turns. 'How is he?'

'In recovery,' I say, not wanting to be drawn into explaining the details.

'We don't know if he's going to recover.' Eloise folds her arms and stands beside Prudence.

'I'm so sorry.' Prudence dries her hands. 'Is there anything I can do?'

'Thanks, you've done enough.' There's an edge to Eloise's words, making her response ambiguous. Does she hold Prudence responsible? I suppose Death Café was her idea but this feels like something more. Does Eloise actually think she poisoned Stevie?

Prudence picks up her bag and retrieves her plate, now devoid of coffin-shaped cakes, from the draining board. Without another word, she stalks from the shop.

'That was a little harsh, don't you think?' I suggest.

'No, I don't.'

'But she kept an eye on the shop for us and tidied up. And she waited for us to come back.'

'Tidied up is one way of putting it.'

'Is there another way?'

'She got rid of the evidence, sterilised the crime scene, took forensic counter-measures — take your pick.'

As is so often the case, Eloise has seen something I haven't, knows something I don't. I suddenly remember why we came back here — to collect a sample of the 'dog friendly' cake that probably poisoned Stevie. But all evidence is gone.

'I'll check the bin.' I push down on the pedal and the lid pops open. 'Empty.'

'She couldn't have done a better job if she'd covered the shop in accelerant and set fire to it.'

'I'm not giving up yet. It might be in the bin out the back.' I rush outside and heave open the wheelie bin. A messy collection of mashed-up home baking lies in a sea of packing chips. The evidence we needed is contaminated and destroyed. Perhaps Eloise is right to suspect Prudence.

CHAPTER 44

Eloise: 4 days until Battle of the Book Clubs

If I didn't know better, I'd think I had a hangover. My eyes are so swollen I can see the puffed skin around them in my peripheral vision, my nose is blocked and I feel my pulse throbbing behind my eyes.

'You look how I feel,' says Garth. I'm propped up in bed waiting to visit Stevie. Garth hands me coffee in the mug that says 'Breakfast with my Best Buddy'. It came with a matching bowl for Stevie and my eyes fill with tears — again. Garth kisses my tangled hair and slides gently onto his side of the bed as if visiting a fragile hospital patient.

'You got him there quickly, love. He's going to be okay.'

I nod, emotions as knotted as my hair, fluctuating between grief, anger and guilt. Garth looks awful. Neither of us slept much.

'We should cancel Battle. This has gone too far,' says Garth.

I snort a humourless laugh that sets my head pounding. 'An old lady dies and several other people fall ill but it's the dog that has us really worried.'

'It's an accumulation of all of those things. I think we're in over our heads, and yes, it's the dog. What would you do if we lost Stevie?' His face is stricken.

I feel sick at the thought of a Stevie-less life.

'We're always in over our heads. We've always bitten off more than we can chew and any other bloody cliché you can think of. But also we're the ones who get results and find answers, and continuing with Battle is the only way we will. We can end it there.'

Garth inhales deeply, closes his eyes and lets his head fall back on the pillow. Usually Stevie would be curled in between us, quietly snoozing until someone says 'biscuits'.

This is absolute shit and someone needs to be held to account.

'We should ring Tama,' I say.

'We should. But I'll text him. I can't talk about this yet.'

As Garth finds his specs and gets into his phone I let my mind play out its many conflicted thoughts. From the Admiral's intelligence and from Pinter's intercepted texts, we can assume that there's an accomplice in place somewhere nearby. Prudence went to live in the UK with her family not long after finishing school. Faith Saxon also has publishing ties to Britain. Pinter could well have been in their orbit, or they in his, at the height of his career as a literary agent.

I make a massive effort to think rationally, to not leap to accuse the nearest vaguely viable suspect. I like Prudence, and Faith seems lovely. Why would either of them want to kill fellow writers and punish us? Could they be so completely in Pinter's thrall?

'It's time to do some serious work on this, Garth. I'm sick of fucking about. I need to find out who hurt Stevie because I'm going to smash their head in.'

Garth puts his phone down and takes my hand. 'I know you're

angry, love. So am I, but we need to work through this calmly. Do you reckon we should get someone to interrogate Pinter? An off-the-books chat somehow?'

'We could ask Paula if that's a possibility, but it would alert him that we're on to him, which he'd love. And why would he talk? He'd much rather watch us squirm.'

'Come on. Stevie is today's priority.' I drag my arse out of bed and head for the shower. Kitty and Phyllis are on duty so I don't need to think about the shop.

Thirty minutes later we're at the vet's surgery. Charlotte lets us in, even though they're not technically open yet.

'He's awake,' she tells us. 'Doesn't look too happy, but I wouldn't either if I'd had my stomach pumped.'

'Is he going to be okay?' I'm desperate for reassurance as we follow her backstage, where the peculiar mix of antiseptic and dog smells tickles my nose with its acrid tang. She just smiles in answer and I decide not to push it.

And there he is. The most miserable pup on the planet, wrapped in blankets in a big old crate lined with newspaper. He looks up and there is the tiniest wave of his tail. Charlotte unlatches the crate door and steps aside.

'Hello, sweetheart. Hello, little boy,' Garth croons in the high-pitched tone he uses only for his pup. 'It's okay. We've got ya. We've got ya, Stevie boy.'

And oh my but those soulful eyes look so many things: reproachful, relieved, exhausted, betrayed. If dogs could cry, he would be weeping pathetically.

'Can we take him home?' I ask.

'I'd like to observe him for a while longer, get him drinking and eating.'

I'm about to offer a million arguments for why he should come home now, but as I draw breath to speak, the person who knows me best interjects.

'He's in the best place he could possibly be, love. Let Charlotte do her job.'

He's right, damn it.

Stevie floops under the pats and starts to nod off, so we stay a few minutes longer and then creep away. He's too weary to pay much attention, which makes it a bit easier to leave him.

'Coffee at Oddbeans?' asks Garth.

'Yeah, go on then.'

I'm a bit more optimistic now I've seen Stevie, alive if very unwell, and have a sudden hunger pang at the thought of food. Coffee and breakfast and next-steps planning sounds good to me. Oddbeans is only a couple of doors down from the vet, and as we walk past the wrecked statue I feel a stab of joy. That was a crazy plan come good. Let's see if I can come up with another one.

The café is warm and steamy, the coffee machine spitting and hissing. We manoeuvre our way around customers waiting for takeaways to place our order — a consolatory doughnut for his nibs and proper food for me. My phone tings as we get ourselves seated.

> Paula: Wotcha. More comms in to Belmarsh from NZ. Says: *I'm very much enjoying the Agatha Christies you recommended.*

'What is it?' asks Garth, beard coated in icing sugar.

'It's another message sent to Pinter's phone.' I read it out to him, my mind so full of that peculiar clarity and strength that anger can give you that I don't register any anxiety at all.

As the coffee arrives, Garth puts down his half-eaten fried dough and licks his sticky fingers.

'What was Agatha Christie's favourite murder weapon?' I ask.

'Not sure I've ever read her, now that I come to think of it.'

'Poison. *Sparkling Cyanide*, *Five Little Pigs* — those are both Hercule Poirot stories, then I think Miss Marple gets in on the act later on.' I do a quick search. 'Oh yes, *A Pocketful of Rye*, *The Mirror Crack'd from Side to Side*. Loved her poisonings, did old Agatha.'

'She's not the only one,' observes Garth, adding a coffee moustache to his real, icing-adorned one. His eyes flick past my shoulder. 'Heads up. The DI's here.' Tama pulls out a chair next to me and his mere presence emanates compassion and dependability. I feel like collapsing on him.

'I was going to join you at the vet and give Stevo a pat but then I saw you walking in here. How is he?'

We fill him in on the Stevie situation, and the text intel from Paula.

Tama waves away Garth's offer to order him a coffee.

'For sure, it's further confirmation of a New Zealand accomplice, but it's still circumstantial. Whoever it is can claim they've just been reading books.'

He's right. It adds to our case, but proves nothing.

Tama gets to his own news, emanating brisk efficiency. 'We've had a breakthrough on the two Belinda Henares. I called an old mate in Waipuk — solid community copper. The Belinda who lived on Pikitea Street who died last year was the daughter-in-law of another Belinda Henare. Divorced, but kept her name.'

'Her daughter-in-law?'

'Yeah, who'd have thought?'

Garth puts down his coffee. 'Actually, it happens more than you think. We've got two Fiona Valentines on our bookshop database and—'

'Thanks, love.' I cut him off before he goes down a rabbit hole, sensing that Tama has more to tell. 'So do we have an address or a number for Mrs Henare senior?'

Tama places his elbows on the table and leans in.

'That's where it gets really interesting. Mrs Henare senior died of heart failure after a bout of food poisoning. In 2016.'

CHAPTER 45

Garth: 3 days until Battle of the Book Clubs

'It's too old and cronky,' says Amelia. 'We should get a new one.'

'Are you talking about Garth or the CCTV?' asks Eloise.

'Oh, how we laughed.' I treat them both to a stare so hard that Paddington Bear would have been proud of it. We are gathered behind the counter, the two of them making unhelpful comments while I battle with the shop's aged CCTV system, which has a menu like a minotaur's maze.

'Maybe you should turn it off and on again,' suggests Eloise.

I wiggle the mouse in an attempt to free the pointer, which has now decided to confine itself to a three-centimetre square at the bottom of the screen. 'Feel free to take over if you think you can do better.'

'No, this is definitely a job for the head of tech support,' says Amelia.

'I'm head of HR.'

'You are not.' Eloise nearly chokes on her coffee. 'You're head of tech support, dumpbin construction and fixing things, but nothing that requires human interaction.'

'Fixing things like defective staff members.' I shoot Amelia a meaningful look, which she ignores, knowing I am (probably) only joking.

The screen on the CCTV monitor changes as the system finally decides to obey me, bringing up the recordings from the night of Death Café. Eloise and Amelia draw closer and I'm taken back to my days in the police, huddling around computer monitors in the control room. Northampton town had one of the most advanced CCTV systems in the country at the time. Monitored 24/7, it was an absolute godsend, reducing crime and generally making people feel safer. It also produced many humorous moments, such as footage of the drunken lad who managed to scale one of the poles and rip down a camera. In the morning, when sober(ish), he denied everything until we played him the video of the camera's last moments, which showed a massive close-up of his drunken face.

There will be nothing amusing on the footage we watch today; even after a day's grace I'm bracing myself for the ordeal of seeing my poor puppy poisoned.

'You don't have to watch, Eloise. I can do it.' I'm worried that it will be even worse for her, reliving the trauma of that night.

'I want to. It might help me remember something important. I've got more context for what's happening.'

Only one camera covers the event space. This makes viewing the video easier but also means there are obscured angles and blind spots. The area behind the till where the cakes were cut isn't shown.

Three pairs of eyes focus intently on the grainy footage. With each passing minute my pulse quickens and my nausea builds, knowing that the inevitable horror is coming closer. Then it happens. Stevie collapses and Reagan waves his arms about, his shouts unrecorded by our video-only system.

Eloise inhales sharply and grips my shoulder. 'Rewind a little bit,' she says. 'Let's see it again.'

My hand trembles on the mouse. I don't want to watch it again. Nevertheless, I do as I'm told, managing to get it to play back at half speed.

'Look there,' says Amelia, pointing. 'Reagan's giving Stevie some cake.'

'Yes, but who gave the cake to Reagan?' I rewind again, a little bit further back this time. Beth comes into view from behind the counter with a large plate of chocolate cake and begins handing it around to the guests, while behind her Prudence passes a piece of cake to Reagan, pointing to Stevie. Reagan dutifully holds it out to our boy.

The grip on my shoulder tightens. 'That fucking bitch.'

'It's not conclusive. You can't even tell what kind of cake it is. Weren't there several?' I place my hand on Eloise's. 'It would never stand up in court.'

'It stands up in the court of Eloise. I'll fucking kill her.'

'We don't see Reagan do anything suss to the cake,' says Amelia, 'so it kinda does incriminate Prudence.'

'Does it though?' I lean back from the screen.

'Yes,' say Eloise and Amelia in unison.

'I'm not convinced. It doesn't feel right that it would be Prudence.' Then again, how often do the most horrific murderers fly under the radar as the nice, quiet, never-a-bother-to-anyone types? 'Let's just take a moment.'

'No, let's take a copy of Ken Follett and beat her to death with it.' Eloise glances at the bookshelf behind the till. *The Armour of Light* is indeed a weighty tome and could adequately replace the lead piping in a game of Cluedo.

'Before we carry out any summary executions — or, better still, go to the police — we should make sure our evidence is solid.'

'It is!' Eloise points at the screen.

'It lacks context. It's like a video clip on the internet showing a copper going hands on. It might look bad but it doesn't show the previous five minutes where the offender has already decked two people and punched the copper first.'

'I have the context. I was there.'

'You didn't look away for a moment? You didn't get distracted by conversation? You saw absolutely everything that happened behind the counter that the camera didn't catch?'

I take Eloise's silence as a no.

'What would we do if we were still in the job?'

Her anger starting to abate she silently considers for a moment. 'Question Prudence. Full background check: previous convictions, local intelligence, look for connections to the other victims and the cold cases.'

'That's more like it.'

Eloise lets out a long sigh and picks up a pencil and a piece of paper. 'We should do that for the others at Death Café, and Adele's poisoning too.'

'Starting with Beth and Agatha,' I say.

'Why those two?'

I open an app on my phone. 'Because my spreadsheet shows they were both at the library event where Adele was poisoned, and Beth and Prudence were at the Will Pickett launch.'

Eloise scribbles a list.

'We should look at Matty too,' I say.

'Matty?' Eloise looks doubtful. 'He's been helping us.'

'Serial killer 101: insert yourself into the investigation. Matty was at three of the poisoning events. He even warned you off the brownies.'

A motorbike roars outside, grumbling to a halt in front of the shop. I immediately go to comfort Stevie. A lump forms in my throat, a watery sheen covering my eyes as I remember he's not here.

The Black Dog rider dismounts and staunches into the shop. 'I need the next Dragon Brothers, Mr Sherlock.'

I know him. He's not a bad sort compared with some of his colleagues. He was even quite polite when he threatened to rough me up the previous time he was in the shop. I wipe the wannabe tears from my eyes. 'Your boy's enjoying them, then?'

'Yeah, we are.' He follows me to the children's section. 'That Pitbull's a wrong'un.'

I straighten, thinking he's talking about Stevie, before I remember that the villain in the stories is called The Pitbull. 'Flynn and Paddy will sort him out,' I say, referring to the book's heroes.

'And Briar, she's hard case.'

The Black Dog grabs my wrist as I hand the book over. His crushing grip is like the jaws of a dog around a bone, even though I don't think he's trying to be intimidating. 'The boss said to tell you they're applying for a search warrant.'

'For where?'

The pressure on my wrist releases. 'Unit 39.'

The Loan Ranger shudders to a halt outside the vet's. My heart skitters like the kittens in the window, and not just because we're going to get Stevie back. Inside, near the reception desk, I'm sure I see the gothic enigma that is Prudence.

'Do you want to wait with the car while I get him?' I ask Eloise hopefully.

'No!' She looks at me like I've suddenly gone mad. Perhaps I have — there was no way she wasn't going to collect our special boy.

'Well, just stay calm, okay?'

The concern on her face deepens. 'What's gotten into you? We're getting Stevie back. This is the good bit.'

'I know, I know.' I open the passenger door. 'I'm just saying we should avoid any drama, for Stevie's sake.'

'I'm not going to hide that I'm pleased to see him if that's what you mean. What's your problem?'

I pause at the door, partly because I'm always confused about whether it's a push or pull and partly because I'm fearful of what's going to happen when Eloise spots Prudence. Deciding that the door is a push, I open it and we walk inside.

Eloise looks around and momentarily tenses before striding straight towards the dark-veiled Prudence. I shadow her, readying myself to drag her away.

'Hi, Pru,' I shout by way of a warning.

Prudence turns, startled. 'Oh, hello. I was just asking about Stevie.'

'Why?' Eloise squares her shoulders and her hands lift above her waist. 'To see if your poisoning was successful?'

'Sorry?' Prudence looks bewildered and genuinely hurt.

Eloise's fingers curl into fists. 'Sorry that you didn't succeed? You're on CCTV handing Reagan the cake that poisoned my dog!'

'But it was the special doggy cake I made — there was nothing in it that would have harmed him! Eloise, you know how fond I am of Stevie. I realise you're upset but—'

'Upset? You have no—'

I grab Eloise's shoulders and pull her backwards. 'Go and see Stevie.'

'Get *off* me!' Eloise tries to shrug free. I've anticipated this and my grip is like iron.

'You said you'd be calm, for Stevie's sake. Now go and see him. He must have heard you and will be wondering where you are.'

'This isn't over.' Eloise glares at the visibly shaken Prudence and stalks off to the recovery area, chaperoned by a concerned-looking vet nurse.

I stand with Prudence in awkward silence. She appears stunned and I want to give her the benefit of the doubt, but my naturally suspicious copper's nature pushes me towards an alternative explanation: that she's been caught in the act, unmasked as the culprit and is trying to appear innocent. Or, worse, she came here to finish the job.

'Do you really think I would hurt Stevie?' Prudence asks quietly.

'Honestly, at the moment I don't know what to think.' I don't apologise for Eloise's behaviour — what if she's right and I should have let her lump Prudence one? 'It was a bit of a surprise to see you here.' I let my words hang. It's not a full-on accusation but there's enough that it requires an answer.

Prudence looks down. 'I was going to come into the shop but then I didn't know what I would say if poor Stevie had died. So I thought I'd come here first to check.'

Raised voices sound from the recovery area, then Eloise bursts through the door, tears streaming down her face.

'It's Stevie. He's gone.'

CHAPTER 46

Eloise: 3 days until Battle of the Book Clubs

We're at home, exhausted and slouched on the sofa, trying to fathom this latest blow. Garth is in a mega-sulk, and for once it's absolutely justified. Stevie *has* gone, but he's not been dognapped, or gone to live on a metaphorical farm. He's been sent to the veterinary teaching hospital in Palmerston North because they want to keep a close eye on him, and they have the resources on hand if he takes a turn for the worse. Which doesn't bear thinking about.

'I'm so sorry, love,' I say again. 'I didn't mean to do that to you. I was in shock.'

'The problem, Eloise, is that you have most of a conversation in your head and expect me to pick it up at the point where words come out of your mouth. You really need to consider how what you say affects other people.'

That was an exceptionally long statement for Garth. He is very upset indeed. My anger flares at the criticism but I take heed and keep my mouth shut. He's right. A deep breath and a clear, calm explanation that Stevie has been transferred in order to get the best care possible would have saved Garth the trauma of thinking — even briefly — that his precious one was gone for good.

I take a few deep breaths through my nose and wake up my laptop in preparation for our scheduled meeting. My hands are shaking. I look over to the green chair. It's going to take more than deep breathing to keep my mind off the big gap where my dog should be.

'I still don't see why Tama just couldn't come round here,' says Garth. 'It seems stupid to Zoom him in when he's only in Napier.'

I keep my irritable sigh internal. We've been through this at least seventeen times: Tama is busy. It's his day off. Coming over to us would add at least an hour's travel plus faffing about having a drink and listening to Garth talk about Dungeons and Dragons. I'm glad I've stuck to my guns and spared him that.

We're scheduled to Zoom with Tama and Paula together at 7pm. It is now 6.57pm.

'Open the chat room then,' says Garth, shuffling his bum closer to mine and plonking his coffee on my copy of the new Carl Shuker. I think of what happened to the dog in his previous novel, *A Mistake*, and my eyes well up, yet again.

'I will, at 7pm.'

'But you'll need those three minutes to log in and be ready to let them into the chat. Do it now.' I will only forgive this snippiness for so long, shock or no shock.

'Oh look — there's an email from Duncan in Canada. We could have a quick squiz before we log on. Might be—'

'No, Eloise. Concentrate on one thing at a time. Now, will you please log in?'

I apply every fibre of my being to the task of ignoring this incessant pedantry. It doesn't matter. It's not worth killing him over three minutes. I actually quite like him on the whole and would miss him. I open the chat. We stare at it. Tama arrives at 7.03pm and I let him in. He has a glass of red on the go. Bloody good idea.

'Nice day off?' I ask.

'We're not here to socialise, Eloise,' says Garth.

'Yeah, it's been pretty cruisy to be honest,' says Tama. 'Tidied up the deck, fixed that door hinge Chloe was on about. Had a beer. Easing into my evening nicely.' He gives us a 'cheers' with his glass. 'More importantly, how's Stevie Pup doing?'

'Not out of the woods yet is what they keep saying. I'm furious, Tama. We have to get this sorted soon as.'

Tama nods solemnly but says nothing. What is there to say?

We wait, talking about nothing until Paula's name pops up in the room, which it does at 7.06pm. Garth is trying to suppress his vexation at her tardiness but I can feel the tension in his leg, jiggling next to mine as we huddle over the screen.

There's a digital crackle and a bit of snow on the screen, which recedes to reveal my old mate Paula.

'Morning, Sarge,' I say. 'Nice hat.' She's wearing what looks like a satin beret adorned with pink, yellow and green flowers on an orange background. She's a vibrant, welcome blast of life in the midst of our very shit day.

'It's a sleep cap, you muppet. I took my braids out and I'll have to shave my hair off if it gets tangled. It's a living nightmare.'

'Well, it's certainly . . . arresting,' says Tama, grinning his cheekiest of cheeky grins.

'Yeah, yeah, I see what you did there. This is the Kiwi cop then, yeah? Hello from Blighty.'

'Kia ora. I've heard a lot about you, DI Taylor.'

Paula sits back and folds her arms. 'Have you really?' she says, slowly.

'So,' says Garth, all business. 'What do you have for us, Paula?'

'Oh right, that's the niceties done, is it, Garth? Suits me.' She sits up straight and starts tapping on her keyboard. 'Okay. I haven't had time to look at this but I do have a digital file of the list you wanted, so I'm gonna share my screen, all right?'

A document appears and the fancy logo of Distinction Literary Services relegates our four little faces to the side of the screen. I scan the first paragraph and it makes me so angry that I feel dizzy. I take a measured breath and Garth pats my leg.

> Distinction Literary Services deals with only the most outstanding writers and manuscripts. If I choose to represent you, your reputation is assured.

Pinter. What an absolute cockhead of an arrogant bastard.

'I'd forgotten what a twat he is,' says Paula. '"I'm the best, so you'd better be too." What a load of bollocks.'

'Well, it worked for a while, until his hubris made him deadly,' I say. 'Right, if you scroll down slowly, Paula, then we'll see if we can spot Prudence Ballion or Faith Saxon.'

'Or anyone called Deirdre,' says Garth.

Good point. Prudence might have used her Goth Girl pseudonym.

There are about fifty clients on the list, which seems a lot for one literary agent. Pinter worked independently, deeming himself too much of a cut above to have partners. The slow scroll jerks down the screen.

'Maddox Alexander. That's a fancy one. What do you think he writes?' offers Tama.

'There are three Harriets on this list. When do you ever meet a Harriet?' adds Paula.

'Carole Nwadike. I remember her. He didn't represent her for long,' I note.

'Not good enough for him?' Tama says, and I can hear the grin in his voice.

'Nope. That's why he set fire to her, along with her manuscript.'

That stops the chat. Tama exhales, grin gone, mutters something that gets lost as he breathes into his wine glass. We've told him a bit about Pinter but not all the gory details. It's too much — for all of us.

We get to the end and Paula scrolls back up, a little faster. No sign of a Prudence or a Faith, or a Deirdre for that matter. I lean back in my chair.

'Hold up, hold up, go down again really, really slowly. Aaaaand stop.' Garth has spotted something and waits for a beat until we catch up. I shock forward.

'Elizabeth Borden. Lizzie. Fucking hell.'

'Language, Eloise.'

'Who's she then?' says Paula.

'If it's the same person — and the coincidence would be astounding if it wasn't — she is the New Zealand author who had her publishing contract cancelled after her work was called out as plagiarism. According to Faith Saxon, at least. Lizzie Borden is a pseudonym, obviously. We don't know who she is.'

'The plot thickens,' says Tama.

'Indeed,' says Garth.

'She got very shitty about it too, according to something we found on Twitter.'

Paula nods. 'Well, you would, wouldn't you, if your career went down the bog on one person's say-so.'

'Indeed,' repeats Garth, a sure sign he's mentally chewing on something.

'So was it Lizzie who tried to murder Stevie and has all the other poisonings on her hands?' I ask. 'We need to find out who she is, Tama. We need to find her now.'

I'm about ready to get in the car and stop every woman on the street until I find her. Garth places his hand firmly on my thigh, holding me in place.

'We do, Eloise, we do,' says Tama. 'But we need to do it methodically, and when I'm not drinking merlot. I'll get the name rolling around our databases and maybe you should talk to Faith and see what she remembers about this person.'

He's right. Faith is a good place to start.

'What have you found so far in relation to this Lizzie apart from the thing about losing her publishing contract?' asks Paula.

'Just that bit of snark on Twitter having a go at the judges. It was anonymous,' I say. 'And an absolute shit ton of irrelevant stuff that pops up when you search the internet for Lizzie Borden.'

Paula nods. 'Okay, well, good luck. I'm going to get some conditioner through these curls, darlin's,' she says. 'Keep me updated.' She leaves the meeting the only way she knows how — abruptly. The rest of us exit shortly after.

'I'm ringing Faith,' I say, unlocking my phone to find her number.

'Just . . .' Garth reaches out to hold my arms. 'Just give it a minute, Eloise. Let my brain sift through all that information first. Please.'

His request grounds me. We've had a hell of a day and yes, Lizzie, whoever she is, might be out there poisoning someone as we speak, but it's more likely that she isn't. I get a weird image of a nasty old woman, hunched over by evil, sitting in a meanly lit, under-heated room plotting the downfall of everyone who ever wronged her. Garth gently rocks me, trying to soothe. 'Go and open a bottle of wine while I think. I might have half a glass too.'

It's so unusual for Garth to be my drinking buddy that I shake myself back to reality, trying to extricate myself from spiralling images of my unwell puppy.

We shall reconvene in the incident room with wine and make a plan.

CHAPTER 47

Garth: 3 days until Battle of the Book Clubs

Wine poured, we open the email from Duncan. There are the usual pleasantries, which we both skip over, zeroing in on the meat of the email, and what rancid flesh it is.

> Fortunately, I kept records of everything related to the competition, as it was a right furore at the time and caused a good deal of bad feeling among the committee. Lizzie Borden's entry, 'Last Day at the Library', was in the top three selected and passed on to Faith to judge. However, she discounted it when she recognised some of it as being plagiarised from her own novel, *The Poison Pen*, written under a pseudonym before she hit the big time.
>
> Lizzie denied it, of course. She sent death threats to Faith and also threatened to kill her cat. Faith didn't want any

publicity or to get the police involved because she didn't want to escalate things but it seems her agent at the time may have contacted Lizzie's publisher-to-be. That's what presumably led to Lizzie's contract being withdrawn.

'Fuck-a-doodle-doo!' says Eloise.

'I couldn't have put it better myself. Have you read *The Poison Pen?*'

'Yonks ago, when they re-released it under her real name. Can't remember much other than that I enjoyed it, and it had a great cover.'

'What was it?' I ask.

'I don't recall. But it must have been good because at the time I remember I thought about getting it as a tattoo.'

'A woman walking away?' I suggest perhaps one of the most overused book-cover tropes in the industry.

'No.'

'A woman looking at the Eiffel Tower?'

'No.'

'A woman walking away *and* looking at the Eiffel Tower?'

'Yeah. In a red coat.'

'Really?'

'No, you twat. Now shut up and let me think.' Eloise closes her eyes and her face scrunches. 'Foxgloves.'

'Foxgloves? I think I'd prefer a woman in a red coat, walking away, a suitcase in one hand, staring at the Eiffel Tower.'

'I said shut up and let me think.' Without opening her eyes, Eloise punches me. 'It was foxgloves, but the flowers were made to look like the feathers of a quill, with the stems morphing to a point like an ink pen nib.'

'That does actually sound cool. Even if it didn't have the Eiffel

Tower.' I point to the bottom of the email. 'Look. Duncan's included an attachment.'

Eloise clicks on the file and it opens in a new tab. It's Lizzie Borden's short story.

Unable to take our eyes from the screen, we devour the prose, which is dark and well written. The macabre tale tells of a woman wronged who slowly poisons a librarian by dipping the librarian's pen in a lotion prepared from foxglove petals. The lotion's toxicity is slowly increased over time and the sickening results recorded in precise detail in a notebook by the poisoner, who visits the library every day. Finally there's a day when the poisoner waits all day, notebook poised, but the librarian never shows.

'Wow,' I say. 'A librarian like Belinda Henare.'

'And foxglove poisoning would cause heart failure.'

'Also like Belinda Henare.'

Eloise pulls a downwards smile. 'Good story, though. No wonder it was a finalist.'

I scooch from the bed over to our incident room wall. 'That certainly gives us another piece of the puzzle.'

Eloise takes a glug of wine. 'Except this jigsaw is 3D and spreads across ten years and two continents.'

'You make it sound so hard.'

'We don't have the resources of the police, we have a lot of unanswered questions, we only have three days until Battle of the Book Clubs and, worst of all, my wineglass is empty.'

'That is troubling. How on earth did that happen?'

'No idea.' Eloise shrugs. 'I could have sworn it was full a minute ago.'

I top up her glass and return to the incident room wall. 'Let's look at what we have, starting with the cold case and moving forward.'

Eloise squints at the board. 'In 2016 Kiri Wereta, Belinda Henare and Lizzie Borden were shortlisted in a local writing competition. The judge, Faith Saxon, ruled out Lizzie Borden and awarded Kiri and Belinda joint first place.'

'Lizzie Borden threatened Faith, who ended up moving to the US, which was a wise move because we believe Lizzie then poisoned Kiri and Belinda.'

'Except, thanks to Tama, we suspect that she got the wrong Belinda Henare.'

I pick up a whiteboard marker, fiddling with the lid as I try to organise the information in my mind. 'Come forward to fourteen months ago and the *correct* Belinda Henare is poisoned — also by Lizzie Borden? — and then a year later a copy of *The Cause of Death* is sent to Belinda's address on the first anniversary of her death by serial killer Arthur Pinter. Why?'

'We know from the interview provided by the Admiral that Pinter mentored a writer who turned the tables on him. We also know he is communicating with someone in New Zealand who is poisoning Battle of the Book Clubs members. I don't think it's unreasonable to assume it's the same person.'

'I know! I know what it is! Give me the pen.' Eloise impressively rolls from the bed without spilling her wine, snatches the marker from my hand and draws a ring around Faith Saxon. 'The winning team of Battle gets to have dinner with Faith. That's when Lizzie's going to kill her.'

CHAPTER 48

Eloise: 2 days until Battle of the Book Clubs

I should be trying to figure out who the hell Lizzie Borden is but my brain currently has the consistency of a soft French cheese. Tama's search is drawing a blank, that being the problem with aliases. Chrissy is picking me up in half an hour to visit Reagan, who can only be described as very poorly indeed. At least the hospital bed that Chrissy rented has enabled him to stay at home, with his wife Anna looking after him and the nurse calling in to dispense pain medication.

'You coming to see Reagan?' I ask Garth, who is making coffee.

He goes still and looks out of the window. 'No,' he says quietly. He looks at me and I see everything he's not saying. We share a smile and I lean in for a hug. He wraps me up and rests his chin on my head, whispers a 'thank you'.

'Are you doing okay?' I ask. 'It's a lot, with the poisonings, and Stevie, and Battle looming. I'm feeding off anger at the moment but you're looking a bit . . . shell-shocked.'

'That's a good way to describe it.' He ponders for a moment. 'I'm okay, but me going to see Reagan wouldn't do him any good — or me. I don't want to insert my misery in to that situation, and, just between you and me, I don't want to see him dying.'

'I'll tell him that. It'll make him laugh.'

'Don't you dare!' He shoves me away with a smile. I shove him back.

'It's all a bit shitburgers at the moment, eh, love?'

'Yup.'

I take the coffee he hands me and collect my thoughts. Brain cheese or not, I reckon I've got time for a quick call to Faith Saxon. She's not fully off the suspect list yet, so I need to tread carefully, but if our latest theory is correct, she's the hunted rather than the hunter. I pull the wheely chair up to my desk and wonder how the fuck it gets so messy in here. I'm constantly filing invoices and statements but there seems to be paperwork everywhere.

Pen in hand, paper at the ready, I dial. Faith answers on the second ring.

'Eloise, is that you? I saved your number from last time. Is that weird?' Her warm, easy tone relaxes me immediately. Is it an act? It doesn't sound like an act.

'It's me, all right. How are you?' Doesn't hurt to soften up a suspect with a friendly opening.

'I'm glad you rang. I've been working on this paragraph for an hour and getting nowhere. Distract me!'

'Well, I can certainly do that. I'm after info about Lizzie Borden.'

There's a rapid inhalation and I can feel the shock down the phone line, or waves, or whatever they are these days. Perhaps *she* is Lizzie Borden and is horrified at being rumbled. I bite my tongue to let whatever this is play out.

'Sorry. I'm sorry . . . I'm trying to compose myself,' she says. 'Do you know what that woman is to me? What she did?' Faith is clearly shaken and I feel chastened. I've caused this distress.

'I know that you accused her of plagiarism and she lost a publishing contract.'

'Yes, that's right.' Faith's tone has taken on some anger, an emotion I'm familiar with right now. 'It was a massive shock to recognise my own writing — like swathes of it lifted directly from my work and dumped in her story. And it was so unnecessary. The parts she wrote herself were great — quite ingenious, actually — and I feel sure she could have come up with something completely original.'

'I don't quite understand why *you* feel so wronged by her actions, though, Faith,' I probe, gently as I can. 'She's the one who suffered for what she did.'

'Yes, but she absolutely went for me! I received threatening letters, phone calls — I don't even know where she got my number and address from. It was insane. I tried to be brave about it but in the end I just packed up and fled back to the US. It was such a relief to get away.'

'Did you leave because of Lizzie?'

'Not entirely. I was awarded a fellowship, so I was going anyway. When the stress of the threats became unbearable I brought it forward a bit. Gosh, just hearing her name like that has given me a panic attack.'

Oh, I feel really awful now. Poor Faith. I give myself a shake and a reminder not to blindly trust what she's saying.

'Why are you so interested anyway?' Good question, Faith.

'She has a connection with someone from our past.'

'Someone you'd rather stayed in the past?'

'Correct. I'm so sorry to bring this up for you, Faith, but do you have any contact details for Lizzie, or know of any way we could find her?'

'I don't think I do, no. She was so cagey about everything, right from the beginning. I always assumed Lizzie Borden was a pseudonym, because of . . . you know. Her email address kept changing and her social media profiles kind of came and went.'

'Your agent contacted the publisher-to-be. Would they have details?'

'We fell out about that. I hadn't asked her to do so. And I'm afraid she passed away not long after.'

'Oh. I'm sorry . . . would there be someone else at her agency I could speak to?'

'She *was* the agency. That was another reason I went to the States, to seek new representation. It really was the most terrible time. You can't imagine what's it's like to be hounded by a psychopath.'

'A psychopath?'

'Oh yes, I think so. Lizzie threatened to kill my cat. Only a psycho behaves like that.'

'Brace yourself. He's not looking pretty.' Chrissy is as organised as ever. She's done Anna's shopping and picked up our coffee order from the café near Reagan's house. 'Although he'd say he wasn't that pretty to begin with.' It's true. Reagan's ability to laugh at himself, as well as his delight in winding up others, has served him well.

We pull up the drive and Eva, Reagan and Anna's daughter, comes bounding down the steps to relieve Chrissy of the coffee; there's a hot chocolate in there for her somewhere. I marvel at her resilience, how normal she looks even at this stage of the game.

The sliding doors open into the living room and Reagan is laid nearly flat out in a recliner, his bed close by and freshly made. His eyes slide to us as we enter.

'Well, look what the cat dragged in!' His voice is a whisper, his face swollen and red, but we'd know that sly grin anywhere. It's the one that belies the words; he's pleased to see us all right. Anna gets up from her perch on the bed to hug Chrissy and take the groceries. Eva hands out the coffees and disappears back to her room.

'She's looking okay.' It sounds like a statement but Chrissy's look to Anna turns it into a question.

'She's up and down, eh, Reagan?'

He nods, adds, 'She'll be just fine with a mum like you.'

He's prepared his family so well, found the joy in every minute, the fun in the absurdity of dying in your forties. Eva will have a file of beautiful memories to carry her through life.

'How's Stevie?' croaks Reagan.

'Oh he's getting there. Thank you so much for raising the alarm so quickly that night. You saved his life, Reagan.'

Chrissy bustles about unpacking the shopping, throwing out the odd question to Anna. It all feels so . . . mundane. The man is dying right in front of us but the loo roll still needs putting away.

'You look as knackered as Reagan, sweetheart,' Chrissy says to Anna. 'Why don't you curl up on that bed while he's out of it?'

Anna nods and I stand to leave, placing a light hand on Reagan's arm. His eyes remain closed as he slurs, 'I won't see you again. Glad to know you.'

God he's a heartbreaker.

'The pleasure has been all mine, my friend.'

CHAPTER 49

Garth: 1 day until Battle of the Book Clubs

The vet nurse comes through the recovery room door with Stevie on a lead behind her. His tail is as curled beneath him as is doggily possible and his head scans nervously from side to side. On seeing us he emits a whine, his eyes reproachful, but his tail unfurls a little, giving a half-hearted wag. I do hope that he somehow understands that we were trying to do the best for him. Eloise drops to her knees and gives him a big hug, pushing her face into his soft fur. He tolerates this for a long moment before pulling his head aside.

'Hello, mate.' I pat his flank; he feels thinner. 'Shall we take you home?'

His ears prick up and he pulls towards the door. I take the lead and let him drag me to the car while Eloise gets medication and instructions from the vet nurse.

By the time Eloise joins us, Stevie is ensconced in the rear footwell, curled into a tight ball.

'They couldn't identify the cause but all his bloods and other tests have come back clear, so he should make a full recovery,' Eloise reports. She eases the Loan Ranger out of the vet's car park with an uncharacteristic degree of care.

'We can't ask for more than that.'

'Yes we can. We can catch the bastard who did it to him.' The Loan Ranger surges into the traffic on Napier Road, any consideration of careful driving forgotten.

'It's too risky. We should cancel Battle of the Book Clubs.'

'If we cancel, we'll never find out who the culprit is. And it won't prevent Faith's murder; it will postpone it at best.'

They're valid points, and perhaps we're not encumbered by the same duty of care that we had in the police — not legally, at least. 'It just feels wrong to use Faith as bait.'

'I was used as bait to catch Pinter.'

'And you nearly died.' I shake my head. 'Also, you were a copper and had a choice in the matter. Perhaps we should warn her?'

'Faith didn't cope well with Lizzie's threats last time. If we tell her our suspicions she'll cancel and bugger off back to America. Then Lizzie will still be at large and free to try again. Our best bet is to see this through and catch her in the act. *Before* the act.'

'Then I reckon we need to brief Tama, so he has our backs.'

'He's going to be there anyway as part of Chloe's team.' Eloise swings the Loan Ranger onto our drive. 'And if we let him know what we're up to he might force us to cancel.'

'Or he might provide some proper support, surveillance teams and the like.'

'We had surveillance teams last time, Regional Crime Squad and the tactical unit, and it didn't make any difference. It was you and me who caught Pinter in the end, and it'll be you and me who catch his proxy this time.' Eloise yanks the handbrake on.

'On that op Pinter was our only suspect and the wheels still came off.' I pat Stevie's head as he pushes it between the seats. 'We've got four possible suspects this time. How are we going to cover that all by ourselves?'

'We're not. We're going to have a little help.'

'ESM?' I ask.

Eloise nods. 'Emergency Staff Meeting.'

My legendary vegan Bolognese waits on the table, garlic bread has been pulled from the oven and sliced, and Stevie is doing zoomies around the front room proving to Kitty, Amelia and Phyllis that he is well on the mend.

'So who's the secret superstar author that we're launching this time?' Phyllis shuffles, getting comfortable on one of the three sofas next to Kitty. The last time we had an ESM it was for the book launch of Isabella Garrante and the staff clearly think we've gathered them to announce something similar.

'If only it was that simple,' I reply ironically. There was nothing simple about that launch; however, despite all the mystery, drama and threats, nobody's life was actually on the line. But if we stuff up this next event somebody may get murdered and the blame may well fall on us.

'We need your help to catch a killer,' Eloise says with a bluntness more akin to my MO.

'Fantastic,' says Amelia. 'Is this a new quiz round for tomorrow?'

'No new round,' I say. 'We're deadly serious. With the emphasis on deadly.'

'Oh, exciting!' Amelia clasps her hands together. 'And just a tiny bit terrifying.'

'I caught the last one.' Phyllis swings an imaginary hurley stick. 'I think I'm on a winning streak — happy to bag another.'

'And I caught Basil.' Kitty's face remains impassive, making it uncertain whether she is speaking with pride or regret.

'You're all aware of at least some of what's been going on.' I look at each of them in turn; they're resolute, excited and terrified and I feel like an absolute cad for drawing these wonderful people into our investigation. 'The back-of-book blurb is that we believe an author with the pseudonym Lizzie Borden is an accomplice of Pinter's and is going to try to murder Faith Saxon at Battle of the Book Clubs.'

There's a sharp intake of breath from Kitty. 'An accomplice?'

'Murder Faith Saxon? Wow!' says Amelia.

'Her writing's not that bad,' says Phyllis.

I nod, trying to look confident despite knowing that this 'blurb' is pure guesswork and there's still a very real possibility that we are the targets.

Eloise sits next to me on the arm of the sofa. 'We need your help to make sure this doesn't happen. The tricky thing is that we don't know who Lizzie Borden is, but we have four suspects in the frame that Team Tomes will have to shadow. You all know about Prudence and the video where it appears that she may have poisoned Stevie. She was also at the Will Pickett event where Damian was poisoned, and she was living in the UK when the accomplice was recruited.'

'I still can't imagine Prudence hurting Stevie,' says Phyllis.

Amelia shudders. 'She's always given me the willies.'

'Next we have Agatha, the librarian.' I check my spreadsheet. 'She was at Damian's and Adele's poisonings, and has a strong dislike of Faith Saxon who years ago bailed on an event Agatha had arranged.'

'Agatha's so good-natured, I can't see it being her,' says Kitty. 'She's in Forest and Bird.'

'That's the thing with serial killers, they tend to blend in. They often seem nice,' I say.

'Which brings us to lovely Beth,' says Eloise. 'In our book club, cares for the elderly, and was present at Damian, Adele and Stevie's poisonings.'

'And last but definitely not least,' I say, 'Matty. He was at the poisoning of Lily, Damian and Adele.'

'Oh no,' says Phyllis. 'I've so enjoyed my Dublin chats with him.'

Eloise folds her arms. 'We have no evidence that isn't circumstantial against any of them, so we need to catch whoever it is in the act.'

'Easy enough.' The unflappable Phyllis starts to serve tomatoey sauce and pasta onto plates.

'It's like an episode of *Midsomer Murders*!' Amelia negotiates an end bit of garlic bread. 'No. Wait. *Mid-Havelock Murders*. Will there be a handsome young detective? Or better still, an officer in uniform?'

I try to bring the conversation back on track before anyone mentions truncheons or Amelia goes down a firefighter rabbit hole. 'This is serious business, team. From our investigation we think this Lizzie has killed at least four people so far, and tried to kill at least three others.'

Amelia, not looking the least spooked, pulls out her phone. 'I'll set up a group chat so we can send each other secret messages on the night.'

Kitty is feeling less robust. 'I'm not sure that I'm really up to this sort of thing.' She worries at the ends of her scarf. 'In books it's fine because it's safe, but this is too real.'

'That's all good, Kitty,' I say. 'We know it's a big ask, and Eloise and I don't want you doing anything you're not comfortable with.'

Stevie, who has stopped doing zoomies, slinks up to Kitty, perhaps sensing a fellow nervous soul. He puts his head in her lap and looks up at her with sad golden eyes.

'Sorry, pupper, I'm just not cut out for this.' Kitty rubs the velvety patch on the top of Stevie's head. Then her eyes widen. 'Wait a minute. This Lizzie, is she the one who poisoned Stevie?'

'We think so,' says Eloise.

Kitty's soft, gentle face suddenly hardens. 'Well, bugger her! I'm in.'

CHAPTER 50

Eloise: Battle of the Book Clubs

The Function Room is full, abuzz with excited wine-drinking readers. The queue for the bar snakes through the cabaret-style tables towards the loos, even though we sent out pre-order forms. Most of the battlers are repeat offenders; after a glass of something and a speech from Chrissy to remind them why they're here, the quizzlers pull out purses and wallets, buying raffle tickets by the handful, determined to make a serious difference to the lives of young people affected by cancer.

Tama and Chloe bustle in, a bit late and flustered, searching for their table amid the boisterous chatter of the crowd. Never have I seen Tama look so out of place. He's already sweating, trying to follow Chloe and get his jacket off. He glances over and gives me a chin salute, eyebrows raised questioningly. I reply with the double thumbs up. He doesn't look reassured.

Garth is checking in the teams, making sure we have their correct team name and, most importantly, that they've coughed up the entry fee. I give him a nod and move through to the quiet ante-room where my loyal team of crime fighters has gathered. It was all we could do to stop them donning camouflage and balaclavas.

'So, one more time. I'm on Faith, and Garth is on Prudence. Amelia?'

'I shall be marking Agatha. She's drinking pinot noir and has ordered three bowls of hot chips for the table. Seated at said table as of three minutes ago.'

'Impressive work. Kitty?'

'I'm keeping an eye on Matty. He hasn't arrived yet. I feel a bit sick actually, Eloise.'

'I'll get you a cider in a minute and you'll be right as rain. Phyllis?'

Phyllis's eyes are narrow with gumshoe determination. 'I'm on Beth. Butter wouldn't melt with that one. She's been here since five o' clock helping Chrissy put the pens out, so she has.' Phyllis has always loved Beth for her charming nature and generosity, but now she's a suspect, it looks like all bets are off.

'Good. And what are we looking for?'

Amelia shoots her hand in the air and I nod to her to go ahead.

'Anything out of the ordinary, especially involving food or drink. We are to report to you immediately in person, or by text to the group chat.' Amelia all but salutes. It's like she's been training for this day her whole life.

'Oh yeah,' I fish my phone from my jeans back pocket and turn it on to vibrate.

'I'm not sure I want a cider,' says Kitty, 'seeing as we're looking for a poisoner.'

'All the recent victims have been on a quiz team — apart from Stevie of course,' I say reassuringly. 'You're quite safe, Kitty.' Phyllis nods a 'Sure, y'are', and Amelia gives Kitty's shoulder a pat. She straightens, shored up by team spirit and a loyal heart.

'Right, let's get in there. Remember to keep hydrated; there's a Sherlock Tomes tab at the bar.'

Determined to set a good example, I join the bar snake and take the opportunity to scan the room. Agatha is exactly where Amelia said she was, seated with her team, Destroyers of the Universe, laughing and flapping her arms about excitedly. They're strong contenders to win, consisting mostly of librarians and writers. Amelia sidles up and joins the chat, while Agatha grabs the wine bottle and offers it around, topping up glasses enthusiastically. Amelia is offered a glass and waves it away, citing duty with a point at her Sherlock Tomes tee-shirt.

Garth is now up at the podium, checking the microphone and faffing with the laptop. Kitty is by the door peering out to the car park and I take this to mean there's still no sign of Matty. Prudence's team, Book of the Dead, is a mix of Death Café crew and ring-ins; although more subdued than the librarians, they seem to be having a good time. There's an open cake tin on the table, containing what look like heavily iced chocolate muffins. Prudence is adorning the table with strips of black lace, scrunching it around the giant-papier-mâché acorns Chrissy has dotted about.

At the front of the queue, I order a sauvignon blanc, mainly because I can see they need to open a fresh bottle, guaranteed unadulterated. Armed with alcohol, I dodgem my way through the mostly settled teams and take my seat at the front table, next to Faith Saxon. My phone buzzes just as I'm about to sit on it:

> Kitty: M just in. At the bar.

I look over and there he is, checking the tags on the pre-ordered bottles of wine. He selects one and unscrews the cap while walking over to join the Quill and Ink table. He arrives to exclamations of welcome from his (mostly older, female) team members. Bringing the bottle to his face he mimes swigging straight from it, to great hilarity from the team. There are so many people between us I can't see what he does next, dammit. I glance over to the door. Kitty ambles closer to him, so blatantly casual that she might as well be whistling.

'Gosh I'm nervous,' says Faith, safely contained in the seat next to me.

'Well, at least you're up first so you can get it over with.'

She throws a rapid nod/grimace my way and does look genuinely rattled, fingers fluttering about in her handbag. Because she has to make a speech, or because she's planning dastardly deeds? I keep an eye on the handbag but she only drags a hankie out of it and dabs at her nose.

It's time.

'Good evening and welcome,' booms Garth, giving it a beat for the assembly to realise he's talking and quieten down, 'to Battle of the Book Clubs for the Mighty Oooooaks!'

A cheer goes up as if Muhammad Ali had just walked into the ring.

'Eight rounds of ten questions, from the sublime to the obscure, *Hairy Maclary* to *War and Peace*, *Fifty Shades* to *Pride and Prejudice*. And all for an essential cause, the Mighty Oaks.'

And the crowd goes wild, again. My phone vibrates.

> Phyllis: Beth is in play.

She is, too, heading for the loos from her perch at the Book of the Dead table. It's an odd time to go — when we're about to start. Prudence thinks so too, her eyes following Beth with a typically unfathomable stare. I tune back in to Garth.

'. . . without further ado, please welcome the Bay's most famous novelist, Faith Saxon!'

A sizeable number in the audience are Faith faithful, judging by the racket that goes up. She seems buoyed by this as she makes her way to the microphone.

'These actually aren't my own boobs,' she begins and there's a moment of spontaneous laughter that gives way to awkward mumbling.

'Titter if you like, pun intended, it's fine. I've been surgically flat-chested for years now and these perfectly pert and enviable baps are prosthetic. Let me tell you the story.'

And she does. By the end of the tale of mutated genes, a mother gone too young and a chemo story from hell involving an incidence of projectile vomiting in Wellington's poshest restaurant, everyone's faces are aching with tears and laughter. What a damn fine storyteller she is.

'So yes, you've paid your entry fee, but I now want you to buy enough raffle tickets to paper every inch of your table because Chrissy and her team are the only thing, the Only Thing, keeping these families sane right now.'

Wow. Good lass. Even if she turns out to be a poison-toting murderer from the very bowels of hell, the girl did well.

There's a break in proceedings as the Mighty Oaks volunteers seize the moment to do a bit of tin rattling and Eftpos machine waving.

Beth has missed the whole speech as she is only now making her way back to her table. Another buzz from the Bat Phone.

> Garth: Pru just sprinkled something glittery all over those cakes on her table. Garth.

Oh my god, that's not good at all. I'm about to move when there's a follow-up.

> **Garth:** Beth and P have just scoffed a cake and not died. Yet. Garth.

The crowd settles down for round one, Spot the Author of Aotearoa. The large screen on the wall shows a fabulously doctored black and white photo of an unsmiling woman wearing a clown's red nose and a rainbow wig. It's the jauntiest, most irreverent image of Katherine Mansfield I've ever seen. It's pure genius by Garth to begin with such an engaging round. There is much mirth.

A text comes in halfway through round two, The Dog Did It.

> **Amelia:** Agatha isn't doing anything interesting at all. Just drinking too much and laughing. Can I swap with someone?

I look towards the bar to see her staring at me intently. She gives me a 'Come *onnnnn*' look: wide eyes, imploring hands. I return it with the 'what can I do?' pursed lips with shrug, and head towards her for a chat.

While I've been distracted with this little exchange, and moved as far away from the person I'm covering as is possible in this room, I see Prudence is on the move. She's holding a champagne flute in her left hand and is just metres away from Faith Saxon, sashaying through the maze of tables and reaching into her capacious skirt pocket. Whatever it is she's withdrawn is in her right hand and is edging closer to the glass.

I break into a run, weaving through the crowded room full of merry bibliophiles, contriving to trip over a chair leg and go flying into Prudence just as she is about to reach Faith. Her glass and I both tumble, landing on the carpet in a damp, inelegant heap. I look up to find Prudence glaring at me, a Death Café card in her hand. Faith is cackling, covering her mouth as if to shove the sound back in. There are yelps of surprise from around the room.

'I'm all right!' I call. A cheer goes up.

'Faith,' says Prudence frostily, gathering her composure. 'Before we were so spectacularly interrupted, I was going to invite you to Death Café. Let's talk later.' She looks at me as if I'm completely bonkers, before turning and drifting back to her table.

Garth attempts to rein the crowd back in. 'Thank you, Eloise, for the light entertainment. And now, back to the quiz.'

CHAPTER 51

Garth: Battle of the Book Clubs

I flick tabs on the laptop so the spreadsheet showing the scores projects onto the big screen. The room momentarily quietens as the teams figure out their positions, my technical skills having failed to get the names to sort by score. The lull is replaced by chatter and laughter from the bottom teams who are in it just for fun now, and by serious discussions among the top four teams, who mathematically at least are all in with a chance.

All of our suspects' teams — Quill and Ink, Book of the Dead and Destroyers of the Universe — are in the top four.

I leave the scores up a little longer than usual while I scan the table of the second-placed team, Tequila Mockingbird. Have we missed something? The Admiral waves at me from the table with his cane, taking my prolonged stare as a sign of greeting. Next to him is another face I recognise: Will Pickett. Damn, could it be one of them? Is there another connection that we've overlooked?

'Now, moving on to round seven,' prompts Eloise over the microphone, dragging me from my panicked thoughts. I bring up the Heroes and Villains PowerPoint and flick to the first question. Eloise reads it out and my mind again races, although not trying to figure out the name of D.V. Bishop's heroic detective. The Admiral was a hero when he saved me from the Black Dogs, and he managed to procure us that Pinter audio, but could he be a villain too? I really don't want to think ill of him — he's a charming old stick — but from the stories he tells he's had a shadowy past, including working in naval intelligence. And how the hell did he get that audio file?

My phone vibrates.

> Phyllis: Beth and Pru arguing. If looks could kill!

From their animated gestures and the looks on their faces, the 'discussion' is clearly intense. They're too far away for me to make out any words, and I suspect Phyllis can't either. The general hubbub is loud, and they're arguing in heated whispers. Then Beth leans back and folds her arms, scowling, while Prudence's black-painted lips curl ever so slightly upwards as she writes an answer.

I flick to the next question, and while Eloise reads it out I message Amelia.

> Me: What's the haps with Agatha? Garth.

Destroyers of the Universe are at the back of the room and I can't see much. I'm relying on Amelia to be my eyes and ears and she doesn't disappoint.

> Amelia: Agatha hasn't stopped drinking. I reckon she's pretty rinsed. Can I please swap?

I'm tempted to say yes and put Amelia on Tequila Mockingbird, only I have no idea of what or who we're looking for. Could we have it all wrong and none of our suspects is Lizzie Borden? What the hell were we thinking?

I don't put this in the group chat. It's like at work: when the bills are pressing or there's some other drama, Eloise and I have to project calm and confidence as the custodians of Sherlock Tomes. My fumbling fingers struggling to override the phone's autocorrect, I reply:

> Me: No stick with Agatha, just in case. Garth

Agatha may be drinking like a fish, but that doesn't make her incapable of murder. I've seen Eloise tuck away a fair few gratis wines and then still go on to present the national book industry awards without anyone being any the wiser.

Eloise reads out the answers of the previous round. I pay no attention, more concerned with the overall points tally. Quill and Ink have dropped to fourth; the other three top teams are neck and neck. Not that that gets Matty off the hook. We've assumed the killer has hobbled the other top teams to ensure that their team wins but there's still a big element of chance, especially with some of the oddball rounds we like to throw in.

The final round is Say What You See, for which Meryl painted us some artistic representations of book covers. The first one shows an arrow pointing up, a red jewel, and a beautiful picture of a tūī. It's probably the easiest one of the bunch and I expect most teams will get Ruby Tui, although they may not know the title, *Straight Up*.

As the round continues, I try not to get distracted by Meryl's excellent artwork, keeping my eyes on Prudence and the Book of the Dead team. The altercation seems to have simmered down, the members tightly huddled, deep in discussion.

The answer sheets are collected, and our two helpers from the Readers and Writers Festival committee begin the final scoring. Eloise is organising the drawing of the raffle. Chrissy hurries over to Faith and I edge a little closer to the author. Not that I suspect Chrissy, but my normal unhealthy paranoia appears to have reached new heights.

'Faith, can we prevail upon you to present the raffle prizes?' asks Chrissy.

Oh fuck. Let's just paint a target on her prosthetic chest, why don't we.

'Of course. It would be my pleasure.' Faith stands and makes her way towards Eloise.

I trail her, trying to look natural. I've never been on close protection detail and have only a basic understanding of how it works. You need to be near enough to intervene if required but not so close that you intrude. If your VIP gets killed, you got it wrong.

The first few raffle winners are named and I can hardly hear the yells of delight over the hammering of my heart. The next ticket drawn is Agatha's. My heart ratchets up a significant number of BPMs and I become lightheaded as I track Agatha's weaving approach towards Faith. In the police you get used to dealing with drunk people and I don't think she's putting it on. That doesn't mean she won't try something, but it might give us the edge if she does.

Eloise is totally invading Faith's personal space, their shoulders touching as Agatha draws nearer.

Faith holds out a fancy presentation case containing two bottles of local wine. Agatha grabs it with one hand and I see a flash of something in the other as she lunges forward. I step across her, blocking the way so she hurls the rolled-up pamphlet at Faith instead. 'You were shposed to come to my talk!' she yells.

'Not really the time or place, eh, Agatha?' I say.

Agatha wipes away a tear. 'But I really liked her.'

Faith unrolls the pamphlet. It's an old flyer for the event Agatha arranged. 'Oh, that was you,' she says. 'I'm so sorry. Things were . . . complicated. I promise I will come and do a talk soon.' Faith leans in to give Agatha a hug and there's nothing Eloise or I can do to prevent it.

'Thanksh,' slurs Agatha, returning the hug a little too enthusiastically before wobbling back to her table.

I glance over to the scoring station and I'm given the nod. 'The results are in,' I whisper to Eloise.

Eloise checks that the mic is off and turns away from the tables to hide her words. 'Well, nobody's dead yet, so I'm taking that as a win.'

'Great stuff, keeping positive. Okay let's do this.'

I head back to the laptop and, hiding the projection, flick to the spreadsheet showing the results. I switch on the microphone. 'Okay, book-loving whānau. It's been a close-run competition, right up to the last round.' I pause to let the noise die down, and for dramatic effect. 'The winner of this year's Battle of the Book Clubs is . . .'

CHAPTER 52

Eloise: 30 minutes after Battle of the Book Clubs

Book of the Dead are beside themselves with joy, and a not insubstantial dollop of hubris. We march in tactical formation behind the somewhat inebriated winners to their prize: an afterparty with Faith Saxon at Rosie's Café. Prudence looks enigmatically smug and Beth is hugging anyone she can grab.

Garth and I flank Faith, surreptitiously guarding her. On we go through the fragrant steam of Rosie's, past the help-yourself beer fridge and out to the garden where a long wooden table is set for us. Fairy lights swoop, candelabras drip, the ambiguous harmonies of a bossa nova play out into the dark. The unicorn's playground illusion is so convincing that you can't tell that there's a concrete car park just the other side of the fence.

There's a bit of jostling as victors, celebrity author and Team Tomes find their seats. Amelia body-blocks a confused Prudence as she goes to sit next to Faith at the head of the table. I slip behind

Amelia to slide into prime position on Faith's immediate left. Prudence recovers and fluffs out her skirt to sit on my left, Amelia settling next to her, pleased at having finally engineered herself a new, more interesting target.

Phyllis brings up the rear with a flushed and jubilant Beth on her arm, crab-stepping between table and bench to form a barrier between Faith and Beth. After a timely wine delivery, glasses are filled diligently by Garth. Everyone settles.

'To this year's champions, Book of the Dead!' An appropriate amount of ovation occurs before everyone falls upon platters of bread, cheese and the saltiest olives in existence.

The evening so far is a roaring success and I have to keep reminding myself that one of the people present is a conniving, cold-hearted killer. I am uncharacteristically quiet and sober, trying desperately to listen in to every word of cross-chatter and monitor every flick of cutlery. I can see Garth is struggling too, convivial crowds being up there with shark attacks on his list of situations in which he would prefer not to be found.

It's a long, thin table and I relax into listening, snatching floating words and letting them drift again.

'. . . really lovely woman in Gore who recommended them. Best socks I've ever owned.'

'No, no, it was the little dog, not the big one. He's an absolute sook.'

'Why would you put so much salt on something that's preserved in brine?'

'. . . broke my ankle. Yeah. Absolute pest really. There's a parcel I was supposed to pick up in Waipuk a month ago and of course I couldn't get there!'

I do my best not to spin around at this last comment. The voice belongs to Beth.

'People were so kind, though, sending meals and messages.' She pauses to sip her wine and I can't quite make out her teammate's question. 'Yes, an old friend in the UK.'

I lean across the table and cut some cheese, concentrating hard. 'He's, umm, he's incapacitated, so we try and cheer each other up with the odd project.'

My heart is thudding and a flush of dangerous, feral rage begins in my stomach and burns wild through my torso. The heat chills and turns to an icy determination. Never before have I been so clear-headed. The chaos around me fades and I have perfect energy, perfect focus.

As Beth leans in to pour more wine, the floaty material of her blouse billows in the breeze, revealing a mark on her collarbone. A sly, slim blade slides into my heart. The mark is a tattoo, writing on a scroll in neatly executed Times New Roman. A similar tattoo sits upon my ribs, engraved by the most evil being I have ever met. I feel it sting like an answering call.

Several possible plans of action flicker across my mind in seconds but the space is crowded, full of innocent people, and the evidence, although compelling, is still circumstantial. I manage a tricksy bit of gymnastics and release myself from the bench.

'You all right?' asks Faith.

'Just going for a wee.'

She nods and turns back to her conversation with Chrissy, who has wandered over for a chat — something about wigs. I catch Amelia's eye and she gives a slight 'I got this' nod.

There is so much noise, so much animated chat that no one else notices me leave. I put my arms around Garth's back, all so natural, so warm and fuzzy. A couple of team members, faces aglow with wine and good company, throw affectionate smiles our way.

'Come with me,' I say, my voice low. 'Keep it jaunty.'

He attempts a fake laugh in response and clambers from his spot. Taking his hand as if we were just two tipsy booksellers having a fabulous literary night out, I lead him towards the loos to an alcove with a washing machine and I pull him in. It's gloomy and smells of late-night laundry.

'It's Beth.'

'Are you sure?'

'She has Pinter's tattoo.' I point to my collarbone. 'It's her, Garth. Beth is the Kiwi stooge.'

'Beth...' Something dawns on his face. 'Elizabeth. Lizzie. Beth. Oh my god, how has it taken us this long to see that?'

'She fucking poisoned my dog.' I'm spitting, freshly furious.

The door to the main room opens and a waiter strides past carrying a champagne bucket, distractedly glancing our way but staying on task.

'You guys okay?' he hollers, on the move.

'Yep, just making secret plans,' I reply and he laughs.

'We'd better get back and find out what her endgame is. And keep an eye on Faith.'

'It's not Faith, it's me! It has to be. Her "little project" from Pinter is to fuck up my life — or kill me. Or... no! She's after you! She's trying to take away everything I love. Poisoning Stevie, ruining our reputation, and now she wants you dead — as revenge against me!'

'Calm down,' says Garth, inadvisedly. He swiftly recognises his classic mistake as I prepare to erupt. 'I mean... we have a job to do, Eloise. Let's get in there, put on normal faces, and observe. Then, when the time is right, we act.'

I nod, force air into my lungs, feel my heart rate begin to slow. There's a percussive bang as a cork explodes from a bottle, accompanied by a celebratory cheer. I look at my partner in crime.

'Time to rejoin the party.' He takes my hand, we mentally shake ourselves out and skip back to the throng, full of piss and vinegar.

'Woo-hoo! Who's getting this party cranking with the champers?' I yell above the din.

Beth is centre stage, pouring the gush of bubbles into flutes, instructing the excited gathering to grab a glass. She's whipping up chaos, all white teeth and affability.

'Go, go, go! Pru, that's yours; Kitty, grab this one . . . whoops!'

The cynic in me suspects a deliberate shake of the bottle, causing it to boil over onto Beth's sleeve halfway through filling a glass. She tinkles a laugh and puts glass and bottle down, dipping below the table to rummage in her bag. I feel a hand on my arm — it's Kitty, sensing my tension and having come over in support.

'Gather the troops.' I force a whisper into her ear over the din.

'Team Tomes photo! Over here, Amelia, Phyllis!' she yells. No one but our faithful soldiery notice anything amiss. They extricate themselves and come to join us.

There's something in Beth's hand as she fusses over her dampened sleeve. She's deft, and it's flicking in and out of my vision, hampered as it is by candlelight and commotion. She swipes the rim of the half-filled glass with an oddly handled napkin, pours a little more champagne in and gives herself an organisational shimmy. Then she's on the move, heading towards Faith. I'm briefly blindsided by relief; she's after Faith, not Garth.

'A glass for the star of the evening!' trills Beth. Faith is delighted; she reaches out her hand and Garth strides in, emitting an authoritative 'No!' It's so unexpected that the hubbub dies. He grabs the glass, sloshing froth down its sides.

'What is going on here?' Beth attempts a little laugh, as if it's a game, part of the evening's competitive, quiz vibe.

'Lizzie Borden.' Garth states this suddenly, forcefully, straight at Beth. The mask flickers, sweetness fouling to a snarl, and I know we're right. She repossesses herself, brazening it out.

'Is this another quiz question? Haha, let me see . . .' She plunges her hands into the pockets of her skirt, casual and thoughtful.

Faith stands up, face white, hands shaking.

'Preserve the evidence please, Amelia,' says Garth, handing the glass to his loyal aide-de-camp, never taking his eyes from Beth.

'On it, boss.' Even in the midst of this madness, I see him grow a little taller at the words.

'Lizzie Borden? What the hell?' Faith stares at Beth, joining the dots. Garth has his arms out and wide at hip height, hands palm down, a levelling gesture to indicate calm authority. He speaks slowly, deepening his usual tone.

'I would like everyone apart from my team and Beth to quietly and calmly . . .'

The waiter chooses this moment to burst through the door carrying several plates of food, yelling a jaunty, 'Here we go, folks!'

Garth turns to look. In a move so fast it'll come to haunt my dreams, Beth has a syringe to his neck. It's all gone so violently south that no one says a word. Her left hand is bleached white as it grips his upper arm, her right thumb on the plunger, pustulent liquid in the barrel, the needle pricking my husband's neck, a jewel of blood surrounding the steel. It would take nothing for her to depress that plunger and end everything.

I grab a wine bottle. I'm not the best shot and Beth is using Garth as a shield; I dare not throw it. Then in my peripheral vision I see Phyllis inching stealthily along the edge of the long table towards them.

'Please, Beth.' I adjust my grip on the bottle. 'Why are you doing this?'

'Because she ruined me. This is the ending to a very long and macabre story, Eloise. You could sell lots of copies in your shop.'

The needle presses deeper into Garth's flesh. 'I couldn't get to Faith in the States. You poison the odd cat or two and suddenly your visa's declined.'

I have to try to talk her down. 'I understand about Faith, but why Kiri and the two Belinda Henares?'

'They took my place. I took their lives. It was a bit gutting when I read in the paper that I got the wrong Belinda. How was I to know there were two of them? But I got the right one eventually. Oh, he loved that. Hasn't let it go all this time — even sent me an anniversary present for finally getting it right.'

Beth sways slightly and it occurs to me that not only is she very, very angry, but she might be a little tipsy too.

'Who's he? Pinter?' I want to hear her say it.

'Who do you think? There's only one man who holds sway over you and me both, isn't there, Eloise?' She gives Garth a shake to emphasise her point. His eyes never leave mine. I need to keep Beth talking for just a moment longer.

'What about Miss Mooney? She never did anything to you.'

'Who?'

'Erma Mooney,' I say slowly. I need to be careful; she's getting bored with me. 'Lily, Damian, Adele. You tried to kill them all. And Stevie.' My voice cracks and she rolls her eyes.

'Oh yes. The Battle team people were a bit of insurance, really, to smooth the path to my team's win and this little soirée with Faith. Something to tell Arthur about later, too.' Her use of his given name is like an endearment, her obsession stroking it like a pet. 'He was well ahead of you, of course. Knew Fiona Kidman wouldn't be available long before you did. He still has contacts, you know. Not everyone abandoned him.'

'But . . .' I struggle to process her words and she loses patience with me. She adjusts her grip on Garth's arm and he winces as the needle pushes further into his neck.

'Now. Prudence, open that gate over there, unless you want Garth to become a member of Death Café in a very literal sense.'

Glowering, Prudence stalks over and unlatches the gate, pushing it open.

Beth smirks with the red-hot confidence of a woman who thinks no one can stand in her way. But she hasn't met my team when one of its members is under threat. To my left Kitty appears terrified, like a frightened Basil, yet below the table I see her slide her phone from her pocket and text 111.

Beth takes a step back, dragging Garth with her. 'Now everyone is going to stay exactly where they are while Garth and I take a little walk.'

'You won't get away with this, Beth,' I shout, pointing and gesticulating to keep her attention firmly on me. 'You'll be caught, and we'll soon have Pinter back in solitary where he belongs.' Her eyebrows rise at the name and I see something possessive, almost jealous in her psychotic gaze.

'Ha! You know nothing, Eloise. Let me help you understand the pain of losing someone who is everything to you.' Her thumb twitches on the plunger and my heart stops.

'Eloise!' Phyllis's shout slices through the air. I toss her the wine bottle. It barely lands in her hand before she's scooped it, flipped it and hurled it with extreme prejudice in a moment of lightning-fast poetic fluidity. It smacks Beth squarely on the side of her head and she drops as though dead on the spot. I fucking hope she is.

CHAPTER 53

Garth: 2 days after Battle of the Book Clubs

The Loan Ranger idles as we wait outside the Hastings nick. The sun is near setting, casting a surreal light over the city. Tama was none too impressed that we'd kept our secret plan from him, using words such as reckless, ill-conceived and foolhardy, interspersed with quite a lot of swearing. Having given him a couple of days to mellow, we've offered to take him for an after-work pint as recompense, to which he has begrudgingly agreed.

I tap the Loan Ranger's dashboard lovingly. I've grown to like the vehicle and am disappointed at the prospect of having to return it. 'I suppose I should be grateful that you didn't crash into anything in the process of unveiling another murderer.'

'Serial murderer,' corrects Eloise.

'Although, at least my injuries would have garnered me some sympathy.'

'Everyone was very concerned. You even got cake.'

'Yes, from Prudence, which I dare not eat.'

'I'm sure it'll be fine. She's forgiven us now that she knows what we were dealing with.'

'It's in the shape of a poison bottle.'

'That's just Pru having a joke. Once I'd apologised I actually think she was quite taken with the idea that we thought she might be a murderer.'

'It suits her gothic persona I suppose.'

'Maybe. Although on the lighter side, she's offered to help out the Mighty Oaks.'

'I'm sure Chrissy's delighted about that,' I say with all due sarcasm.

'She actually is.' Eloise folds her arms. 'Pru's going to be on the board and she and Tracey are donating a hundred grand.'

'Good grief! And they say there's no money in books.'

The glass doors swing open and out walks a distracted-looking Tama.

'What's up, chuck?' asks Eloise as he gets into the back seat.

Buckling up, he shakes his head. 'I don't know. It's weird.'

I pull away from the kerb. 'Good weird, or bad weird?'

'Just weird. There's something cracking off. They've got a search team in and some brass from Professional Conduct but I couldn't find out what's going on.'

I check the rear-view mirror, my guilt deepening as I see the worry lines on Tama's face. 'That does sound weird.' I don't dare look at Eloise.

'If it wasn't for Professional Conduct, I'd think it was a drug or gang thing.'

'Well, you've done nothing wrong, so no need to fret,' says Eloise.

'Nothing apart from having a lock-up full of case files, and off-the-books investigations with a couple of meddling bookshop detectives.'

I nudge Eloise. 'Do you remember the good old days of being coppers?'

'You mean the ones where people were actually grateful if you cleared up four murders?'

'Yes, those were the ones.' I take a right, which is totally the wrong direction for the pub. Fortunately Tama is too distracted to notice. 'In those days I even think that sort of thing might have helped you get a promotion.'

Eloise folds her arms. 'You know what? I think they would.'

'Enough! Before I arrest you both for inciting a police officer to give you the bash.' Tama shakes his head. 'I rue the day my wife joined your book club.'

'No you don't,' says Eloise.

'You're right. I don't.' Tama smiles.

'Which means you can spill the deets on what's happened with Beth,' says Eloise.

'She's a piece of work.' Tama shakes his head. 'Didn't say much to start with but when we searched her home and found incriminating diaries, poison preparations and a garden stocked with toxic plants she cracked.'

'She coughed to the book club poisonings?' I ask.

'All of them. Lily and Miss Mooney were apparently easy, with thallium added to their meds at home. Beth hadn't needed her moonboot for a week before it officially came off, so she was able to move about quite easily without anyone suspecting her, and being home help to both of them she still had keys. Damian and Adele were trickier. Damian was poisoned by a bit of pre-cooked deathcap quiche added to the food on his plate at the Will Pickett launch, and an injection of ethylene glycol in Adele's water bottle did for her — or would have done if she'd drunk more of it.'

'All of that just to get at Faith?' Eloise turns to look at Tama.

'She was supposed to be the grand finale. The lab found enough oleander preparation in her champagne glass to floor an elephant.'

I try not to think about how close we were to that happening.

'What about Stevie?' asks Eloise.

'Rat bait squished into the doggy cake Prudence made for him when no one was looking. She said Pinter was furious.'

'His only redeeming feature.' Eloise lets out a cynical laugh. 'He loves dogs.'

My grip on the steering wheel tightens. 'So what's the deal between her and Pinter?'

'She once tried to poison him after he ridiculed her writing. He recognised a kindred spirit and took her under his wing, as an author and a killer.'

I turn into the street where the storage unit is located. The gate is open, and parked inside the yard are two police cars, a police van and a blue hatchback. Unlike in the movies, where the faux coppers don't have to worry about draining the battery, the bar lights on the police vehicles are not illuminated.

'What the fuck? We need to get out of here!' Tama ducks down and looks over his shoulder.

'No, no, we need to brazen this out. Trust us, we've got this, Tama.' I pull to a halt as directed by a uniformed officer and wind down the window.

'We're conducting a search. You need to turn around,' instructs the officer.

I wave my keys. 'It's my storage unit, so I have a right to be here,' I say.

'I can't let you in,' says the officer.

'Detective Inspector, perhaps you could have a word?' says Eloise.

Tama takes a deep breath and exits the Loan Ranger. 'Constable Johnston, are you sure about this?'

'Orders from Professional Conduct, sir.' The constable looks towards the storage unit, clearly hoping that someone senior will come and resolve this problem.

'Lawful orders? Even they have to respect the law.' Tama puffs out his chest and gives the constable the hardest of stares. 'You have a choice to make and it's one that is going to affect the rest of your career. Let us in, or arrest me.'

The officer's officious confidence melts like a candle under a blowtorch and he stands aside.

I park up and we join Tama. 'You don't have to be here,' he says. 'I got you into this, it's on me.'

Eloise places a reassuring hand on his arm. 'When I took Pinter down it wasn't entirely by the book but the DI put her head on the block for me.'

I scan my key fob and we enter the security air-lock. 'Different DI, different country, but it's time to repay the favour.'

The internal doors slide open. Forty metres away, around the entrance to unit 39, stand a posse of police and Fedora Fatale. One of the officers is struggling with a set of bolt croppers trying to cut free the padlock.

'Stop!' I yell. 'I have the keys.'

Our footsteps echo as we approach, the expressions on those gathered ranging from annoyed, to confused, to amused.

'And who are you?' asks a serious-looking man in a suit, who is clearly in charge.

'Well, as you're the one about to break into my storage unit, I might well ask you the same question.' I wasn't a huge fan of senior officers when I was in the job and my opinions have not changed.

'Superintendent Elliot.' The officer flashes a warrant card. 'And this is DI McGregor's unit, not yours.'

'On paper, yes. But he's loaned it to me.'

Tama's protest is cut short by Eloise's elbow in his ribs.

'It doesn't matter,' interjects Fedora Fatale. 'The evidence inside will show that proper procedure has not been followed and that under the circumstances my client, Franklin White, should be released.'

'The keys, please,' says Superintendent Elliot, holding out his hand.

I toss the keys to the constable with the bolt croppers, who is sweating profusely. The padlocks I recently installed are Abus Rock models with shackle guards, and nothing short of a gas axe will open them without a key.

Both padlocks are removed in a matter of moments. Tama is hardly breathing, his hands trembling as the constable grabs the roller handle. The glow of fluorescent light seeps from beneath the door. Superintendent Elliot gives a curt nod and the door is hauled upwards.

There is a moment of stunned silence. Then, from behind his Games Master screen, Gordon says, 'Great. You're here.'

'Yeah.' Sim strokes his beard. 'It's time to battle the Scroll Lord.'

Inside the unit there are no filing cabinets, no walls covered with witness statements, no charts of evidence, just a single table with screen, map, figurines, dice and four seated geeks ready for a game of Dungeons and Dragons.

'Grab a chair, Tama,' I say. 'We have a mystery to solve.'

EPILOGUE

Eloise

Is that a woodpecker? There's a tapping on the inside of my skull. Then a chaos of barking and someone is shaking me.

'Wake up, Eloise. It's your phone. It's Paula.'

I reach over to grab the shrieking, buzzing thing, knocking it to the carpet. Fully awake now, I swing my legs out of bed and retrieve the phone.

I swipe the green icon and put it on speaker. 'Sarge, what's up?'

'Um, hello, mate. Sorry to wake you.'

'You okay? You sound a bit weird.' She's not usually one for apologies, our Paula.

'Yeah, yeah. Look. Listen. Is Garth with you?'

'Of course he is — it's about 3am!'

'Cool. Course. Nice.'

Okay, this is really odd. I'm starting to think I'm still asleep and dreaming. I wait, listening, watching Garth listening, hearing Paula's raggedy smoker breath and Stevie's disturbed little huffs.

'Okay. So. Thing is.' She gulps in a big breath before landing the punch.

'Pinter's escaped.'

ACKNOWLEDGEMENTS

The response to *Dead Girl Gone* has been phenomenal, exceeding all expectations. Thank you to everyone who has bought it, borrowed it, recommended it, and come to visit us at Wardini Books. Never has a flower box been so photographed. And massive thanks to all the booksellers who have loved our peek behind the curtain of bookselling and supported our book, and us. We have never worked in an industry that is so collegial.

Thank you, again, to Catt Walsh, Amy Janes and Phill McCaughey. Your bookselling skills, beautiful personalities and willingness to be fictionalised are a daily inspiration.

Thank you, Adele Broadbent, for letting us poison you, and for being a fabulous writer, reviewer and team member. We must acknowledge that it was ex-Wardini lad Nigel Olsen whose penchant for giving everyone a nickname was the origin of Adelios Broadbentios. Kia ora, Miguel, from Louburger and G-Man.

Thanks to Dame Fiona Kidman for being a genuine Battle of the Book Clubs guest and for letting us use her in our book, although in the end we didn't have the heart to poison her.

Thanks to Emma and Marie at the Havelock North Business Association for helping us with promotion.

We had some necessary medical advice from Emma Merry, Craig Ellis, Lou Trent and Cynric Temple-Camp, and from Alanda Rafferty and the team at VetEnt in Havelock North. Thanks to

Monique Dalley and Ross Pinkham for their NZ Policing advice. Any inaccuracies or liberties taken are entirely down to us.

Thank you to our publisher, Grace Thomas, and the team at Penguin Random House New Zealand. Your support has been extraordinary and we're so glad to be part of your crew. Thank you also to Dorothy Tonkin and the team at Penguin Random House Australia for doing us proud across the ditch.

A debt of gratitude is due to our editor Rachel Scott. Thank you for wanting more Stevie (I mean, who doesn't?) and for helping us make sense of things.

The Mighty Oaks is based on a Hawke's Bay organisation called The Acorn Project (do you see what we did there?). Its founder, Kerrie Waby, is an awe-inspiring human who, with her team, works tirelessly to ease the load borne by families going through a cancer journey. Kerrie introduced us to the Davis family: Reagan, Anna and Eva. We only met Reagan briefly, but his courage, resilience and humour shone so brightly that the fictional version wrote himself. Thank you, Davis family, for sharing your story with us.

For more information on The Acorn Project, and to donate, go to https://www.theacornprojecthawkesbay.org.nz/

ABOUT THE AUTHORS

Gareth and Louise Ward are the real-life owners of independent bookshop Wardini Books, with stores in Havelock North and Napier, New Zealand.

Louise is known among the staff as *Fearless Leader* and Gareth as *a bit of a dick*; he is, however, the author of the Tarquin the Honest and The Rise of the Remarkables book series, as well as being the bestselling and award-winning author of *The Traitor and the Thief* and *The Clockill and the Thief*.

Gareth and Louise met at police training college in the UK and are both ex-coppers. Louise has one murder arrest to her name, is an English Literature graduate and as an ex-teacher inflicted Shakespeare on inner-city twelve-year-olds. She regularly reviews books on RNZ.

Both are obsessed with their rescue dog Stevie, avoid housework and gardening, and live in the cultural centre of the universe that is Hawke's Bay, Aotearoa New Zealand.

The Bookshop Detectives: Tea and Cake and Death is Gareth and Louise's second book together.

Read the first book in The Bookshop Detectives series!

"When we opened Sherlock Tomes people warned us that we'd made a terrible mistake. People warned us that e-readers were taking over. People warned us that we'd never compete with Amazon. The one thing they didn't warn us about was the murders..."

Introducing... the Bookshop Detectives!

When a mystery parcel arrives at Sherlock Tomes bookshop in small-town Havelock North, New Zealand, husband-and-wife owners Garth and Eloise (and their petrified pooch, Stevie) are drawn into the baffling case of a decades-old missing schoolgirl.

Intrigued by the puzzling, bookish clues the two ex-cops are soon tangled in a web of crime, drugs, and floral decapitations, while endeavouring to pull off the international celebrity book launch of the century.

With their beloved shop on the chopping block and the sinister suspect who forced them to run away from Blighty reemerging from the shadows, have Garth and Eloise Sherlock finally met their Moriarty?

Powered by Penguin

Looking for more great reads, exclusive content and book giveaways?
Sign up to our newsletters.

Scan the QR code or visit penguin.co.nz/newsletters